PRAISE FOR J.

"I quickly became caught up in the lives of Hochstetler's characters and felt their joy, pain, and struggle to either hold tight to their faith or open their heart to God. Warning: The deeper you journey into this painfully honest tale, the more you'll need a ginormous box of tissues close by. Very recommended!"

— *Tamara Leigh, author of* The Redeeming

"The characters are so well drawn, they've stayed in my mind long after reading the book, almost as if they were real people that I've known for a long time. Being the daughter of a Vietnam Vet, I also appreciated Hochstetler's gentle handling of one of the most tumultuous times in our country's history. And even though it's set during the Vietnam era, there are lessons to be learned and truths to be taken away from this beautifully crafted story for today. Highly recommended."

— *Kaye Dacus, author of* Follow the Heart

"*One Holy Night* is powerful yet gentle in both its method and message. Set in the 1960s amidst the divisiveness of an unpopular war, a family's very faith and foundations are tested as memories and cultures collide. Hochstetler's "lighting the past . . . and leading you home" signature couldn't be more appropriate than in this sacred tale of hope rising sweetly from the ashes of sorrow."

— Kathi Macias, author of *Last Chance for Justice*

"Amazingly, Hochstetler tackles several big issues—love, loyalty, war and death—while maintaining a positive thesis. Family can survive. Human love is grander in weakness than in strength. And faith is, by necessity, stronger in tragedy than in triumph. *One*

Holy Night is a miracle story with an inspirational message that will warm your heart with love. It is a wonderful statement of faith and a gift of hope."

—Kathy Harris, author of *The Road to Mercy*

"Author J. M. Hochstetler has crafted a story that will drive us to tears but also lift our spirits at the same time. It is a 'family' story that all readers can enjoy and one to which they can relate in some way. Each person described in the story comes alive and takes his/her place in the order of things. The author even brings in side characters to flesh out the story and she does it with inventiveness and skill."

—Jackie Cooper, author of *Back to the Garden:*
The Goal of the Journey

"This life-changing story will move you to tears as you experience the humility of a young Vietnamese woman, her husband's desire to see his father heal, and the trials that bring them together in one desperate attempt to save another's life."

—Michelle Sutton, author of *Surprise Love*

"Within [these] pages you will discover the most beautiful modern-day essence of Christ's nativity, mercy, and grace you've read in a very long while. . . . As the story unfolds its final scenes, the reader is left with renewed hope in God's sovereign design for each of our lives and His miraculous ability to bring good out of even the darkest circumstances. [Hochstetler] richly captures the turmoil surrounding the lives of those affected by the Viet Nam War, and the many emotional conflicts that raged on as a result of that war."

—Kim Ford, *Window to My World* blog

"*One Holy Night* contains a miracle that can change even the hardest of hearts. I was impressed at how Hochstetler let her characters talk about their faith to unbelievers without proselytizing. It's a perfect novel for Christmas with a story full of hope and love."

—Christy Lockstein, Christy's Book Blog

"What makes [Hochstetler's] writing so compelling is the combination of real life characters and riveting plots. Reading becomes a journey and an adventure."

—Linda Mae Baldwin, *The Road to Romance blog*

ONE
HOLY NIGHT

J. M. Hochstetler

Elkhart, Indiana 46514
USA

For Vicky

Joseph also went up from Galilee, from the city of Nazareth, to Judea, to the city of David which is called Bethlehem, because he was of the house and family of David, in order to register along with Mary, who was engaged to him, and was with child. While they were there, the days were completed for her to give birth. And she gave birth to her firstborn son; and she wrapped Him in cloths, and laid Him in a manger, because there was no room for them in the inn.

—Luke 2:4-7

For God so loved the world, that He gave His only begotten Son, that whoever believes in Him shall not perish, but have eternal life.

—John 3:16

PROLOGUE

November 19, 1966

MIKE MCRAE DROPPED HIS BATTERED DUFFEL BAG on the concrete floor and glanced through the bank of windows to where the wide-bodied army transport sat waiting on the snow-dusted tarmac. Waiting to take him and his buddies halfway around the world to war.

Viet Nam.

The name hung between him and his family as they gathered in the spare, unadorned military terminal, trying to pretend that this trip was nothing out of the ordinary. But it seemed to Mike almost as if he were gone already, that he had moved beyond the point where he could reach out and touch them. Their faces, loved and familiar, blurred before his eyes as though he looked at them through a mist.

His father cleared his throat before shoving a dog-eared, plain, tan paperback book into Mike's hands. "Thought you might be able to use this sometime," he said, his voice hoarse. "You and Julie used to like to sing some of these old hymns when you were kids. Remember?"

Mike looked down at the book he held. It was his father's old service hymnbook that he'd gotten as a young Marine at Sunday worship aboard a ship headed out to the South Pacific during World War II.

9

Frank McRae wasn't much of one to attend church, and the gift surprised Mike. Maybe spiritual things meant more to his father than he had thought.

It evidently surprised his mother too. "Oh, Frank, I didn't think you paid any attention. Julie taught you those songs when you were just a toddler," she added, lightly touching Mike's shoulder. "The two of you sounded like little angels—" She stopped, her voice choking.

Mike could feel the heat rising to his face. To cover his embarrassment, he flipped open the worn cover and stared down at the inscription on the title page. No date, just the owner's name: Frank McRae.

It was Mike's turn to clear his throat. There was suddenly a lump in it despite his skepticism about anything that had to do with faith or religion.

"Well . . . cool. Thanks."

Blinking back an unexpected prickle of tears, he glanced over at his mother, Maggie, who was thin and wan from surgery and chemotherapy for ovarian cancer. His sister, Julie, hovered near her, still in her white nurse's uniform after coming straight to the airport from the hospital where she worked. Behind her stood her husband, Dan, holding their daughter, Amy.

"I know you've got a lot to carry already, but—"

Mike waved his father's words away. "It isn't heavy, Dad, and who knows. You lugged it through all those battlefields, and you made it home. Maybe it'll bring me good luck too."

On impulse, he pulled a pen out of the breast pocket of his fatigues, clicked it open and added his name below his father's, added the date too. Squatting down, he zipped open his bag and squeezed the hymnal in among his clothing.

When he straightened, his mother stepped forward to give him a fierce hug. "When you get there, let us know you're okay and what unit you're assigned to. Write as often as you can."

"I will, Mom." He struggled to keep his voice from choking up. "Love you."

"Love you too."

"You get well, okay?" he whispered in her ear.

"I will. I'm going to beat this cancer, God willing."

Inwardly Mike sighed, though for her sake he managed not to grimace. He and his mom had always been close, but he got awfully tired of all this God talk. On the other hand, if there really was a benign force somewhere out there in the universe, he supposed prayers couldn't hurt.

Julie crowded in to put her arms around him as well. "I'm sure going to miss you, little brother." She was crying openly, not making any attempt to brush away her tears.

"Aw, you're going to be too busy with this little princess to think about me," Mike returned awkwardly, reaching over to tickle three-year-old Amy under the chin.

She leaned out from her father's arms, reaching for him. Dan surrendered the child, and she wound her arms around Mike's neck, nestled her golden head against his shoulder, giggling, as he tugged on her braid.

Mike was relieved to see that Amy, at least, seemed not to comprehend the dangers he was heading toward or the length of the separation that lay before them. He turned to clasp Dan's hand in a handshake he hoped would say everything he couldn't.

Dan pushed his hand away and embraced him without speaking, pounding him on the back at the same time. Only Frank held back, frowning, as he stared through the windows at the plane.

Outside Mike could hear the engines revving up, signaling that it was time to board. The last of his buddies were heading outside. Hastily handing Amy back to Dan, Mike kissed his sister and mother, shook his father's hand, then zipped up his parka and grabbed his duffel bag.

"Thirteen months," he said, forcing a grin. "See you all back here next Christmas."

"Don't forget to tell Terry hello from all of us. Remind him Angie and the kids want him to stay safe and to hurry home. Give him a kiss from Angie," Julie added with a wicked grin.

"Yeah, right!" Mike chuckled in spite of himself, then hefted his bag. "It sure will be good to see a friendly face when I get there. With luck, I'll end up in Terry's platoon."

"It'll be more than luck," his mother said. "I'm going to pray about it. And we'll be praying every minute until you're home safe with us again."

Mike gave her a crooked smile, then with a quick wave to all of them, turned and strode out the door and across the tarmac. By sheer willpower he kept his stride steady, refusing to let himself turn to look back at them. He knew that if he did, he'd never make it to the plane.

Every step of the way he could sense their eyes following him, and their love. When he reached the stairs, he ran up them, not letting himself think about what he was leaving behind or what lay before him.

Hurriedly he moved through the open door into the plane's dim interior, feeling, like the severing of an embrace, the moment when he disappeared from their sight.

CHAPTER 1

"MOM?" CLOSING THE FRONT DOOR behind her, Julie Christensen stamped the snow from her boots onto the welcome mat in the foyer. "Hello—it's me!"

"Come on in, honey," her mother called from the kitchen. "I'm just putting a hotdish in the oven. I'll be right out. Are the streets still bad?"

Jiggling awkwardly from one foot to the other, Julie pulled her boots off one at a time with her free hand and dropped them onto the mat to drain. "The plows have cleared all the main streets now, but they're still icy in places. I barely got through to the hospital this morning, though. That was quite a blizzard."

She could hear the oven door open and close. "Your father got to the office late," her mother responded. "He called to say there were a lot of fender-benders."

Julie went into the living room on white-stockinged feet. "I brought in the mail. There's a letter from Mike."

Maggie pushed through the swinging kitchen door, wiping her hands on a dishtowel. "Well, it's about time. It's been three weeks since the last one came, and he had hardly anything to say then."

When Julie held out the letter, her mother dropped the dishtowel on the arm of the easy chair and reached eagerly for it. She frowned as she studied the handwriting on the outside.

15

"He's still . . . okay."

Julie's heart constricted. She knew what her mom really meant was *He's still alive.*

"Of course he's okay," she reassured her hastily. "We'd hear right away if he wasn't."

Maggie looked up. "He's only written three times in the past three months."

Julie dropped the rest of the mail onto the coffee table. "Don't forget the letter he sent Dan and me last month."

"All right, four then."

"They've been involved in several operations."

"That's about all he's told us." Maggie sighed. "I want to know how he's doing—really. What it's like over there. How his health is."

"Mom, he's a guy. Guys don't talk much about stuff like that."

Maggie gave a short laugh. "I know. Your father's the same way. How was work today? Is Diane Henderson doing any better?"

Julie hesitated. Diane had been fighting breast cancer for more than a year, and Julie was tempted to gloss over their friend's condition. But when her own mother had been diagnosed with ovarian cancer the previous fall, Julie had promised she would always tell her the truth and not conceal anything, no matter how unpleasant it was.

She shook her head. "Not good. I'm afraid she isn't going to make it through the night. Steve and the girls are with her, and their parents are on the way. I said goodbye to her before my shift ended, but I don't know if she could hear me."

Her movements unsteady, Maggie went to the fireplace, grabbed the poker and prodded the sizzling logs, releasing a shower of sparks that swirled upward and out of sight. Squatting down, she laid another log on the fire, jerking back from the heat as the flames licked at the dry bark. The wood began to hiss and pop, the sound loud in the quiet room.

When she finally stood up and turned around again, Julie could read nothing in her face. As usual since she had lost her abundant chestnut curls to chemotherapy, her mother had tied a bright scarf around her head.

The loss of her hair bothered her more than the terrible bouts of nausea she suffered during treatment, Julie thought. Even now that an inch-long, silky growth of new hair covered her scalp, she still kept her head covered even at home.

Pulling off gloves and muffler and unzipping the parka she wore over her starched, white nurse's uniform, Julie threw them onto the sofa, then went to give her mother a quick hug. "How've you been today? Are you feeling all right?"

"I'm fine."

"You look tired. You haven't been overdoing it, have you? Are you sleeping okay?"

At the barrage of questions, Maggie raised her hands. "Now who's the mother here? I'm supposed to be asking you that. You've got a three-year-old at home, a husband who's a pastor, and you work all day on a cancer ward. With that much stress, it's a wonder you're not sick—"

"Mom, you're always doing that." At her questioning look, Julie burst out, "You always change the subject if it's about you! You always think you have to take care of other people, and you act as if *you* aren't important at all!"

Maggie raised her eyebrows, but before she could protest, they heard a car pull into the driveway. At the same instant the mantel clock tolled four o'clock. Julie went over to the window.

"It's Dad. What's he doing home so early?"

"I hope there's nothing wrong. He hardly ever makes it home before six-thirty."

The engineering firm owned by Frank McRae and his high school buddy, Larry Bringeland, had landed a major contract with the State of Minnesota that had been taking most of his attention for the past eight months. He usually worked late on the job site or at his office in Minneapolis, thirty miles southeast of their home in the small bedroom community of Shepherdsville.

He's more worried about Mom's appointment tomorrow than he'll admit.

Julie bit her lip to keep from blurting out what she was thinking. Her mother was already nervous enough about the appointment at University Hospital the next morning, where she was scheduled to receive the results of tests to determine whether she was finally cancer-free. She didn't need any more anxiety.

After a moment Julie heard her father come into the kitchen, banging the back door behind him. When he appeared in the doorway, he first glanced at Maggie, then apparently reassured, grinned at Julie.

"Thought I'd find you here. You girls have a good day?"

Maggie went to give him a kiss and help him to slip out of his overcoat. "You're home awfully early. We ought to celebrate."

He chuckled. "Sounds like we're on the same wavelength. We finished our last meeting early, so I decided to take you out to dinner."

"But I just put your favorite hotdish into the oven."

"Stick it in the fridge. It'll keep till tomorrow." He crossed the room to warm himself in front of the fire.

Seeing the look he gave her mother as she went into the kitchen, Julie smiled. After twenty-five years of marriage, they still acted like young lovers.

"We're not going anywhere until we read Mike's letter," Maggie insisted. She handed Julie the letter and sat down on the sofa. "Why don't you read it so we can all hear it together."

Eagerly Julie tore open the thin air-mail envelope. Pulling out several creased, humidity-stained sheets of paper, she unfolded them and stared down at the pages thickly scribbled with Mike's free-flowing handwriting.

February 19, 1967
Nha Trang, South Viet Nam

Dear Mom and Dad,
    When you arrive in the Nam, the first thing you notice is the intense heat, followed by the stench of sweat and fuel and refuse that permeates everything. Next is the sound—

*a vibration that raises the hair on the back of your neck—
the roar of helicopters and jet fighters taking off and land-
ing, and the occasional whump of artillery fire. Gritty red
dirt coats everything, from your boots and fatigues to your
food. You chew it with every bite you eat, breathe it in with
every lungful of air.*

*It's a strange feeling—as if you've dropped into an al-
ternate reality, a parallel universe that revolves along its
own separate course on a totally different plane from life in
the real world. Ten months, and I'll be home. That thought
is the only thing that makes life here bearable.*

*Sorry I haven't had much to tell you up till now. It's
taken a while to get oriented and figure out what what's
going on. I have some great news to share, though! I got that
transfer to the medic unit I asked for. Instead of running
sweeps through the jungle and setting up ambushes, my
job will be to accompany the medics during our operations, get them in to the wounded, then get them and the
casualties back out to safety.*

"Thank God!" Maggie said, relief flooding through her. "At
least he'll be a little bit safer with the medics."

She saw Frank open his mouth as if he was going to
say something, but he abruptly closed it again without
speaking. Tilting her head, Maggie gave him a questioning
look.

"I still can't get over Mike's joining the army instead of
taking a student deferment," Julie broke in. "I never thought
my little brother was cut out to be a soldier."

Wondering at Julie's quick change of subject, Maggie said thoughtfully, "Mike has taken his share of detours, but he's always been a good boy at heart."

"He's too easily influenced by the wrong crowd," Frank said, frowning.

Maggie gave him a reproachful look. "Oh, Frank, he's just idealistic. All the kids are nowadays—you know that. They think political action will solve the world's evils. And Mike has always acted as if he could change the world on his own."

When Frank only shrugged in response, she motioned to Julie to continue, irritated at his stubbornness.

I'll never get used to killing another human being, but at least now I'll be helping to save lives. I know you faced the same thing in the South Pacific, Dad, and I keep wondering how you got through it. But back then you knew who the enemy was. Here in the Nam you never really know for sure who's a friend and who's an enemy. You can't afford to trust anybody outside the guys in your platoon, otherwise you could end up dead real quick.

Frank's gut clenched. Leaving the fireplace to move restlessly around the room, he passed his hand over his face, wishing he could as easily wipe away the stark images that haunted his thoughts at unguarded moments.

"All those years I spent chasing Japs through the jungles of the South Pacific, thinking we were going to fix it so no son of mine would ever have to go through what my buddies and I did. Or die like Bobby did." He gritted his teeth. "And now Mike's a grunt in Viet Nam, and those people over there are no different from those lousy, stinking—"

His gaze met Maggie's, and the pain that shadowed her face silenced him. "You know I don't like hearing you talk like that," she said, her voice muffled.

He rarely brought up his wartime experiences. He knew how his hatred for the enemy he had faced during World War II shocked his wife and daughter whenever it boiled briefly to the surface, like now.

The truth was, at times the violence of his anger shocked him as well. Maybe that was the problem, he thought now. If he was ever going to lay the demons of the past to rest, he had to confront them.

But even after all those years, the emotions were so raw that just the thought of intentionally unleashing them made him feel sick to his stomach, as if he teetered on a precipice. Plunging over the edge would surely destroy him. And so as always before he pushed the jumbled feelings and images down deep, out of sight and feeling.

Cocking his head, he winked at Maggie. "Honey, the last thing I want to do is to make you unhappy."

He kept his tone light, but he meant what he said. Since he had first known that he was going to marry Maggie Clayton, he had worn his love for her on his sleeve. Her recent illness and the possibility that he might lose her had only intensified his feelings.

His breath shortened at the thought that Maggie might lose her cruel struggle, but he resolutely pushed that fear away as well. It was a month since she had completed her second course of chemotherapy, following surgery the previous September. Her oncologist had assured them she had an excellent prognosis with this new drug, and Frank refused to entertain any doubts about her recovery.

"Go ahead and read the rest of the letter, Julie," he prompted gruffly.

Julie complied.

I'm getting along okay. I have to admit I miss Terry already. Seems like he's been gone a couple of weeks instead of only a couple of days. It's going to take some time to get used to the new platoon and especially to my new squad leader. He's okay, but he hasn't been with the platoon much longer than me. After two tours of duty, Terry knew his way around. He looked out for me, showed me the ropes and how to survive in the jungle.

I hate to admit that base camp feels pretty empty without him, but when you see him, don't tell him I said so! Don't want him to get a swelled head.

One thing that's helped is that I've grown kind of attached to a little orphan kid who works off and on at the base as a translator. Well, she's not a kid, I guess. Her name is Thi Nhuong, and she's seventeen, but she's so small and delicate, kind of cute, with eyes that are always smiling. Everyone else calls her Merry, but I always call her by her real name. I know she likes that.

Anyway, she's great fun to be with. She lost her whole family in the war when she was only nine years old, and she was raised—if you can call it that—by a cousin. She was on her own by the time she was thirteen, and from what she's told me, she had it pretty rough. But in spite of all she's been through, she seems so joyful at heart.

"I sure hope Mike doesn't get it into his head that he's in love with that girl!" Julie's father exploded. "I'm not going to stand for my son getting mixed up with some . . . some gook! She's probably a prostitute—"

Before Julie could blurt out an angry remark, her mother cut him off with quiet vehemence. "How can you say such a thing? You don't know this girl. If Mike cares for her, I'm sure she's exactly what he says she is."

"You'll notice he's giving us very few details."

"Maybe there's nothing to tell. World War II has been over for twenty-two years, Frank, and the Japanese are our allies now. It's time you let go of your anger. Besides, the Vietnamese are a completely different people."

"All those slanty-eyed people are alike—sneaky and cruel. Look, the war was barely over before the Chinese went Commie. Then so did Korea, and we ended up in a war with them."

"*North* Korea," Julie interjected.

He ignored her. "Now we've gotten dragged into this war with Viet Nam—"

"*North* Viet Nam. And Congress has never officially declared war."

He rounded on Julie. "Then what are we doing over there, blowing up the place and getting our men slaughtered? Most of the South Vietnamese support Ho Chi Minh and the Viet Cong, and those who don't are in it for all of the money and power they can get from us. We're playing right into their hands.

"Mike was right the first time, and he needs to take his own advice. You can't trust any of those people ever—period! They'll knife you in the back as soon as look at you."

"Dad—!"

"*Please*, the two of you!" Maggie cried. "Enough! You're not going to settle this, so leave it alone."

Staring at her father, Julie bit back an angry reply. From her grandparents she had learned that he had idolized his older brother, Bobby, who died in a Japanese prisoner-of-war camp after enduring the brutalities of the Bataan death march. Now she wondered how much he knew about the horrific experiences his only sibling must have been subjected to. He'd never opened up about the subject, a sure indication that it must be unbearably painful to him.

"You've never shown the least prejudice against Terry and his family—or any of the black engineers you employ," she pointed out, keeping her voice neutral. "Why do you hate the Japanese so much?"

Frank folded his arms across his chest. "Black people have fought and died to preserve our freedoms in every war we've ever been involved in. Jordan Williams served honorably as a pilot over Europe during World War II, and Terry's served two tours of duty in Viet Nam. They're decent, honest men.

"The Japs—excuse me, the Japanese," he amended sarcastically, "are different. They have nothing in common with us. You didn't see what I saw during the war, but if you had, you'd find it pretty hard to forgive too."

"You're right—we didn't experience what you did. But Mom's right too. At some point you have to forgive or your bitterness will eat you alive."

He turned his back and moved to the window to stare outside, his hands clenched in his pockets. Julie glanced from his rigid form to her parents' wedding picture on the mantel. In spite of the white strands that now lightly streaked the hair at his temples, he was almost as youthful in appearance as he had been when the photograph was taken, following a spur-of-the-moment ceremony in San Francisco just before he shipped out for the South Pacific a few months after Pearl Harbor.

He had been all of nineteen, a year younger than Mike was now, wearing the neatly pressed uniform of the Marines. Under his rakishly canted hat, his curly red-gold hair gleamed in the muted, sepia tints of the yellowing photograph as he smiled proudly down at his new wife, his clear blue eyes sparkling, dimples deepening at each side of his mouth.

At forty-five he was still as handsome, though he carried a few more pounds than the lean youth in the picture. Julie had been completely in love with him from the age of not-quite-three, when he had stepped off the airplane that had brought her back the flesh-and-blood daddy she had never met to replace the photos that couldn't quite satisfy the longings of her young heart for a father of her own.

It was the one memory from her early childhood that stood out with vivid clarity, and one she would always cherish. No matter how much she disagreed with her father on some issues, no matter how annoyed she became with some of his attitudes, she knew she would always adore him.

Her gaze shifted to the picture on the opposite end of the mantel, next to the one of her taken in white cap and uniform after her graduation from the University of Minnesota Nursing School. It showed another young man, this one in army uniform but with the same disarming grin, blue eyes, and dimples as the one in the wedding picture. The only difference was that Mike had inherited their mother's rich chestnut curls, closely cropped in this picture. It had been taken after her brother finished basic training and just a few days before he left for Viet Nam.

"Let's hear the rest of Mike's letter," her mother said, her voice ragged.

Guilt stabbed through Julie. *Dad and I have to stop this. These arguments are taking too much out of Mom. She needs to focus every ounce of energy she has on getting well.*

She frowned down at the pages in her hand.

I hope both of you are getting along okay. Mom, I have my fingers crossed that the chemotherapy is doing the job and that you're not having any more bad side effects from it. What's the latest report from the doctor? Good news, I hope! I'll keep thinking positive thoughts on your behalf.

Dad, I know how tough this must be for you, but remember to take care of yourself too. You know how much Mom depends on you. We've always leaned on each other, and we'll stick together through this till Mom's well again.

Gotta go. Gonzales is bugging me about the lamp keeping him awake, and I need to get some sleep too. Tell Jules to give that niece of mine a big smooch and tell her I'll bring her a pretty silk dress from the Nam when I get back to the world (in time for Christmas, I hope!). And Dad, punch that big lug Dan for me just for general principles and to keep him in line. Tell him he'd better take good care of my best sister and niece until I get there.

Don't forget to say hey to Terry from me. I bet he'll be home before you get this letter. And give Angie, Terrance, and Shawna hugs and kisses from me, too.

As they say, keep those cards and letters coming! Seriously—your letters make me feel like I still have some connection to the world. I'll write again as soon as I can.

Love you all,
Mike

Julie folded the letter and put it back into the envelope, fighting back the aching sense of loss that overwhelmed her every time she thought about her little brother in an environment so alien and so far from home and family. Suddenly she felt too weary to deal with any more emotion.

"I'd better go. Dan promised to have dinner ready by the time I got home, and he and Amy will be wondering where I am."

"Have you heard whether the weather's cleared in Juneau enough for Terry's plane to take off?" Maggie asked. "After that long flight, he must be crazy to finally get home."

Julie laid the letter on the coffee table with the rest of the mail. "I'm hoping Angie got some news today. If Dan has heard anything, I'll let you know."

She kissed her mother goodbye and grabbed her parka, muffler, and gloves. Frank walked her to the door and waited while she pulled on her boots.

"Are you sure you don't mind driving your mother into Minneapolis to the hospital tomorrow? Larry can ride herd by himself for a day if he has to."

"You need to be there with that big project going on." Julie zipped up her insulated parka and wound the muffler around her neck. "Tomorrow is my day off anyway, and Amy will be at nursery school. I have a whole list of questions I want to ask Dr. Radnor."

He tugged a stray red-gold curl that had escaped from the pins that held her hair back. "It sure helps to have a nurse in the family," he teased.

He accompanied her outside onto the sidewalk in front of the expansive, white frame, Dutch Colonial-style house. It was growing dark, and the air was already so icy it burned her lungs with every breath.

Directly across the street a white, wrought-iron archway defined the entrance to Shepherdsville's town park. Beyond it Julie could make out the sprawling native stone pavilion and the playground that were the park's main attractions. Fifty yards from the pavilion's far end, the graceful stone arch of a footbridge spanned icy Shepherd's Creek, which bisected the park.

She turned abruptly to face her father. "You didn't seem all that sure that Mike's transfer to the medics is a good thing."

His face settled into hard lines. "I didn't want to say anything in front of your mother, but medics have to go right into the worst of the fighting to take care of the wounded and get them out. I saw plenty of them gunned down. It seemed like the Japs deliberately aimed for them."

Julie shivered in the sharp wind. When she pulled open the door of her battered, bright orange '62 Beetle convertible, it gave a protesting creak.

Frank lightly kicked the VW's rear tire. Nodding at the faded, mud-splattered sticker on its back bumper that prominently featured a peace symbol and the words "Give peace a chance," he growled, "Why don't you scrape that thing off? Since Dan's so gung-ho for non-violence, I'd think he wouldn't want to be associated with the tactics of those student demonstrators who are leading all the riots."

Julie slid behind the wheel, slammed the door shut, and rolled down the window. "Now, Daddy, you know you hate this war as much as Dan and I do."

"I don't believe this country has any compelling interests in Southeast Asia that justify our getting involved in their civil war. That doesn't mean I agree with being disloyal to our government and giving aid and comfort to our enemies."

She engaged the clutch and twisted the key in the ignition. The engine reluctantly coughed to life.

"If anyone actually advocates giving aid and comfort to our enemies, it's a very small minority. Please, Dad, let's not argue about this right now. I need to get home."

To her surprise, he leaned in through the window and gave her a light peck on the cheek. "Love you anyway," he said with that disarming smile she could never resist.

She grinned back at him. "Love you too, you old galoot. Take care of Mom, and I'll see you in the morning."

Waving goodbye, she put the car in gear.

CHAPTER 2

THE DRIVE FROM HER PARENTS' HOME on Park Street to her own home around the corner on Church Avenue, two blocks away, took only a couple of minutes. The 1930s two-story white frame bungalow where she and Dan lived with their three-year-old daughter, Amy, was across the street and one house up from Bethlehem Christian Church, the growing congregation Dan pastored.

The car's heater had barely begun to stir to feeble life by the time she dodged around the head-high bank of snow piled along the street by the snowplows, pulled into the driveway, and braked to a halt behind Dan's dented and rusty, but dauntless, Volkswagen van. For once the door of the garage was closed, disguising the overflow that prevented its use for the vehicles it was designed to accommodate. This was balanced by Amy's snow-crusted purple scarf, pink hula hoop, red sand pail, and yellow shovel scattered across the trampled field of white in the front yard.

Breathing a white plume into the brisk air, she slammed the Beetle's door behind her, then tilted her head back to take in the broad sweep of indigo sky overhead. Lower down, beyond the green-black silhouettes of the tall pines in the backyard, the intense fires of sunset were fading. High above, a few brilliant starpoints of light already blinked out of the darkness.

She pulled her muffler up over her nose and mouth to ward off the searing cold and hurried up the snowy walk to the brick front porch that ran the width of the house. After stamping the slush off her boots, she let herself inside.

In the cozy living room to her left, a fire crackled on the hearth. To her right, on the other side of the central stairway with its carved oak banister, the long table in the dining room was partially set for dinner. The aroma that wafted from the kitchen door at the room's rear mingled with the fragrance of wood smoke from the fireplace. She could hear her stomach growling.

It looked as if every light in the house was on. Ramsey Lewis's "Wade in the Water" played softly on the hi-fi. Everything felt warm and welcoming after the frosty twilight that gathered outside the wide front windows. For a moment a sense of peace and hopefulness relieved the hard knot of worry that had taken permanent residence in her stomach since her mother's diagnosis and Mike's departure for Viet Nam.

Just inside the living room Dan was on the phone, two-year-old Shawna Williams balanced on his left hip while he propped the receiver against his ear with his right shoulder and scribbled on a notepad with his free hand. He waved at Julie as she hung her parka in the closet and kicked off her boots.

When Julie came toward them, the tiny child removed her thumb from her mouth long enough to reach out both arms, her dark eyes sparkling. She clasped her hands over her mouth and squealed at the funny face Julie made.

Transferring Shawna to her own hip, Julie returned Dan's quick kiss. As she moved away from him, she tickled the back of Shawna's neck beneath the stiff braids trimmed with colorful beads that gleamed like jewels against her jet black hair. Shawna wriggled and squealed in delight.

Just then Amy and Terrance roared down the stairway and into the room. Terrance flew a model airplane high in one hand to the accompaniment of the appropriate noises. Amy followed hot on his heels while Judge, their giant Saint Bernard, bounded alongside.

Detouring, Amy attached herself to Julie's leg. "Mommy, Shawna and Terrance are staying for dinner, and Daddy's making lasagna!"

Julie reached down to brush her daughter's fine blond hair out of her flushed face. "Ummm—my favorite."

"I helped make it!" six-year-old Terrance announced.

Julie smiled at the contrast the two children made—the boy's vivid, dark coloring beside her daughter's pale gold. "Then I know it's going to be wonderful!" She rolled her eyes and drew out the word *wonderful*, sending the children into a fit of giggles.

Dan finished his conversation and hung up the phone. "That was Mrs. Beal. I need to go see her and her husband tomorrow."

"It was so sweet to see little Callie come down to the altar Sunday."

Carrying Shawna, Julie followed Dan into the dining room. He gave her an exuberant grin as he went to finish setting the table.

"Jimmy decided he wants to be baptized at the same time. This has to be the best part of being a pastor."

Julie returned his smile, thinking how lucky she was to have this solidly built six-footer in her life. He was thirty-three to her twenty-four, square-jawed, with fair hair just beginning to thin on top and wire-rimmed glasses that gave him a bookish air. She had never known anyone as good natured and loving, or one who was steadier in a crisis—a quality she was more grateful for every day.

It hadn't taken long after Dan Christensen was called as pastor of the small congregation she and her mother attended for him to become her anchor. She was a member of the church choir, and Dan had taken to lingering on Wednesday evenings after choir practice ended. Before long, he had begun driving her the short distance home, making the trip last as long as possible while their relationship blossomed. Right now just being near him helped her fight her way back to a measure of confidence that everything was going to be all right.

"Where's Angie?" Julie shifted Shawna to her other hip.

Their friend Angela Williams, Terrance and Shawna's mother, ran Little Lambs Nursery School and Daycare where Amy attended nursery school two days a week.

"The weather cleared long enough for Terry to get a flight out of Juneau last night. He was supposed to come in from San Francisco this afternoon, so Angie drove to the airport to pick him up. They should be here in half an hour or so. I made enough lasagna and salad for everyone."

"Great! It'll be so good to have Terry back."

Julie glanced over at Terrance, who at mention of his father had run to the window to check for approaching cars.

"They aren't here yet." Disappointment tinged the boy's voice.

"Your mom was going to call if the flight didn't come in on time, so they must be on their way back by now," Dan reassured him.

Satisfied, Terrance resumed his own miniature flight pattern with Judge trailing in his footsteps. "When I grow up, I'm going to be a fighter pilot like Grandpa," he announced.

"I'm going to be a nurse like Mom," Amy answered importantly as she trailed after him into the other room.

"Oh dear, I promised to take Mom to the hospital to get the results of her tests tomorrow," Julie remembered. "Angie was going to keep Amy at Little Lambs for the whole day, but with Terry just getting home—"

"My mom said she'd be glad to drive down and stay with Amy until I'm finished with my calls. You know her— she'll take any excuse to spend time with one of her grandkids."

Julie smiled at the thought of Dan's bubbly mother. She set Shawna down and the two-year-old ran to join Amy and Terrance in the living room.

A cartoon soundtrack from the TV suddenly blared its annoying cacophony over the music on the hi-fi.

Wincing, Dan went to the dining room door. "Kids, if you're going to watch TV, please turn off the hi-fi."

"Okay, Daddy," chirped Amy's voice.

The music switched off, and the voices of Sylvester and Tweety took over.

Turning back to Julie, Dan sobered. "Hey, Brown Eyes, what's the matter? Is Mom all right?"

Julie concentrated on straightening one of the napkins on the table. "She seems to be. I don't know what it is—maybe just my own experience at the clinic—but I keep having this bad feeling."

She stared down at the plate in front of her, but she didn't see it. "I wouldn't worry as much if the survival rate for ovarian cancer wasn't so terribly low. I'm just afraid that Mom's going to end up in the same losing struggle as so many of my patients. They try to convince themselves that this time the chemo or radiation actually defeated the cancer . . . only to find out that it's spread."

Without speaking, Dan pulled her into his arms. He felt solid as a rock to her, like a safe haven in the storm. For several minutes she clung to him, her face buried against his shoulder, tears trickling down her cheeks in spite of her determined efforts to blink them away.

"If only Dr. Banks had taken her symptoms seriously at the beginning. But Mom is always so busy taking care of everybody else that she doesn't think about herself. She acts as if symptoms will go away if she just ignores them long enough."

Dan gently tipped her face up until her gaze met his. "Honey, I know it's hard not to worry when it involves someone we love. Okay, maybe it's impossible. But all we're guaranteed is today. Beyond that, we have to trust the One who's in control of it all. Today your mother is all right. And Mike is all right. Cling to that. We can't know what tomorrow will bring, but God will give us grace for whatever the future holds. And he'll carry us in his arms when we can't go any farther on our own."

Julie snuggled back against his chest. "I know you're right. But no matter how much I tell myself to trust, I'm still afraid."

Dan kissed the top of her head. "So am I. We're afraid of the unknown. It's hard to face the fact that we aren't in control of what happens to the ones we love. But God is still good. And a good God will use even the hardest experiences we have to go through for our ultimate good."

Julie sighed, then nodded, peace settling over her once more. Suddenly remembering Mike's letter and her father's reaction to it, she pulled out of Dan's arms and briefly recounted what had happened.

"Dad's probably jumping to conclusions," Dan returned thoughtfully, "but I do believe God brings people into our lives for a reason. He's certainly in control of Mike and Thi Nhuong's relationship—whatever it may lead to."

Smiling down at her, he released her. "You'd better go change. The lasagna's almost done, and Terry and Angie should be here pretty soon."

Julie's spirits lifted as she ran upstairs to exchange her nurse's uniform for tight-fitting jeans, bulky sweater, and loafers. After unpinning and brushing her red-gold curls loose around her shoulders, she went back downstairs just as Dan came through the kitchen door carrying a bowl of salad.

At the same moment, both became aware of the sound of a car approaching up the street. Headlights glinted in the front windows as it turned into the drive.

The children scampered out of the living room. Running for the door with Judge crowding on his heels, Terrance shouted, "They're here!"

CHAPTER 3

DAN SNAPPED ON THE PORCH LIGHT as Terrance tore open the door. Catching the scent of their visitors, Judge began to bark, his deep woofs heavy with warning. Amy and Shawna hung back, suddenly shy.

Angie was first through the door, bundled in a furry coat, boots, and mittens, the tawny brown of her cheeks rosy from the wind. Julie didn't have to see her smile to feel the happiness that surrounded her friend like a visible glow.

Behind her came a tall, ebony-skinned soldier in fatigues and heavy army-issue parka with the hood thrown back. At six feet five inches, he towered over Dan, who reached to clasp his hand before the children got to him. Terry gave him a high-five.

"Do you need to call your folks?" Julie asked Angie.

Angie shook her head. "Terry's whole family met us at the airport, and we'll stop by my folks' house on our way home. They're all planning a big get-together for tomorrow noon, so we don't have to rush away tonight."

"Great!" Julie whisked their coats into the closet and hurried into the living room to snap off the TV before rejoining them.

"How was Alaska?" Dan asked.

Terry's deep voice held a smile. "Believe it or not, it was even colder than here—if that's possible."

Judge nudged between them, tail wagging. Laughing, Terry fended off the dog's welcoming assault.

41

Dan gave Judge a light swat on the hindquarters. "Judge, settle down! Go to your bed!"

His tail drooping, the massive Saint Bernard gave his master a look of dignified reproach before padding off to his bed in the kitchen.

Terry turned his attention to the children. Her face crumpling with fear, Shawna clutched her mother's leg. Amy was hiding behind Dan, trying to appear totally uninterested in their visitor. Even Terrance edged behind Angie's skirt.

"Now, you two!" Angie scolded as she picked Shawna up. "Your daddy's gone the long way around the world to get here. Aren't you going to welcome him home?"

"Aw, it's been a year, honey. They probably don't even remember me."

Julie shooed everyone into the dining room. "All Terrance has been talking about for the past few weeks is you coming home. I remember what it was like when my daddy came home from the war. I'd never seen him before, and I didn't know whether to be excited or scared. Just give them time. Before you know it, it'll be like you never left."

Terry reached out to tickle Shawna's chin, but she pulled away and buried her face against her mother's neck. Grimacing, he squatted down to study his son, his dark eyes intent, searching for some connection. For a long moment the boy hesitated, eyes downcast. Then he threw himself into his father's arms and wound his arms around Terry's neck. Terry gathered him close.

"I missed you, Daddy," the boy whispered against Terry's bulging shoulder. "I didn't think you were ever going to come home. I thought you forgot us."

His words were full of such grief and pain that both of them were suddenly crying.

"I know, my man." Terry's voice broke. "But I'm here now, and I'm not going to leave you ever again. From now on I'm staying home to take care of you and Shawna and your mom."

"Promise?"

"Promise." He held out his hand, and Terrance slapped the large palm with his small one, grinning shyly as he rubbed the tears from his eyes with his other fist.

Julie glanced over at Angie in sudden understanding. The depth of her happiness was due to more than having her husband home at last. This time he meant to stay.

Scooping the boy up in one arm, Terry rose. Julie reached out to give him a hug. As he engulfed her with his free arm, she tip-toed to give him a peck on the cheek.

By now Amy had found her courage. She pushed her way between them and was rewarded with a grin. Curving his hand around the back of her head, Terry pulled her gently to his side.

"Hey, Princess, it's been a long time since I've seen you. You've grown, my girl! Wait till your Uncle Mike gets a look at you. He told me to give you a kiss from him." Bending down, he suited action to word.

Julie brought the conversation back to the subject that interested all of them the most. "Does this mean you'll be stationed stateside from now on?"

Terry glanced from her to Angie, who was beaming. "We talked about it on the way home. I'm going to take a discharge. I've done all the soldiering I ever want to do."

"I thought you intended to make a career of the army," Dan reminded him.

Terry looked around the dining room as though really seeing the pleasant scene for the first time. Finally he met Dan's questioning gaze.

"I've had enough of war, of killing men and seeing my own men get blown apart for no good reason. If that's what this country is all about, then I don't want any part of it."

Dan raised an eyebrow. "Do many of our soldiers feel that way?"

"You'd be surprised how many do." The muscles in Terry's jaw hardened. "I've begun to understand why you're a pacifist."

Julie lightly tapped a spoon against one of the glasses. "We can talk about it later, guys. Is anybody hungry here?"

Brightening, Terry drew in a deep lungful of the rich aroma wafting from the kitchen. "I don't know about the rest of you, but I haven't had a decent meal since I left Saigon—and that was a week ago. It's been either airline food or roast moose since then. If that isn't the famous Christensen lasagna I smell, I'll eat my boots."

Dan glanced at his watch. "I'll have you know, I've been slaving over a hot stove all afternoon. And if we don't sit down right now, dinner's going to be charred."

Terry wasted no time seating Angie and the children at the dining room table. "No way, man! I've dreamed about your lasagna ever since I left. When your choice is either C rations or the chow served up by the company cooks, you stop looking forward to mealtimes."

He squared his broad shoulders and stretched. "Man, it sure feels great to be back in the world again!"

Julie smiled as he settled his tall frame onto the chair next to Angie's. Physically Terry never seemed to change. He hardly looked a day older than he had six years earlier when he graduated from high school a year ahead of her and Angie.

He was all muscle, without an ounce of fat on his lean frame. His smile was disarming, and in spite of his size, his manner was invariably gentle. Yet Julie felt even more strongly now an indefinable difference in him that she had first sensed after his return from his first tour of duty in Viet Nam.

While she helped Dan get dinner on the table, she reflected that beneath Terry's obvious delight at being home lay a deep disillusionment, an edginess, as if all his assumptions about life had been swept away in the chaos of battle, leaving him at a loss for the first time in his life about what direction to take.

She glanced across the table at the children seated on either side of their parents. Little Terrance was the perfect junior image of his father, with some of his mother's sweetness in his features, while Shawna was a miniature replica of Angie's beauty. Fascinated by this mysterious being she had been told was "Daddy," the little girl allowed herself to be lifted onto his lap and after a moment of hesitation happily accepted a bite from his plate.

While they ate, Terry had them laughing at his adventures during the unanticipated layover in Juneau on his way home. Chuckling at their reaction, he suddenly sobered and patted the front of his shirt.

"Oh, I almost forgot." Pulling an envelope out of his breast pocket, he extended it toward Julie. "This is for you. From Mike."

Julie took the letter and threw Dan a questioning look. He nodded for her to open it.

When she tore the envelope open, a picture fell into her lap. She picked it up and turned it to catch the muted light from the chandelier above their heads.

It was a black-and-white photo of Mike in army fatigues standing in front of a large stained and tattered tent. His arm curved around the shoulders of a slender Vietnamese girl whose waist-length black hair rippled over her shoulders as though stirred by a slight breeze. She wore a long, silk tunic with a mandarin collar over flowing white trousers. She and Mike squinted into the bright sunlight, smiling shyly at the camera, and the glow in their expressions told Julie they were very much in love.

Studying the young woman's face, Julie decided that she liked what she saw. The girl wasn't pretty in a glamorous way, but her face held a sweetness and an innocence that tugged at Julie's heart.

"I suppose that's Thi Nhuong," she said to Terry, holding the photo for him to see.

When he nodded, she passed the photo to Dan and briefly summarized what Mike had written about Thi Nhuong in the letter to his parents. "What do you know about her?" she concluded.

"If Mike hasn't answered your questions in his letter, I'll fill you in on everything I know."

Eagerly Julie unfolded the letter and skimmed its contents.

Dear Jules,

I wanted to be sure this got to you, and Terry volunteered to deliver it personally since he was going in that direction anyway—the lucky slob! It's hard to think about all of you still in the grip of winter while we're sweltering over here. Even though it's February, it's mid-90s or higher every day. The heat and humidity leave everything soggy all the time and it wears you down. So the thought of a good old-fashioned, rip-roaring Minnesota blizzard sounds like heaven to me. I keep reminding myself that I'll be back there in a few months, and believe me, I'll never complain about the cold again!

By the way, I really appreciated your last letter. Please keep me informed on how Mom's doing. When she writes, I know she makes her condition sound like it's no big deal because she doesn't want to worry me. So I depend on you, Sis. You and I have always told each other the whole truth even when it wasn't good news. It's hard enough being so far away from all of you. I don't want to be kept in the dark about things that affect our family, thinking everything's going along all right if it isn't. And I'll do the same—whether things are going good or bad here, I'll always let you know.

But none of this is the real reason for my letter. There are some things I want to tell you that I don't want Mom and Dad to know just yet, especially since Mom has so much to deal with already.

If you read the last letter I wrote them, you're probably wondering what's going on with me and the girl I mentioned, Thi Nhuong. Don't tell the folks, especially not Dad, just yet, but we're going to be married as soon as I can get off for a couple of days. I'll break the news to them when it seems like a good time.

I can't wait until you get a chance to meet her. I've really only known her for a couple of months, but when it's the right thing, you just know down deep inside. I watched you and Dan fall in love, and it's the same way with me and Thi Nhuong. *She's like my little sister and my best friend and the love of my life all rolled up into one person. I know it sounds trite, but I can't even think about living without her any more. And even though we know that with my unit being involved in so many operations we won't get to spend a whole lot of time with each other for a while, our future's together.*

So when my tour's over, I'm bringing her home with me. She's a little worried about that still, but I've told her all about our crazy family. I keep reminding her we're going to have the rest of our lives to spend together. I know I can count on you and Dan and Mom to make her welcome, and Dad will come around after he meets her. She's the best person in the world!

I hope you and Dan are doing okay and that Amy's being her usual sweet self. Thanks for the pictures you sent. I have them tucked away in my pack so I can look at them at night before we settle down, just to remember that the people I love are safe and that somewhere in this world normal life still exists.

Write me soon, Jules, and tell me how you feel about me and Thi Nhuong. I want to know that at least my big sister approves and that my wife will get a rousing welcome when I bring her home.

Love you,
Mike

Julie handed the letter to Dan to read and turned back to Terry. "This seems a little sudden. What do you think of Thi Nhuong? Mike says they're going to be married. Do you think he's making a good decision?" She waited with trepidation while Terry thought over his answer.

"Yes, for the most part I do," he said finally. "Mike's grown up a lot since he went into the service, and Thi Nhuong is steady and level-headed, smart, and one of the kindest, sweetest people I've ever met. She's a little thing, but she's tough as nails. She won't let anybody run over her."

"Pretty high praise, coming from you." Dan motioned toward the letter he held. "It sounds like Mike's got it bad."

"From what I saw, he does." Terry finished his last bite of garlic bread and leaned back in his chair.

"You said for the most part you approve," Julie pointed out. "What don't you approve of?"

Again Terry hesitated. "There's a big difference in culture. And Thi Nhuong is at least nominally a Buddhist, though I never saw any outward evidence that she practices her religion."

Absently Julie rearranged the salad on her plate. "Honestly, Mike doesn't claim to be a believer. When we've talked about it, he insists that faith comes so easily to me, that I just accept everything I'm told. He says it's different for him, that he can't help questioning the Bible's claims, and that he has to see objective proof before he believes. I could tell he didn't believe me when I told him I've gone through times of deep questioning too, and that I still wrestle with a lot of issues, but in the end this is the only system of belief that makes sense to me."

"Everyone has to arrive at their own conclusions in their own way," Dan interjected. "But if he and Thi Nhuong come to different conclusions, then that's going to affect their marriage."

"I know Mom will welcome Thi Nhuong with open arms no matter what," Julie said, "but I can't see Dad accepting this. You know how he feels about Asians. And a Buddhist—"

She shook her head doubtfully. "Dad hardly ever sets foot in a church, but in his eyes Christianity is the American way. Thi Nhuong is going to represent everything he despises."

"Maybe Mike's right, though," Angie offered. "Surely he'll come around in time after he gets to know her."

Julie exchanged a dubious glance with Dan. "How is he going to get to know her if he refuses to meet her?"

No one ventured an answer to her question.

AFTER THE DISHES WERE CLEARED from the table, Dan shepherded everyone into the living room. Turning the lights down low, he stacked several LPs onto the changer while Julie added a couple of logs to the fire.

All of them settled onto the floor close to the warmth. Full and drowsy, the children cuddled around Judge and were soon sound asleep.

After some discussion of the growing opposition to the war, especially among college students, Dan said, "If you ask me, President Johnson is making a huge mistake in building up our forces in Viet Nam so drastically. We keep digging ourselves in deeper and deeper, and there's no end in sight."

Terry shifted to ease his back against the edge of the sofa. "You hear all this talk about a buildup, but from what I've seen, almost all our units are still short of men. We have operations going on day and night, so everybody's strung out all the time. As soon as new recruits get to where they have some idea of what they're doing, they're rotated back to the States, and inexperienced troops are brought in to replace them. Then we start all over again. It doesn't make any sense."

"Some of the news reports claim there are coffeehouses on some of our bases that are hotbeds of anti-war activity," Julie put in.

Lying on her stomach, Angie picked at the fringe of the cushion she hugged beneath her. "Honey, didn't you say some of our soldiers are even publishing underground newspapers opposed to the war?"

Terry nodded. "I'm sure not the only one who's disillusioned with this mess we're in. Morale is on the skids."

Dan heard the changer click. The familiar, plaintive melody of the Beatles' song "Yesterday" filled the firelit room.

He glanced over at Terry, saw he had closed his eyes. His face shadowed, Terry began softly to sing along.

After the second verse, he stopped and rubbed his hand over his face. Dan caught the worried glance Angie directed toward her husband and remembered her confidences the previous year about the frightening nightmares that had tormented Terry after he returned from his first tour in Viet Nam.

"So now that you're taking a discharge, what are your plans?" Dan asked abruptly, wanting to change the subject.

Terry focused his gaze on Dan. "I didn't really make up my mind till I was on the way home, so I haven't had time to think a whole lot about it yet. All I know is I'd like to do something with my life that makes a positive difference to somebody."

"Have you ever thought about going into the ministry?"

Terry shot him a dirty look. "You think the firstborn son of Bishop Jordan T. Williams has never had occasion to think about the ministry? The idea was thrust upon me a time or two."

Dan chuckled. "As a missionary kid myself, I know the feeling. So . . . why not?"

"Because being a PK was bad enough. No way I could ever live up to my father's reputation. He took over leadership of the largest African American church in Minneapolis the year I graduated from high school, and you know how he's built it from there. I'd always be walking in his shadow, always be Bishop Williams's son. That's why I decided to do something different in the first place."

He looked away, frowning. "Can't say that's turned out all that well," he muttered.

"Maybe there's a reason why it hasn't," Dan suggested. "Maybe it was never what you were meant to do. Haven't you ever felt the call of God on your life?"

Terry shrugged. "Maybe. Maybe not. How do you know it's God and not what somebody else wants you to do or what you want to do for your own selfish reasons?"

"Sometimes you have to take a step of faith and see what comes of it."

"And what kind of step of faith do you have in mind?" Terry was clearly suspicious.

Dan glanced at Julie before plunging ahead. "Bethlehem Christian has grown to the point where we need a youth minister. We have a lot of preteens and teenagers who need direction and programs that build real commitment. I need someone to take over our youth program and make a difference in the lives of these young people. I'm convinced you and Angie are who I'm looking for."

It was Terry and Angie's turn to exchange glances. "I don't have any experience in that kind of ministry," Terry protested.

Sitting up, Dan leaned toward him, face and body tense. "You have experience in mentoring young people. Look at the impact you had on the guys who used to hang around you back in high school and even after you graduated—Mike included. Not one of them joined a gang, and most of them have either gone on to college or are working in productive jobs. I've seen how you relate to your own children and to Amy and others."

Dan turned to Angie. "It's the same with you. You have experience with youngsters from Shawna and Terrance and from running Little Lambs. You're already teaching the girls' junior high Sunday school class. God has given both of you a talent and a heart for young people. What I'm suggesting is that you give it a try for a couple of months. Then if that's the direction you're being called to go, Terry, apply to the seminary and get the formal training you need."

Terry hesitated, but Dan had to suppress a smile at the excitement in Angie's eyes. She reached to squeeze her husband's arm.

"This might be what you've been looking for. It's what I want to do too."

"You'd be a natural," Julie agreed. "Both of you."

Terry began to chuckle. "Looks like I've been set up. Well, I guess it can't hurt to at least pray about it and help out at the church in the meantime."

Dan pounded him on the back, the exuberance he always felt when someone took a deliberate step of faith boiling up. "You'll never regret it. I know the kids you'll be working with won't."

CHAPTER 4

ENTERING HER PARENTS' KITCHEN, with its yellow and white striped wallpaper and tall, old-fashioned white cabinets and woodwork, was like stepping into sunshine. The cheerful room perfectly reflected her mother's personality and enfolded Julie, as always, with a warm glow that was especially welcome after the cold and snow outside.

As soon as she opened the door from the garage, the rich aroma of freshly baked cinnamon rolls drew Julie inside. She inhaled a rapturous breath, instantly recognizing the unmistakable scent of Olivia D'Angelo's specialty. At the sink her parents' next-door neighbor was pouring coffee into a cup while Julie's father sampled the rolls, hot out of the oven.

"Save some for me!" Julie ordered.

Olivia laughed and set the full cup on the counter. "There's plenty."

"Oh, no there isn't." Frank licked glaze from his fingers and washed it down with a sip of the hot coffee. "I told Livy she'd better make two batches because I'll likely finish this one off by myself."

"You do and you are dead meat!"

Throwing him a fierce scowl, Julie bent to give her mother a peck on the cheek. Seated at the table, Maggie was sipping a cup of tea, neatly dressed and ready to go, a colorful, striped silk scarf wound around her head, her coat on the chair beside her.

"Love the scarf! Is it new? Looks like Joseph's coat of many colors."

Although her mother smiled in response, Julie could feel her anxiety.

"And it's very becoming, too," agreed Olivia.

"Not as becoming as hair." Maggie directed a pointed glance at Olivia's lustrous black hair, which she wore gathered into a fat, loose braid that hung down her back to her slender waist.

Olivia carried the plate of rolls over to the table. "Yours is already growing back, and it's going to be more beautiful than ever. Coffee?" she offered Julie.

"Just half a cup." Julie returned her smile, pleased to see fresh color in her friend's warm olive complexion.

Thirty years old, Olivia owned and ran Angel Florist, a small flower shop just off the square in downtown Shepherdsville. Nine months earlier Rob Piero, her husband of ten years, had suddenly decided he needed to "find" himself. He had left his wife and a promising career and had taken off for California to pursue the search.

At first there had been frequent letters and telephone calls, fervent apologies and overblown promises. Contact had steadily dwindled over the past months, however, as Rob had moved from place to place. For the past six weeks Olivia had heard nothing from him.

Devastated by Rob's abandonment and confused by the mixed signals she was receiving, Olivia had wrestled with whether she should give up on the marriage or hold onto the hope that the relationship could still be mended. During those difficult months, she had grown very close to Julie's parents and to Julie and Dan as they spent hours listening, comforting, offering counsel and encouragement.

This morning, however, Julie sensed a new peace in her friend. She gave Olivia a questioning glance as she set a steaming cup beside the plate of rolls.

"Rob called last night," Olivia explained. "He admitted he's living in Haight Asbury with some of his old drug buddies, including this woman he was involved with in college before we started dating. He wants me to file for a divorce so he can marry her."

Dismay flooded over Julie, and she reached for her friend's hand. "Oh, Livy."

Olivia squeezed her hand. "I was so upset I prayed about it most of the evening, trying to discern what God's will is in all this. Finally I came to some peace about it. I decided to keep on waiting, to do nothing until I receive definite guidance."

Julie nodded and tried to give her an encouraging smile in return, but a mouthful of coffee didn't help her swallow the lump in her throat. She managed to murmur something about God being in control, but the words sounded hollow.

In all the time she'd known Olivia and Rob, they had seemed perfectly happy until the day he had simply walked away. What purpose could God possibly have in that?

"Rob's a fool. He doesn't know what he's giving up." Frank gulped down the last of his coffee and eyed the clock as he finished off another cinnamon roll. "I'd better get moving or I'm going to be late."

He gave Julie a quick goodbye hug. "Call me as soon as you leave the doctor's office. I want to be the first to hear the good news."

Julie assured him she would call, though she wasn't equally certain that the news would necessarily be good.

But as though no other possibility entered his mind, he bent over Maggie. "It will be a good day—you'll see. We're going to celebrate tonight."

WHILE FRANK MADE the forty-minute drive to his office in Columbia Heights, a small community on the north side of Minneapolis, his thoughts kept returning to Maggie's appointment that morning. In spite of the upbeat attitude he was always careful to display in front of her, anxiety nagged at him. He couldn't keep from sorting through all the possible outcomes and asking himself what if.

Finally he switched on the radio hoping for some distraction. As on most mornings, the top news concerned the latest developments in the war and the increasingly vocal and violent student opposition to American involvement.

He shook his head. *What is the world coming to? People don't support the government or the men in uniform like they did when I went to war. We've lost all respect for the values I grew up with—the values that made this country great.*

Against his will his thoughts drifted to Mike. Why did it always seem as if there was competition between a father and his son? He'd been close to his own father, but Frank remembered his teenage determination to do better than his father did, to accomplish more—and something different.

As Frank puzzled over it, his thoughts went back to the summer Mike had turned seventeen. He spent his summer break in South Dakota working on the ranch Maggie's uncle owned. When he returned, he was an inch taller than Frank's five foot eleven. A lean, muscular, suntanned young man Frank hardly recognized had stepped off the train that late August day.

In the year that followed, Mike added another couple of inches in height and ideas that Frank either didn't understand or disagreed with. And the tension between the two of them had intensified.

It wasn't that Mike was lazy or any more rebellious than a typical teenager, Frank decided. Mike worked with passion at what interested and challenged him, and Frank respected that. But Mike also questioned things Frank had always taken for granted and took on causes Frank felt were better left alone.

In some ways, Frank had to admit, he was disappointed in this son of his. In other ways, if he was totally honest, he envied Mike for a freedom of spirit that seemed out of Frank's reach.

He knew that much of the reason Mike had joined the army instead of either waiting to be drafted or filing for a student deferment was because he wanted to make Frank proud, because he believed that was what Frank wanted him to do. And Frank hadn't discouraged the idea.

Certainly he believed that a man was obligated to defend his country. He'd always insisted that obligation held regardless of whether one was in complete agreement with the government's policies or not.

But Frank couldn't help believing that this was a very different war from the one he had served in. That earlier war had clearly defined enemies who threatened the very existence of the United States and its allies. That war had one overriding goal: to win at all costs. There could be no compromise, no alternative, no negotiation without risking the destruction of their freedom and everything they held dear.

But any way he turned the issue around to look at it, the current conflict in Viet Nam appeared to him to be a purely internal matter, a civil war that outsiders had no business sticking their noses into. And ever since Mike had shipped out, Frank had asked himself if, after all, there weren't valid reasons to oppose the government's actions.

His disturbing thoughts were cut short when he turned into the parking lot of the engineering firm he and his closest friend had founded after returning from the South Pacific. McRae and Bringeland Engineering occupied the top floor of a modern, three-story brick and glass building located on a tree-lined street on the edge of an old residential district.

Ordinarily, Frank couldn't wait for the day to begin. He loved his work and looked forward to each day's challenges. And with the state highway contract they'd landed, there were plenty of them.

This morning, however, his steps lagged as he entered the building and took the elevator to his office on the third floor. An unwelcome sense of uneasiness nagged at him. Perhaps it had been a mistake to agree to Julie's suggestion that she take her mother to her doctor's appointment, he reflected unhappily. It had seemed like a good idea at the time since the highway project was at a critical point. But something told him he should have gone with Maggie, just in case.

Pushing the disquieting thoughts resolutely away, he breezed into the outer office and greeted the receptionist as he always did. After mentioning that he wanted her to put any calls from Julie or Maggie through to him without delay, he went into his office to begin the business of the day as though nothing at all concerned him.

MAGGIE SPENT MOST OF THE DRIVE to Minneapolis staring silently out the window. Julie tuned the radio to a local easy listening radio station, and when Henry Mancini's "Moon River" came on, Maggie felt her stomach unclench a little.

She tried to persuade herself that the cancer was gone this time. Something in her body didn't feel right, however, and a numbing fear kept filtering into her mind in spite of her efforts to keep a positive attitude.

The building housing the doctor's office nestled along the bluffs of the Mississippi River just a few minutes east of downtown. The parking garage was linked by a walkway to the sprawling hospital complex on the University of Minnesota campus. On arrival she and Julie were ushered into the examination room and took their seats just as the oncologist, Dr. Radnor, came in.

Closing the door behind him, he walked behind the desk and put several x-rays up on the light screen on the wall. "I'm afraid the chemotherapy didn't give us the hoped-for results," he said as matter-of-factly as though they were discussing the weather.

Maggie struggled to focus on the x-rays while he illustrated his points. "There's a mass here on the small intestine, and the blood tests confirm malignancy. Unfortunately, surgery isn't an option since it's located just above the valve between the small and large intestines. Our next step is radiation—thirty treatments over the next six weeks to shrink the tumor, then another course of chemo."

In response to Julie's anxious questions, the doctor emphasized that the mass was small. There were no indications that the cancer has spread elsewhere, and cases like this often responded well to radiation.

As she listened to them talking, Maggie could feel anger heating her face. "After my surgery you told me the chemotherapy would kill any cancer cells that were left," she broke in. "Now you're telling me it hasn't worked and I have to go through radiation, then more chemo, with all the side effects involved in that. I'm beginning to feel like the cure is worse than the disease! What are my chances of beating this—really?"

All the doctor could offer was more bland words of reassurance. Feeling as though she were groping her way through a deepening fog, Maggie went through the motions of scheduling the first radiation treatment before they left.

By now it was almost eleven o'clock. On their way out, Julie stopped at a pay phone in the lobby to call Frank. He had gone out to the job site, she reported to Maggie, but he was calling in for messages as frequently as he could. Julie asked the secretary to have him call them at home in an hour.

The drive back to Shepherdsville was strained. Neither of them spoke more than necessary. It felt to Maggie as though the day had turned even more bleak and cold than it already was, and she couldn't stop shivering.

When they reached the city limits, she said, "You're a nurse. Level with me. What are the odds I'll survive this?"

Julie's glance skimmed her, darted away. Her fingers tightened over the steering wheel.

"I don't know, Mom. How could I know that? No one knows."

Maggie turned to stare out the passenger side window.

When they got to the house, Julie said, "Why don't you go sit down while I fix us some lunch. Dad should call soon."

Nausea clenched Maggie's stomach. "I'm not hungry. I'm going upstairs to lie down."

STRICKEN, JULIE WATCHED HER MOTHER retreat up the stairs, then wandered into the kitchen. She felt as though she had fallen off a cliff. She felt as though *she* needed comfort. She couldn't imagine how her mother felt.

I shouldn't have spoken to her so sharply, she chided herself, guilt flooding over her. *I should have found some way to reassure her, but instead, I only made her feel worse.*

When her father called, she gave him the devastating news in blunt words. For a tense moment he said nothing while she listened to the faint static of the telephone line.

"Should I come home right away?" He sounded as if he was having trouble breathing.

"I'm going to stay with her, Dad. She's lying down right now. We can talk it out after you get home tonight."

Again he was silent. Then he said tersely, "I'm not doing any good here. I'll be home in an hour."

Before she had a chance to reply, the phone went dead.

DAN ARRANGED FOR ANGIE to keep Amy overnight, then hurried over to the McRae's house. Her voice shaking, Julie gave him a detailed rundown of what the doctor had told them, what she had seen on the x-rays, what radiation would entail.

"The mass isn't large, but it's in a bad location," she concluded. "And now that the cancer has spread to another part of Mom's body, it's highly likely that more cells are lodged in other organs, where they could grow for some time before they can be detected."

He tried to swallow, but his mouth had gone dry. "Dr. Radnor thinks radiation and more chemo have a good chance of knocking this thing out?"

"Oh, Dan, I'm a *nurse*!" Julie cried. "I've heard the same happy talk often enough that I have trouble believing it anymore. Too many women on my ward have made what seemed to be good progress at first, only to steadily lose ground and finally lose the battle altogether."

He pulled her into his arms and held her tightly against him. "I'm so sorry," he whispered, wishing he could come up with something more encouraging to say. Taking her face between his hands, he kissed away her tears. "We have to keep on believing that God will heal her. For her sake, we can't give up. As long as she keeps on fighting, miracles can happen."

WHEN FRANK GOT HOME, he had Julie relate every detail the doctor had told them. This was simply a problem like any other, he assured himself while he listened intently. He would find the solution, just as he had for other problems they had confronted.

In the middle of the recital, Maggie came downstairs and into the kitchen. Lifting his hand, Frank motioned Julie to silence.

He studied Maggie as she came to join them at the table. She looked pale and strained, but as far as he could tell, her emotions were under tight control.

"It's obvious that the doctors at University Hospital haven't done me any good," she said into the silence. "I want to see Dr. Dyer at the clinic here and get another opinion."

"Maggie, the doctors at University Hospital are the best in the state," he said calmly.

"Then my prospects don't look very hopeful, do they?"

He heard the tremor in her voice but quickly pushed it out of his consciousness. "According to Julie, Dr. Radnor said that—"

"You know I hate driving so far. The Shepherdsville clinic is just minutes away, and Julie is there. It'll be so much easier to have her near. Besides, we've spent thousands of dollars already, and the cancer has spread in spite of everything they've done. At least the clinic will be less expensive—"

"Expense doesn't have anything to do with it!" Frank banged his fist on the table in frustration, but quickly swallowed his anger when she winced. Forcing his tone to remain even, he said more quietly, "That's what we have insurance for. I want you to get well, and University Hospital is our best bet. They have access to the latest research and the most advanced treatments."

"The clinic is gaining recognition for the work they're doing," Julie pointed out. "Dr. Dyer did his residency at University Hospital and is as good as any doctor they have. It makes sense for Mom—"

"We're not going to change doctors now."

When Julie opened her mouth to speak, Dan laid his hand over hers. "Maggie has the right to make decisions about her own healthcare, Frank. She's the only one who can decide what's best for her."

Frank clenched and unclenched his hands. "If this were an ordinary illness, I wouldn't interfere. But she could die. This is too important for us to play around." He looked over at Maggie, pleading. "I'm only thinking about what's best for you. I know we can beat this thing together, but we need the best doctors available. And we need to trust them and do everything they say."

Maggie hesitated. "Fine," she said at last. "If that's what you think best."

Frank pushed back his chair and stood up, ignoring the blankness that had fallen over Maggie's face like a mask. "Good—we're agreed, then. Dan, I'd like to talk to you for a minute. Can we go into the den?"

Dan followed Frank down the hall into the den. Closing the door behind them, Frank motioned him toward the leather sofa. Wondering what was on his mind, Dan took a seat and waited silently while Frank stood leaning against the desk, staring into space.

Finally he said, "Maggie said you're baptizing the Beal children Sunday."

"I am."

"Well, I want you to baptize me too."

Dan crossed his arms over his chest and leaned back against the sofa. He studied his father-in-law for a long moment before speaking.

"I'd be glad to baptize you if you've accepted Jesus Christ as your Savior. Have you?"

"Of course," Frank said heartily. "Maggie has wanted me to be baptized since before we got married, but you know how it is—first there was the war, and then when I got back I had my attention on building my career. I let too many things slide. But God has been good to us, and I know he's going to heal Maggie, so—"

Dan stiffened, but before he could speak, Frank continued hastily, "I've been praying about it, and I have a real sense of peace I've never felt before. I know Maggie is going to be healed. God wouldn't take her away from her family now when we have so much ahead of us. So the least I can do is to completely turn my life over to him and—"

Getting to his feet, Dan went to put his hands on Frank's shoulders. "Frank, I know you want to believe that Maggie is going to be healed. All of us want to believe it. And it's very possible the Lord will heal her. She has excellent doctors, and our families and friends and the whole church are praying that they'll use all the wisdom and skill they have in treating her. We're all asking the Lord to heal her miraculously, if that's his will.

"I believe in the power of prayer. But none of us can know God's will absolutely. We're human beings—we can't see things from the Lord's perspective. I don't believe it was God's will for Maggie to get sick. It isn't his will for her to die so young and leave her family. But every one of us is subject to the illnesses and evils that are part of living in a fallen, sinful world. And whatever God's reasons, sometimes he doesn't choose to intervene. Sometimes we pray and the answer is no."

Frank shrugged out of Dan's grip. "I know, I know, but I'm committed to cleaning up my act and living a better life and—"

"You can't bargain with God, Frank. You can't bribe him or buy his favor—"

"I do have faith," Frank protested. "Maggie's healing is a separate issue."

"And if she isn't healed? Will your faith hold up?"

"Yes," Frank said, his tone and expression utterly in earnest. "Now will you baptize me or not?"

Dan smiled. "Nothing would make me happier."

Deep down inside, however, he remained troubled.

Frank felt Maggie move restlessly next to him. She wasn't sleeping either. Both of them were awake, and there was no point in pretending otherwise.

He rolled over and curved his arm around her, pulled her close. For a moment he could feel the tension of her body, and then she snuggled against him as always. It never ceased to thrill him—the sensation of her body pressed tight to his and the way she cuddled against his chest as if she had been uniquely made for his arms.

After a moment he said, "Can't sleep?"

She let out a soft breath. "No. Am I keeping you awake?"

"I can't sleep either."

Silence stretched out between them. Finally he said, "It's going to be all right. *You're* going to be all right."

He knew it sounded lame, but he meant it, believed it utterly.

She didn't answer, but the tightness returned to her body. After a long moment, she took a shaky breath, slowly released it.

"It's true," he said into the darkness. "I've been praying, and I can feel it. I'm going to be baptized Sunday, like you've been wanting me to. It's the right thing to do. And we're just going to keep on trusting and going forward until you're well again."

"What else can we do?" she whispered.

The hopelessness in her voice was unmistakable, but he refused to allow it to shake his confidence. Cradling her in his arms, he closed his eyes and smiled, thinking gratefully of all the precious years they had shared until now, and of the long, joyful time that surely still lay before them.

Chapter Five

As always when she was seated in the sanctuary of the church, Julie's eyes were repeatedly drawn to the magnificent stained-glass window behind the altar that soared to the high, vaulted ceiling.

The morning sunshine intensified the vivid rainbow of glowing colors and sent ribbons of light spilling across the pews. Dominating the smaller but equally exquisite windows along the sanctuary's side walls, the central window focused on the image of Mary holding the infant Jesus against a sky filled with clouds. The Christ child's face radiated joy, and he reached out his hand as though beckoning the onlooker to come to him.

Well known throughout the area for the majestic stained-glass windows and ornate interior woodwork imported from Germany in 1889, the graceful old limestone building that housed Bethlehem Christian Church had originally belonged to the local Episcopal congregation. Four years earlier, when they had moved into a beautiful modern sanctuary on the edge of town, the parish had sold the property to Dan's then-fledgling congregation. Julie still marveled at how their church had been blessed with such a beautiful facility for ministry and worship.

The last notes of the praise chorus died away, and the congregation quieted. Setting his guitar beside the piano, Dan left the choir to stand in front of the pulpit.

"Today I have the honor and privilege of baptizing three persons who have accepted Jesus Christ into their hearts and lives as their personal Savior. Afterward, as a congregation, we will accept them into the membership of this church."

Seeing surprised looks on some of the faces in the pews, Dan smiled. "In addition to Callie, Jimmy Beal and Frank McRae have also asked to be baptized. I rejoice with both families to see these individuals become our sister and brothers in Christ."

Julie looked over at her mother. Although she appeared tired and drawn, she was smiling and her eyes were alight with joy as she watched her husband go forward to join the two Beal children.

The congregation moved into the baptistery off the rear of the sanctuary, while Dan led Frank and the children into the robing room to change into baptismal robes. With Terry assisting, he baptized the children first, then Frank, before presenting them to the congregation as new members of Christ's church.

After Frank dressed and rejoined them, he was surrounded by those who pressed to shake his hand or pound him on the back. Angie, Olivia, and several others embraced both him and Maggie. Seeing her mother dab at her eyes, Julie found herself blinking back tears as well.

Though she was pleased by her father's warm welcome into the church, Julie's joy was tempered by the reservations Dan had privately confided. *Your faithfulness still covers your children's weakness,* she prayed silently. *Oh, Father, if there are any barriers that still stand between you and Daddy, please break them down until he can give himself completely to you.*

After everyone returned to the sanctuary for the benediction, Dan went to stand in front of the altar railing. Their closest friends in the congregation already knew about Maggie's test results. Now Dan briefly explained to the rest that Maggie was going to have to undergo radiation and more chemo.

He called her to come up front and asked her to kneel at the railing as the elders gathered around her. After praying with her, he anointed her with oil.

This time when the tears came, her father put his arm around Julie's shoulders. "She's going to be all right," he whispered.

She looked up into his well-loved face. "Yes, Daddy," she agreed in a choked voice. "Whatever happens, Mom is going to be all right."

JULIE AND AMY JOINED DAN in the vestibule by the outer door to shake hands with members of the congregation as they filed outside. Her parents planned to join them for lunch at their house, and after everyone else had gone, they shrugged on their coats while Dan turned off the lights.

He ushered them out through the heavy double doors, and for a moment they lingered on the steps in the pale sunshine, enjoying the wintry view across the tree-shaded campus that bordered the northwest side of Shepherdsville's city park. Julie and her mother started down the steps with Dan following, while behind him came her father holding Amy's hand in his.

"Aren't you going to lock up the building?" Frank asked.

Pausing on the sidewalk, Julie turned to look up at him. "We never lock the church doors."

"That's crazy! Anybody could just walk in, take whatever they wanted or vandalize the place."

Dan led the way across the street. "Shepherdsville doesn't have the crime rate Minneapolis has—at least not yet. And we don't keep anything of great value in the building. The church I served while I was in seminary always kept their doors locked, and one winter we found the body of a homeless man huddled against the main doors. He died of exposure.

"Since then, wherever I've served I've always kept the church doors unlocked and my business card on the vestibule table so anyone who has a need can contact me. Preventing an occasional theft isn't worth a person's life. A church should provide a safe haven."

"Church buildings should be open to anyone who needs to find shelter, whether physical or spiritual," Julie agreed.

Frank shrugged, but his expression remained doubtful. "You're just asking for trouble. When something gets stolen or the building is vandalized, don't say I didn't warn you."

JULIE SET THE CLIPBOARD on the edge of the counter at the nurse's station. "Dr. Peterson changed a couple of Mr. Norman's meds to try to relieve his vomiting."

"I'll add the changes to his chart." Lily Chou, the

young first-year nurse at the desk, reached for the clipboard. "How's your mother doing?"

"She's going in for her first radiation Monday."

Lily studied her sympathetically. "How bad is it?"

Julie told her. Lily looked away, tapping her pencil against the clipboard.

"Doesn't sound so good."

"No. It doesn't." Julie managed to keep her voice flat, matter-of-fact. "I'm thinking about cutting back to part-time, just working on weekends. That way I could drive Mom to all her appointments and monitor her response to the treatments. The only problem is how we'd make it financially without my income."

"Have you talked to Dan?"

"Not yet, but I know he'll support whatever I decide to do."

Lily looked at her watch. "Hey, it's quitting time! Do you have to go straight home?"

"Not this evening. Dan is making calls at the hospital and nursing home, and then he has an administrative board meeting until late. And Mom wanted Amy to stay with them overnight while she's still feeling good."

"Do you want to see if we can get Angie to meet us at the soda shop? We could grab a bite to eat and have some girl talk."

Julie forced a smile. She didn't feel like being sociable today, but on the other hand, the thought of going home to an empty house didn't appeal to her either.

"Sounds good," she decided.

Lily called Angie at the daycare center, and they arranged to meet at the Vikings' Lair, three blocks north of the square and directly across the street from Shepherdsville High School, where all three of them had graduated. Angie was already parked outside when Julie and Lily drove up.

"I sure am glad you came up with this idea!" Angie exclaimed as she joined them. "I don't know what it was with the kids today, but they were supercharged. I need a break!"

They pushed through the chrome and glass double doors into the crowded shop. Built at the end of World War II, the one-story concrete-block building had immediately become a popular hangout. Named in honor of the Shepherdsville High School Vikings, its exterior was painted in the school colors, with royal blue trim and white walls. A glowing neon sign in the front window outlined a burly Viking in battle gear and declared the place to be the Vikings' Lair.

Inside, the shop still retained a worn 1950s style. Its faded turquoise and melon color scheme and scuffed grey and white Formica countertops rimmed with chrome were long past their prime. None of the kids who congregated there seemed to notice any deficiencies, however. The generous burgers piled high with lettuce, tomato, and onion; the thin, crispy fries and onion rings; and the thick malts were as good as they get, Julie reflected, her mouth already watering.

This afternoon, as usual, the restaurant was packed, primarily with high school students and other young adults like her and her friends, many of whom they knew from their school days. It took almost fifteen minutes for their favorite corner booth to become available.

Waiting in line by the front counter, Julie swayed to the rhythms of Diana Ross and the Supremes while breathing in the mingled aromas of grilling hamburgers and onions and the refreshing scents of ice cream and soda. To make the time pass more quickly, the three of them called greetings and waved to acquaintances across the room.

Once they were seated and while they waited for their orders to be delivered, their conversation drifted to their high school years. Part of the same loosely-knit group of girls, Julie and Angie had been casual friends. After graduation, when their circle had split up due to marriages, new babies, and careers, the two of them had discovered unexpected mutual interests.

Newly married, Dan and Julie had moved into the same neighborhood and only a couple of blocks from where Terry and Angie lived. Their marriages, careers, and babies, far from separating them, had drawn them closer together.

Lily had graduated three years behind them. After graduating from nursing school the previous year, she had taken a position at the Shepherdsville clinic, where her lively personality had quickly endeared her to Julie and later to Angie as well.

By the time the waitress finally arrived to plunk plates and drinks onto the table, Julie's stomach was growling. And judging by the way her friends attacked their food, she concluded they were as hungry as she was.

Lily took a long drink of strawberry milkshake, then poked at the thick, pink liquid with her straw. "I always envied you older girls big time—your clothes, the way you did your hair and your makeup, your boyfriends. I never felt like I fit in. My mom is from the old country. She wouldn't let me dress in the modern styles or wear makeup. If she'd had her way, I would have worn traditional Chinese dress to school! And if I'd ever tried to date an American guy, she would have locked me in my room till I was dead." She rolled her eyes and took a bite of her cheeseburger. "Not that any of them were interested," she mumbled through a mouthful of food.

Julie and Angie exchanged astonished glances. "Oh, come on! You must have had guys lining up to ask you out," Julie protested. "You're gorgeous! Talk about envy—I always envied your long, straight, black hair and your beautiful eyes."

"Uh-huh." Angie nodded in agreement as she helped herself to one of Julie's onion rings. "You have that exotic look guys can't resist. If they didn't ask you out, it's because your mama scared 'em off," she concluded, waving the remnant of onion ring for emphasis.

Lily regarded Angie with raised eyebrows. "You've got to be kidding. Asians aren't exactly the ideal of beauty here in Minnesota. I mean, you both have round eyes. You're statuesque with an awesome figure, and Julie has pale skin and curly, strawberry blond hair—"

"Yeah. She's a regular Debbie Reynolds." Angie assessed Julie through narrowed eyes.

Julie wrinkled her nose "Oh, please—I'm trying to eat! You're going to make me lose my dinner. Besides, I always thought I looked more like Ann-Margret."

Angie guffawed. "Get over it, girl! Of course, you *were* homecoming queen our senior year. You'll notice they never chose a black girl."

"You're the one who should have won." Julie sucked up the last drop of her cola. "You could be a model. But they did elect you head cheerleader. I couldn't even get on the squad."

"Well, sure. You know—blacks, athletics. That's why Terry went out for basketball."

Julie gave her a withering look. "He's tall. Not to mention incredibly talented."

"That too." Angie returned a smug smile.

Scrutinizing Julie, Lily decided, "I don't think she looks anything like Debbie Reynolds."

"I meant she's cute like that."

"More like Annette Funicello, but, you know—whiter."

"Exactly!"

Angie stuck out her hand. Laughing, Lily smacked her palm against Angie's.

"Well, excuse me!" Julie objected in mock outrage.

Angie reached over to pat her arm. "It's okay. You can't help it that you were born that way. We don't hold it against you."

The three of them burst into hysterical giggles. It took several minutes before they could meet each other's eyes without doubling up all over again.

Dabbing at her eyes with her napkin, Lily sobered. "Another thing I always envied was your guys. I mean, you and Terry were so tight from the beginning, Angie, and it was obvious you were made for each other. And Julie was dating the captain of the football team."

Julie giggled again. "Well, look how that turned out. He ditched me for Sandra Lamont."

Angie rolled her eyes. "And weren't they a match made in heaven? They got married the minute they graduated, had a baby six months later—and divorced the same year."

"Marry in haste, repent at leisure," quoted Julie.

"You have a wonderful husband," Lily insisted.

"I really do, but I didn't marry in haste. Dan's too deliberate for that." Julie studied her friend for a moment. "I don't know Sam very well, but he seems like a groovy guy. Are you two having problems?"

Tears welled up in Lily's eyes. Her expression reflecting concern, Angie reached over to give her a hug.

Lily blinked away her tears and made a dismissive gesture. "Oh, it's probably just the same things every married couple goes through after the honeymoon wears off. I thought this was going to be so perfect—after all, Sam's Chinese American too, so he ought to understand how I feel about things. Mom and Dad were ecstatic when we got married, and I guess I thought we'd live happily ever after. But Sam's such a perfectionist, and he has this old-world ideal of a woman's role. He wants the apartment spotless and dinner on the table the minute he gets home."

"But you work too, and at the end of the day you're as tired as he is," Angie pointed out.

"You think?" Lily shrugged off her sarcastic words. "Sam works really long hours, so I do understand how he feels. He's been under a lot of stress since he's gotten into handling commercial real estate. He's juggling this huge deal with a developer who wants to build a new shopping center at the edge of town. Sam's trying to arrange everything so he can manage the center if the deal goes through. There's a lot of money at stake."

"Well, if he has any problem understanding how stressful your job is, I can clue him in." Indignant, Julie tore the edge of her napkin into jagged points.

Lily sighed. "He wouldn't listen. He sure can be stubborn. He wants everything to be his way—"

"And you want everything to be your way." Julie gave her a wry look.

"It feels as if we're working against each other instead of together," Lily admitted.

"Your marriage looks perfect from the outside," Angie said, "and I imagine so do ours. The truth is it's never perfect on the inside. It's a struggle to live with another person—especially if that other person has been away as much as Terry has been. And when he finally does come home, he wakes up every night screaming and tearing up the bed with nightmares. It's like there's a stranger living inside my husband, and I can't reach him or understand where he's hurting because he won't talk about all these awful things he went through."

She stopped abruptly and stared down at her plate, frowning. A hard, tight lump in her throat, Julie put her hand over her friend's.

Angie looked up and forced a smile. "Maybe it's worse for us women. We want to mother our man just like we do our kids, organize their lives, tell them what to do, straighten them out. It's a shock when they act like adults who have the right to make their own decisions and do what they want to do."

"Amen!" Julie agreed. "I have to keep reminding myself that just because I want things done a certain way doesn't mean that's necessarily the only way or even the right way to do it. A lot of times I have to bite my tongue and let Dan do things his way.

"For example, he loves to cook, and he's really good at it. Most of the time he has dinner ready or at least started by the time I get home. But I swear the man uses every dish and pot in the kitchen! By the time he's done, he has the sink piled high and the counters covered with mess."

Angie and Lily giggled, nodding in understanding. Julie couldn't help smiling.

"It makes me crazy, but there's a hot meal on the table that I didn't have to cook. And afterward we work together to clean things up, which gives us time to talk. He couldn't be a better father either. So I guess it just depends on your perspective."

"I know you're right," Lily said in a subdued voice. "I know he doesn't mean to, but Sam can be so thoughtless sometimes. He'll make a remark that really hurts my feelings, then he'll say he was only joking and I'm too sensitive."

"He isn't abusive, is he?" Angie asked, alarm reflecting on her features.

"Oh, no." Lily hesitated. "It's just that . . . sometimes I wonder if he really still loves me."

They talked about the situation for a few minutes longer. Both Julie and Angie assured Lily that they would pray for her and Sam and that any time she needed to talk, they would be glad to listen. But Julie had the feeling that, although Lily appeared to feel better for having confided in them, she and Angie hadn't really offered their friend much practical help.

She knew that Lily and Sam attended a small Chinese church near their apartment on the other side of town. Somehow advising Lily to study what the Bible had to say about marriage and then put its principles into practice sounded presumptuous.

Evidently Lily had shared all she wanted to about her marriage for the time being. Changing the subject, she asked whether Julie had written Mike yet about the results of her mother's tests.

Julie dissected the remnants of her cheeseburger with her fork. "I tried to start a letter, but I don't know what to say. Since Mom first got sick, I've always told Mike the truth about what's going on, but this time it feels different. Mike takes his responsibilities so seriously, and he's committed to staying with his buddies. Plus, from his letter and from what Terry told us, he's so in love with Thi Nhuong and so determined to marry her that I can't believe he'd be able to leave her even if he could get permission to come home. On the other side, he and Mom have always had a special bond. If she . . . if she doesn't get well, it's going to tear him apart.

"So how do I write a letter like that?" she concluded.

"You start by telling Mike about your dad's being baptized," Angie suggested. "Maybe that will break through his defenses."

"Sure. And mention Dan's doubts about it." Seeing Lily's questioning look, Julie related Dan's concerns.

Lily gave a short laugh. "I know all about trying to make bargains with God, even though I know it doesn't work that way."

"Why *doesn't* it work that way?" Julie demanded, frustrated. "Why *don't* we have a God who always answers our prayers, especially if it concerns the welfare of someone we love, especially someone who also happens to be a believer?"

Angie finished off her last bite of hamburger. "God does answer our prayers. It's just not always the answer we want."

"How can it be God's will for anyone to suffer and die with a terrible disease like cancer?" Julie shot back.

"I guess if we knew the answer to that one, we'd be God," ventured Lily.

Angie stirred the puddle of catsup on her plate with a wilted French fry. "If the Lord always did what we want, then wouldn't we be in control, not him? I know—I feel the same way you do, but also I know I wouldn't make a very good god."

Julie stared down at her plate. "I keep telling myself all the same things. But there are times, especially in the middle of the night, when none of it makes any sense, and there don't seem to be any answers . . . and it's really hard to keep on trusting."

All of them were silent for several moments, picking absently at their food. Finally Lily asked, "What about Thi Nhuong? Are you going to tell Mike about your dad's reaction to his letter?"

Julie flinched. "I'm going to have to warn him. He has to know. There's no way Dad is ever going to accept his son marrying a Vietnamese woman—and a Buddhist at that."

THE NEXT DAY DAN was working on his sermon when he was interrupted by a knock at the back door. Pulling off his glasses, he rubbed his eyes and pushed aside the commentary he had been studying. The knock was repeated, followed by a low woof.

Getting up reluctantly, he went into the kitchen. Judge was standing at the back door, his tail gently waving. Surprised to see Terry on the step outside, Dan pulled the door open and motioned him inside, then led the way through the kitchen into his study.

"Have a seat." He gestured toward the easy chair in front of his desk. "What's up?"

Folding his tall form into the chair, Terry ruffled Judge's head before returning Dan's inquiring gaze with a rueful smile. "I met with the dean at the seminary this morning. He doesn't think I'll have any problem being accepted for next fall. So I went ahead and applied."

Dan pounded him on the back. "That's great news! I take it you've been doing some praying about our conversation last week."

"You put me under conviction, brother. I keep trying to

weasel out of it, but every sign I've asked for has been to move ahead. When I found out Frank was going to be baptized after all these years, I knew the Lord was trying to tell me something. I hate to admit it, but it sure felt good to help you baptize him and those kids Sunday."

Dan leaned back against the edge of the desk. "I'm glad he finally made the decision."

Terry studied him, frowning. "You don't sound as happy about it as I expected you to."

"I guess I'm not so sure about Frank's motives. He's convinced that the Lord is going to heal Maggie, and he wants to show his gratitude. I hope he's right about Maggie being healed, but I've got to wonder if he's trying to make a deal with God."

"He wouldn't be the first one. I saw that a lot in Nam. But don't you think God is faithful when we make a commitment even if it's for the wrong reasons?"

Absently Dan rearranged the items beside him on the desk. "I believe the Lord is faithful. But I've also seen people make a shallow commitment like that, only to fall away when things don't turn out the way they want them to. Remember the parable of the sower and the seed?"

"It takes a long time and some hard experiences for most of us to understand that faith isn't for the times when life is great and everything is going our way," Terry returned, his tone somber. "It's for the times when we're up against the wall and there aren't any answers, when it feels like God's gone AWOL and is nowhere to be found—or at least he isn't talking to us."

"I've gone through a time or two like that myself," Dan admitted with a sigh. "The only way I got through it was to keep reminding myself of all the things God did for me in the past and for people I knew. Then I made a deliberate decision to hang onto hope and trust in God's ultimate goodness, no matter how bleak the situation looked. It feels like it doesn't make sense, but in the end, I came out of it stronger, even those times when I didn't get an answer."

"Do we ever really get the answers this side of heaven?" Terry scoffed.

Dan leaned toward him, the line of his body tense. "I've come to believe that this is what God wants from us, my friend. In this life we're going to suffer trials and tribulations—that's a given. But will the Lord find us faithful when he returns? There's the test. The Son of God was faithful even to the cross. He didn't get any answers when he was hanging there, but he didn't walk away from the time of testing even though he had the power to do it. He went all the way because he loves us. Do we love him that much?"

"I understand that, man." Terry took a deep breath. "I feel like I've been to hell and back already. But I know I have to go all the way no matter where it leads."

Dan reached out to clasp his hand. "You're going to make one terrific youth minister."

Terry's response was a sober one. "I'm going to give it my best shot, but I'm still wandering in the wilderness. A war like this one lays your soul waste. Just keep praying that the Lord will lead me back home again."

"He's led you this far," Dan reminded him, "and I've never known him to abandon one of his children."

CHAPTER SIX

LATER THAT WEEK before her mother's first radiation treatment, Julie finally forced herself to write a letter to Mike, a task she had dreaded since learning the test results. She could bring herself to give only a general explanation, writing that although the cancer had spread, the mass was small, and the doctor was confident it would respond to radiation.

Next she shared details of their father's baptism, wondering what Mike's reaction would be. Once he reached teenage, he had developed their father's indifference to attending worship services, and none of their mother's efforts to change his mind had any effect. In the hope that the news might get through Mike's defenses, she decided not to bring up Dan's reservations about their father's motives.

Choosing the words with care, she went on to describe their father's response to Mike's last letter. *You need to understand that Dad will likely react very badly if you marry Thi Nhuong,* she cautioned. *You know how he feels about Asians, and he's made it clear he has no intention of changing his mind. And I have to be honest. Mom and Dan and I are also concerned about the cultural differences between the two of you, especially the fact that Thi Nhuong is a Buddhist. I know you don't claim to be a believer now, but if that should change in the future, it could cause a serious rift between the two of you.*

However, if you're still determined to marry her, you know we'll welcome her and make her feel a part of our family. We love you, and we will love and accept whoever you choose to marry.

She concluded the letter and sealed the envelope with a tight feeling in the middle of her chest.

Off and on during that week she and Dan discussed the possibility of her cutting back to working only on weekends. "It's going to be too stressful for you to work part-time and care for Mom and Amy too," he insisted. "I want you to take a leave of absence. We'll find a way to get by on my salary until she's finished with the radiation and chemo and gets her strength back."

At last Julie agreed to the wisdom of his arguments and made arrangements to take time off work indefinitely. Her father, however, solved the problem of their finances.

"I'll pay you whatever it would cost to employ a home health nurse," he insisted. "The peace of mind it'll give your mother and me to have you oversee her care is well worth the price."

After some persuasion on his part, strongly seconded by her mother, Julie and Dan gratefully gave in.

MAGGIE'S FIRST APPOINTMENT was on Monday. At the hospital the technicians used markers to draw across her abdomen and back a series of dots, which they used to align her body for the thirty-second radiation treatment. She had been tense and anxious before the appointment, but the technicians' jokes and good-humored chatter quickly put her at ease, and she was soon on her way home with Julie.

After several more treatments, however, nausea began to overwhelm her. The smell and even the sight of food made her sick to her stomach, and when she forced herself to eat, she often could not keep the food down. She discovered that Julie's suggestion to take medication for the nausea as soon as they arrived home and then lie down for a long nap made the discomfort more bearable.

They settled into a routine. Leaving at six o'clock each weekday morning, Julie drove her into Minneapolis for her appointment and then brought her home. Later in the afternoon either Olivia or one of the women from church would come to relieve Julie until Frank arrived home from work.

To soothe Maggie's nausea, they had tea and toast ready the minute she got up from her nap. They prepared soothing vegetable or chicken broth or mild soups for her dinner and coaxed her to eat as much as she could.

Every day neighbors and friends from church dropped by casseroles, vegetable and meat dishes, breads, salads, and innumerable desserts. By the end of the first week they had so much food that Julie took much of it home to freeze and save for later.

Maggie was grateful for everyone's thoughtfulness, but she had to stay out of the kitchen. The aroma of those wonderful homemade dishes made her feel like throwing up. And at times all the attention made her feel worse instead of better. It was a daily reminder of how drastically her life had changed in less than a year—and of how ill she really was.

She and Frank had planned a cruise to Mexico to celebrate their twenty-fifth anniversary on March 21. But as the date neared, she felt so unwell that Frank reluctantly canceled their reservations.

"We'll go next year when you're well again and can really enjoy it," he promised, holding her tightly. He bent to kiss her. "And then we're going to throw a celebration no one will ever forget."

On days when Amy didn't have nursery school and Dan's appointments made it impossible for him to stay home with her, Julie brought her along to the hospital. Maggie was pleased and touched at how well the small child adjusted to the change in routine and how seriously she took "helping Grandma get better." When Amy ran to bring her medicine or a glass of water, tucked Maggie into bed and kissed her lovingly on the cheek, announcing, "I'm a nurse, just like Mommy!" Maggie's heart melted, and for that moment her misery seemed more endurable.

In spite of all their efforts, however, she could feel her energy steadily ebbing. With Julie in charge of the children's Easter pageant and no chemo scheduled on the weekends, Maggie was determined to go. She felt well enough to not only attend worship on Easter Sunday but also to help Julie and the other teachers with the children, in spite of Frank's concern. But by the time she got home, she was so weak and breathless she was forced to spend the rest of the day in bed.

It became an effort for her to get up in the mornings. Her bladder began to burn constantly as a result of the abdominal radiation. But to her surprise, her spirits revived from the initial depression she had experienced on learning the test results. As her physical discomfort increased, she felt her faith and determination grow proportionately stronger.

On the drive to and from the hospital, she and Julie talked and laughed, made plans for the summer, and often sang their favorite hymns, taking comfort in the timeless words. She was especially touched that Frank was even more attentive to her needs then usual. He was unfailingly patient with her constant exhaustion and nausea. And to her amazement, he insisted on helping Julie with the house cleaning and even did the laundry.

He regularly brought Maggie bouquets of her favorite coral roses. He carried her to bed when she was too out of breath to climb the stairs and checked on her frequently throughout the night. He made sure she had whatever she needed or wanted until Maggie began to be careful about expressing a wish for anything for fear he would rush out and buy it.

Frank kept his promise to attend church too. Each Sunday found him seated in the pew beside her, paying close attention to the sermon. He began to read a passage from the Bible and to pray with her each morning before leaving for work and again at night before going to bed. For the first time in their relationship, they talked about deep spiritual matters.

In spite of the seriousness of her illness, Maggie discovered that she had never been so happy. "If it took my cancer to bring Frank to faith," she told Julie, "then every bit of what I'm going through is worth it."

DURING THE LAST WEEK OF MARCH, halfway through her mother's third week of radiation, Julie arrived home to find a letter from Mike in the box with the rest of the mail. Eagerly she tore open the airmail envelope and spread out the thin sheets on the kitchen table so Dan could read along with her.

March 18, 1967

Dear Jules,

I just got your letter. Thanks for the honest report on Mom's condition. Dad letter didn't give any details, just said she was doing fine and that the Lord promised him she's going to be healed. I suppose he wants to spare me, but I appreciate your telling me the truth.

I hate it that I'm so far away and can't do anything to help out. I know—what could I do if I were there? But at least it'd make me feel better. It's really scary thinking that Mom's going through stuff I don't even know about until after it's over.

I've got to hurry this up because I've only got a few more minutes before today's post goes out. Before I sign off, I just want to let you know that congratulations are in order! Thi Nhuong and I got married a couple of weeks ago while I was on a short leave. An old priest at the local mission married us, and we had a couple of nights together at her pad in town before I had to report back to camp. We're keeping it a secret—only my closest buddies know about it so far. I don't know if this would be legal stateside, but right now I don't care. We can always have Dan marry us again when we get home if there's any doubt about it.

The worst thing is that this makes every separation even harder. Usually Thi Nhuong's very tough. She always has an encouraging word and a smile for me when I have to go. But a couple of days ago she broke down, and I realized for the first time how hard it is for her and how much it scares her every time I leave. She's lost so much in her life that I guess it terrifies her to think that the happiness we've found together might be taken away too. So I try to be really savvy about every move I make so I'll make it back to her again.

I promise I will write Mom and Dad in the next few days and tell them about our marriage. If you go ahead and tell Mom now, please make sure Dad doesn't find out before I write them. I'll try to break it as easy as I can. I appreciate your warnings about his reaction, but even if he's mad for a while, I know once he meets Thi Nhuong he won't be able to resist her for long. She's just that special.

Have I told you how much your letters mean to me, Sis? When we get in from an operation the first thing we all do is check to see if there's any mail. It's like Christmas morning when we get a letter.

So keep on writing. And give my love to the folks and to Dan and Amy.

Love you, Jules—
Mike

Julie brushed away a tear and leaned against Dan's shoulder. "My baby brother's gone and gotten married."

She could feel his dismay as his arm tightened around her. "I hope he's right about your dad. I just have this sinking feeling that it isn't going to be as easy as Mike's hoping it will be."

Julie nodded as she tried to swallow the lump in her throat. "I know you're right. I'd better warn Mom to be prepared for the worst."

THAT SATURDAY WHEN FRANK brought in the mail, he found Mike's letter. He waited to open it until Maggie got up from her nap, knowing she would want to be the first to read it. Each letter they received from Mike was a relief, a cause for celebration. Their son was still all right, still alive. His breath constricted, he focused on Maggie's trembling hands as she tore the envelope open.

March 20, 1967

Dear Mom and Dad,

When I got your letter, Dad, and then Julie's, I admit I was really worried to hear that Mom's cancer has spread. But it sounds as if the doctors have everything under control and that the radiation will do some good. Please keep me updated and know that I wish with all my heart that I could be there with you to help out in any way possible.

Now I have some good news I want to share with you. It's really the best, and I'm hoping you'll be as thrilled as I am! You remember me telling you a little about the orphan I met, Thi Nhuong? We've gotten to know each other very well during the past couple of months. Over the past several weeks it's become clear to me that she's the best thing that's ever come into my life, and I want to share the rest of it with her. Best of all, she feels the same way too, and I actually managed to talk her into marrying me!

Dad, I know how you feel about Orientals, and I don't blame you. From my own experience I can guess what you went through in the war. Seeing that kind of brutality first-hand can really turn you against people. But not all of them are like that, and Thi Nhuong is the most special person I've ever met. I'm hoping that when you get to know her, you'll love her too and see what a good influence she has had on my life.

I grew up with your example before me of what a marriage is supposed to be, and I've found that same relationship with Thi Nhuong. Naturally, there are differences of culture and religion. Thi Nhuong was raised Buddhist, but religion isn't a big deal to her or to me, as you know. And compared to what we have in common and what we feel for each other, there isn't anything we can't overcome. Just being with her has given me a whole new reason for living.

Not waiting for Maggie to read the rest, Frank jerked the letter out of her hand and crumpled it into a ball, his face livid.

"Frank, give this a chance. Maybe it was the Lord's will to bring them together—

"You think it's God's will for our son to marry a *Buddhist?*" he demanded, incredulous. "We're Christians, Maggie, and Mike's supposed to marry one of his own. Orientals have nothing in common with us. They're barbarians!"

None of Maggie's protests or attempts at reason could break through his rage. For the first time in their entire relationship, they could find no compromise, not even any point of toleration in their disagreement.

"As far as I'm concerned, if Mike marries a Vietnamese, he's dead to me," he ground out through gritted teeth.

"If you truly love your son, you'll accept the decisions he makes, regardless of whether you agree with them or not," Maggie countered, the words shaking with her anguish.

"If he really has married that girl, then I no longer have a son. I don't ever want to hear his name again—or hers!"

"Oh, Frank, you're breaking my heart." Weeping, Maggie turned away, her hand pressed over her mouth.

But he did not hear her sobs or her footfalls as she retreated upstairs. His agony and his anger blotted out everything except the stark and brutal images of that long-ago war and, superimposed over them, TV news footage of the battles that were even now raging halfway around the world.

His movements mechanical, he groped into the den, still carrying Mike's balled-up letter, and sat down heavily in the chair behind the desk. He laid the crumpled sheets on its surface and pulled open the center drawer.

He took out the manila envelope he'd kept for years. Inside was the creased and yellowed photograph given him by a soldier who had survived the prisoner-of-war camp where Frank's older brother, Bobby, had died a brutal death.

The image showed a group of men—unidentifiable as American soldiers had it not been for the faded handwriting on the back—captured in film on the day they had been liberated. They stood just inside the prison camp's gate. Or, rather, they huddled against the iron bars and against each other as if the slightest breeze would blow them to the ground.

Each one was hardly more than a skeleton. They were clothed in tattered rags caked with unimaginable filth. It was difficult to believe these were living creatures, much less men, and yet tentative smiles contorted their gaunt faces as though for the first time they allowed themselves to hope that the hell they had endured for three years could finally be over.

Oddly, at that moment in Frank's head reverberated the story he had read the night before of Ezekiel standing in the valley of dry bones, staring at heaps of disconnected, parched remnants of skeletons. "Can these bones live?" the Lord God had demanded of the prophet.

Closing his eyes, Frank shook his head. It was too late for life to rise from the ashes of the past.

He dropped the photograph as though it burned him, grabbed his pen and pulled several sheets of writing paper out of the drawer. His hands shaking, he began to write, fiercely jabbing the pen against the paper with the intensity of his emotion.

Mike,

I'm not going to mince words. I was very disappointed —disgusted is more like it—to receive your letter. What were you thinking to throw us a curve ball like this with your mother so sick? I'll be surprised if this doesn't put her in her grave. But then, you never seem to be able to put others ahead of yourself, do you?

I don't know what you think you're doing or even if you're thinking at all. It's beyond me why a son of mine would want to get involved with—much less marry—one of the enemies of our country and of the Christian religion. But it's your life. And knowing you, you'll do whatever you please and go on your merry way without any consideration for the people you're hurting.

Just don't expect me to bankroll this mistake. If you decide to grow up and change your mind, I'll welcome you home. But if you go ahead and marry that girl, you're both on your own. As far as I'm concerned, you might as well stay over there with the rest of those gooks, since you plan on becoming one of them. I don't ever need to see you again.

He signed his name in full at the bottom of the letter, creased the page into thirds, and shoved it into an envelope. Not letting himself think about what he was doing, he scribbled Mike's APO address on the letter and added postage. Then, without stopping to put on a coat, he carried it out to the mailbox on the corner of the street.

CHAPTER 7

JULIE REACHED TO SQUEEZE Olivia's hand. It was almost midnight. The three of them sat together around the kitchen table. The golden glow from the overhead fixture threw shadows into the corners of the room and reflected in the black rectangles of the breakfast nook's tall windows behind the partially drawn curtains. The silence was broken only by the gusting wind sighing through the row of pines behind the house.

Dan and Julie had been on their way upstairs to bed when they were stopped by a knock at the door. Olivia stood on the porch outside, and they gathered her out of the cold and into their arms. For some time she stood with them just inside the door, waging a futile battle to fight back the wrenching sobs that shook her body.

"We've been so preoccupied with Mom's treatments," Julie apologized now, "though I haven't wanted to pry either. I just want you to know that we've been praying for you too, and for Rob. What happened? Have you heard from him?"

Olivia took a sip of hot coffee to steady herself, set down the cup and pushed it away. "He just called. He sounded like he was high. He said he got a divorce yesterday in Reno and that I'll get the papers in a few days. It's all over. Just like that."

She stopped, then went on raggedly, "I no sooner than hung up the phone when my brother Tony called. He lives in Walnut Creek, and he went into San Francisco this morning to try to find Rob and talk some sense into him. Tony finally tracked him down at a rundown old apartment above a drug paraphernalia shop. This woman he's living with was there too . . . and she's pregnant."

Through her sobs, she continued, "They were both stoned, strung out on heroin, and in bad shape. Tony said it's a good thing he got the divorce, and I need to forget all about him."

Again she broke down. Julie scooted her chair closer so she could put her arms around her. Olivia laid her head on Julie's shoulder and wept.

"Oh, Livy. I'm so sorry."

"I always wanted a baby." Olivia's voice was muffled by sobs. "Rob insisted he didn't, so I kept telling myself that we were just fine, that it didn't matter. But it did. And now that woman is going to have his baby."

Dan handed her a tissue. "Livy, I know it's hard to keep on trusting the Lord when something this bad happens. But that's what our faith is for. God is still in control, and he can bring good out of the worst circumstances. Even out of this."

Straightening, Olivia nodded. She brushed back her hair and dabbed at her tears.

"I keep telling myself that." She laughed shakily. "And I keep thinking maybe I could have done more to make him happy—but what? I don't know what went wrong! I prayed and prayed he would come back . . . and I tried to have faith that he would ... but now what do I do? Do I keep on praying and waiting for him to come back. What if he never does?"

Dan hesitated before saying gently, "Livy, Paul says in First Corinthians that if the unbelieving partner in a marriage chooses to leave, the believing partner should allow him to go, that the believer is not bound in such circumstances. We're called to live in peace with one another, and there can be no peace when two people are unequally yoked."

For a long moment Olivia remained silent, staring down into the black depths of her coffee cup. When she looked up, tears welled in her expressive brown eyes.

"Thank you," she whispered, her voice breaking. Taking a shaky breath, she added, "Every time Rob called, I told him that no matter what he's done, I still love him and I want us to be reconciled, that I am willing to make any changes necessary to restore our relationship. But he refused to listen."

Julie got up to refill each of their cups, then returned to her seat. "If he isn't willing, then he's responsible for his attitude, not you. You can't change another person."

"God doesn't force his children to do what is right," Dan agreed. "It has to be our own free choice. There isn't any way you can make Rob be the husband to you that he should be."

Julie blinked back tears. "No matter how much it hurts, you have to accept that and move on. You're God's child, and God has a perfect plan for you, with or without Rob."

Sitting together in the partially darkened kitchen, they found each other's hands, instinctively began to pray, Julie first, then Olivia, and at last Dan. Of one accord they pleaded for Rob's healing and salvation and for that of the woman he was living with, and for their baby's welfare. With aching hearts they committed Olivia's future to the Lord, asking that his perfect will for his child would be done, that she would find forgiveness wherever she had been at fault and healing from the pain of this broken relationship, and that God's peace would indwell her in the midst of the storm.

For that moment, peace and trusting surrender embraced each of them like tangible, loving arms.

FEELING PHYSICALLY ILL, Julie sat down at Dan's desk and searched through the drawers until she found writing paper. For some time it seemed impossible to begin. She stared blankly out the window, too distraught to find the words she needed to say.

It was Sunday afternoon. A couple of hours earlier her mother had come over to talk to her and Dan, more upset that Julie had ever seen her. Returning home after church, she had told Frank that regardless of his attitude toward Mike's marriage, she was going to write to Mike and give him her blessing. His response had been to blurt out the details of the letter he had secretly sent Mike and to forbid her to write to him.

They had argued for the better part of an hour before she had rushed out of the house and over to Julie and Dan's home.

Trembling with shock and anger, she told Julie, "I don't know if I can live with your father after this. I still love him, and I will until the day I die. I know he's incapable of being rational about this because of what he went through during the war. But how can I forgive him for hurting our son this way?"

Julie heard her out, stunned. She had expected her father to react strongly to the news of Mike's marriage, but to disown his son in such harsh terms—to cut off her beloved little brother so completely—she had not believed him capable of that. She was so dismayed she could hardly speak.

"You can't cut Frank off now, Maggie," Dan had intervened forcefully. "He needs you more than ever—needs all of us. We have to forgive him even for this and trust God to change his heart and bring reconciliation between him and Mike."

Julie wrung her hands. "How can we act as if nothing happened? I love Daddy too, but he's gone too far."

"We have an opportunity to model God's love and forgiveness to your father," Dan answered. "The more anger we direct at him, the more likely he is to dig in his heels. But if we approach this with a gentle spirit and show him we love him no matter what, just as we love Mike—and that God loves him too—it's got to soften his heart in the end.

"And even if it doesn't," he continued, turning to Maggie, "right now your condition is too fragile for you to hold onto anger. You need to concentrate all your energies on getting well. Keeping your emotions stirred up over this isn't going to do you any good."

It had taken considerable discussion before Julie and her mother had been able to put aside their anger sufficiently that they could see the wisdom of Dan's counsel. With Julie's promise to write Mike immediately, Maggie had gone home, quietly determined to love Frank into a change of heart.

At last Julie forced herself to pick up Dan's pen.

April 6, 1967

Dear Mike,

I suppose by the time you get this letter you'll have received the one from Dad. He told Mom about his letter this afternoon, and she just told us. Mom pleaded with him to change his mind, but he refused. In fact, he's forbidden her to write to you.

After talking it over with her, Dan and I feel that she is too weak to fight him on this. She needs to concentrate on getting through these treatments and getting well. So for the time being she'll keep in touch with you through my letters, and all of us will be praying mightily for the Lord to convict Dad and change his heart.

Little brother, I want to apologize for what Dad's done. You must be so incredibly hurt, and I can't begin to imagine what Thi Nhuong must think of us. But please don't believe that either Mom or Dan or I agree with a single word he wrote.

I keep telling myself that something really horrible must have happened to him during the war to make him act this way, though that doesn't excuse his actions. I don't know how I'm going to be able to even speak to him now. The only thing I can do is to remind myself that he is still our father, even though he's terribly wrong on this issue. And if God can forgive him, then we have to also.

Mom and Dan and Amy and I love you so much. So does Dad, in spite of the fact that he's denying it right now. If he didn't care so much, he wouldn't have reacted so strongly.

We know we're going to love Thi Nhuong, and we're praying for the day you can bring her safely home. If Dad still refuses to see you, you have a home with Dan and me. Dan said to tell you that we have an extra bedroom, and we would be thrilled if the two of you would stay with us until you get settled in a job and can afford a place of your own. We're so excited at the thought of having a new sister, and Amy is just ecstatic. She's convinced Thi Nhuong is the present you're bringing her when you come home!

So please, please don't be discouraged. Just remember, you and Thi Nhuong have a family that loves you and longs for you to be with us. Sometimes families go through really unhappy times, but I know we'll get through this and be closer than ever.

Give Thi Nhuong a hug and kiss from us. Tell her we already love her with all our hearts. Kisses and hugs to you too, little brother. Please be careful when you're out on an operation, and know that we're all praying for you.

Feeling miserable, she signed the letter and addressed the envelope, hoping that her words would help to ease Mike's pain a little. Again she thought about their meeting with Olivia just the night before. What blessed peace had bathed their hearts like a healing ointment as they prayed. But so quickly turmoil was once more tearing apart the confidence she ought to feel in God's power to carry his children through every crisis.

At times she felt so frustrated. She was a pastor's wife, after all, involved in her own ministries in the church. She was supposed to be an example to others. Still she struggled with issues of faith and trust. Each time a new trial arose, she found herself questioning God's ability to care for her and her loved ones just as she had during the previous time of testing.

Would she ever learn to simply rest in quiet trust no matter the situation? She needed only to focus on the many prayers God had answered in the past and trust the future to him, she reminded herself. Just like Peter obeying Jesus' summons to come to him across the tumultuous water, she needed to keep her eyes on her Savior's face and not on the heaving waves and the raging winds.

How much easier that was to say than to do!

With a sigh, she folded the letter into the envelope, sealed it, and then went into the kitchen to start dinner.

THE NEXT TO THE LAST WEEK of April, as the days lengthened and spring put forth tentative bloom, Maggie finished her course of radiation. Frank went with her for the last treatment and for the tests the following week that showed that the tumor had shrunk significantly.

"We're going to schedule you for nine courses of chemotherapy using a promising new experimental drug,"

Dr. Radnor told her. "One course will be given every three weeks. You'll have some unpleasant side effects, but this drug has shown excellent results in clinical trials. I expect you to be cancer-free when we finish."

"What did I tell you?" Frank exulted when they left the office. "God promised to heal you, and he's doing it!"

As the cool winds and chilly rains of April gave way to May's southerly breezes and serene azure skies, Maggie went in for her first round of chemo with a renewed sense of hope and resolve. Because of the residual effects of the radiation, however, this time the drugs took an even greater toll on her body than before.

She was ill for days, and her emotions fluctuated like a roller coaster, varying between anger, hopelessness, confidence, and panic. Staring at her once trim and healthy body in the mirror, she told Julie, "I hate what the radiation and drugs are doing to me! Why does it have to be so bad? I just want this to be over."

"I know it's awful, but you just have to get through it, Mom," Julie countered. "Once you're well again, this will all have been worth it. Keep that thought in your mind."

Nausea, coupled with numbness in her arms and legs due to the radiation, was hard enough for Maggie to bear. But she hated most of all that the thick chestnut hair that had finally grown long enough to begin curling attractively all over her head once more began to come off in patches, then clumps. Her eyebrows, eyelashes, all the hair on her body began to fall out.

The lack of any word from Mike heightened her anxiety. Since February several Army units, including Mike's, had been involved in battles along the Cambodian border. Then in April Marine units had begun an assault on two hills in the mountainous region near the Demilitarized Zone around Khe Sanh. The news media were full of accounts of the various operations, and one hundred thousand protesters staged demonstrations in New York, another twenty thousand in San Francisco.

Every day Maggie, Julie, and Dan scanned the mail, fearing a telegram bringing the news that Mike had been wounded—or worse. Gradually dread replaced anxiety. They combed reports in the *Shepherdsville Star* for clues to when and where Mike's unit was fighting. Finally they wrote to him, echoing Julie's earlier letter.

FRANK NEVER TOLD THEM that a couple of weeks earlier he had received a letter from Mike at his office. He almost didn't read it. He wanted to rip it to shreds, unopened, and throw the pieces into the wastebasket. But he couldn't.

For a long time he stared at the envelope that bore his son's handwriting. Finally, setting his teeth, he tore it open and quickly scanned the contents. Against every resolve, he went back to the beginning and read it again, slowly, with uncertainty now, the words tearing through the carefully guarded barriers he had erected.

April 21, 1967

Dad,

I don't know how to answer your letter. It's clear you don't want an answer, but I can't simply let my father walk away from me without at least trying to reach out to you one more time. Because I love you. And I think, deep down inside, you still love me too, in spite of the hard things you wrote.

We've both been in battle, and we both know the bitterness and the hatred that can come from the brutal things we see human beings do to each other. I don't want any part of that anymore—not in my relationship with you, not in my relationship with anyone. I want to live in peace. I want all of us to live in peace together.

But I can't leave Thi Nhuong no matter how much you want me to. It isn't that I love her more than I love you and Mom. The love I have for her is different, but just as real, just as deep. She's the partner of my life, just as Mom is yours. The way you feel about Mom is the way I feel about Thi Nhuong.

Dad, you can curse me if that makes you feel better. You can turn your back on me and refuse to ever see me again. But from what I remember of the Bible you say you believe in, it claims God's love for us is unconditional. And so is my love for you.

Your son,
Mike

For agonizing moments Frank wavered. The ache to break down the barriers between them and clasp his boy to his chest came very close to overpowering the anger he had harbored for so long. Yet, as always, darker images inevitably blotted out the one of Mike's mischievous grin that always caught at his heart.

Gaunt, broken men leaning against the gate of a prisoner-of-war camp. Bobby covering the broken body of a comrade with his own, only to be bayoneted by an enemy whose features surely had been contorted in demonic glee.

The beep of the intercom on his phone startled him. His hand shaking, he jabbed the button.

"Yes?" he rasped.

The voice of his secretary, Susan, came across the wire. "Frank? Are you all right?"

"Yeah, fine. What is it?"

There was a pause before she answered. "Larry asked me to check with you. The team from the state is here, and they're all waiting in the conference room. Your meeting was scheduled for ten o'clock."

Feeling numb, Frank glanced at the clock on his desk. It was seven minutes past the hour. He prided himself on never being late for a meeting.

He cleared his throat. "I'll be right there."

He shoved back his chair and got to his feet, looked down at the letter he still held. With a raw, guttural sob, he instinctively clenched his hand into a fist, crumpling the thin pages into a tight ball. Striding out the door, he passed Susan without acknowledging her concerned look and went down the hall toward the conference room at the far end.

Before entering he made a quick detour into the restroom. Feeling as though it burned his flesh, he dropped the balled up letter into the wastebasket beside the sink.

Then he turned on the faucet full force and scrubbed his hands until he could no longer feel the sensation of the paper against his skin, as if hot water could erase the plea that echoed in his heart.

CHAPTER 8

"HEY, BROWN EYES. Is everything okay?"

Julie transferred her moody gaze from the landscape flowing by outside the windshield to Dan. It was shortly after eleven o'clock in the morning. They were in the Beetle, with Amy in the back seat, heading for Dan's parents' home just north of East Bethel, about forty miles northeast of Shepherdsville. Because all of them were involved in responsibilities at their own churches every Sunday, Dan, his siblings, and their families gathered at their parents' home the third Saturday of the month whenever possible.

Julie forced a smile. "I'm just feeling a little stressed out, that's all."

"We don't have to go if you don't want to."

She reached over to touch Dan's arm, and he took his hand off the steering wheel long enough to squeeze hers. "No, I want to go. You know I always love getting together with your family."

She sighed. "Honestly, right now it's a relief to spend some time in a normal environment. Oh, I know your family has had its share of crises, but for the moment all of them seem to have everything under control."

"I was afraid taking care of your mom was going to be too much of a strain for you. I know you have a lot of experience working with cases like this, but taking care of someone this close to you just makes it that much worse."

"Honey, I'd have to go through this with her anyway. If it was your mother, would you try to keep your distance—or would you want to be involved in every part of it?"

Dan glanced over at her, his forehead creased with concern. "Of course, you're right. I just worry about you."

"Knowing at least as much as the doctors do about what's going on will make it easier in the long run. So often we try to spare the patient and family by not telling them everything. But I'm convinced that actually makes it harder if your hopes are raised and then the patient doesn't recover. It's better to face the truth from the beginning."

She was silent for a moment. "Mom took care of me when she was all alone, when I was too little to take care of myself and Dad was off in the South Pacific," she said then. "No matter how hard this is for me, it's harder for her. I have to do whatever I can to help her make it through."

Dan stared down the road ahead of him. "Do you think she's going to die?"

The words were quietly spoken, without emotion. When Julie answered, however, she couldn't keep her voice from trembling.

"The odds are that she's not going to make it. But I know she's trying to fight this with everything she has, and I know God can do a miracle if it's his will."

"There are a lot of people praying for her. My mom told me the whole family is holding your folks and Mike up before the Lord every time they pray, and so are their churches."

Julie gave him a grateful look. "It makes a difference knowing they're praying for Mom—and for Mike and the situation with Dad too. The other day Dad mentioned to me how much it means to him that the church has been so supportive. He's really grateful for your folks' visits too.

"You were right. I can tell that the faithfulness of so many believers is softening his heart little by little. At least it's making him think about his attitude."

In a little more than forty-five minutes after leaving Shepherdsville, they turned into the driveway of the expansive white frame farmhouse owned by Niels and Anna Christensen. Its neatly manicured lawn shaded by hundred-year-old oaks, maples, and elms nestled amid gently rolling fields that stretched to the tree-dotted horizon.

No sooner had they rolled to a stop than several children varying in age from early elementary to teen swooped down the steps of the porch to greet them with cries of welcome. Amy was the first to jump out of the car, and Henrik, her oldest cousin, caught her up, swinging her around in the air until she squealed with delight.

In spite of the heaviness of her heart, Julie couldn't help laughing. Amy's older cousins took as much delight in her as she took in them, and they babied her shamelessly. Julie had hardly gotten out of the car before they carried Amy away with them.

Dan's two sisters and their husbands had been enjoying the fresh breeze on the green wicker rockers and chairs on the wide, plank-floored porch with its ornate posts and spindles. They followed their offspring to the car to greet Julie and Dan and relieve them of the dishes they carried.

Both of Dan's sisters had married ministers, one currently pastoring a church in St. Paul, the other on the opposite side of Minneapolis in Maple Grove. Rachel, his older sister, had earned a Christian education degree and was involved in the children's ministry of her church. Hannah, who held a masters degree in music, was the choir director at the church her husband, Carl, served.

Dan's three brothers were absent from the gathering. The two oldest, John and Peter, had returned to the mission field in January, one to Africa, the other to India. His third brother, David, who served a large urban congregation in Milwaukee, was unable to come this Saturday.

As they climbed the stairs to the porch, Dan's parents stepped outside to greet them with welcoming smiles and hugs. They were plain people, sensible and solid with an unshakable faith each of their offspring had personally claimed after the usual youthful rebellions.

After serving on the mission field for forty years, Niels and Anna had retired seven years earlier and returned to Minnesota. For another five years they had served a rural church near East Bethel before finally retiring from the ministry two years ago.

Even at the age of seventy-two and seventy-seven they were still in excellent health. Anna was energetic and full of fun, tireless in the kitchen, where she was usually to be found bustling cheerfully around, whipping up something good to eat. She was equally tireless in assisting her husband in serving the church. Her perfect counterpart, Niels was even-tempered and steady, deliberate in everything he did.

To Julie they were giants of the faith, and she loved them without reservation. From her second date with Dan, when he had brought her home to meet them, they had treated her with the same indulgent affection as they did their daughters. Julie had quickly grown as close to them as she was to her own parents.

The women carried the food into the spacious, sun-filled country kitchen with its old-fashioned painted bead-board walls and glass-doored cabinets. Dishes of hot potato salad, lettuce and fruit salads, pies, plates of cookies, and baskets of hot rolls vied for space on the crowded counters and the kitchen table.

Julie had brought Danish apple cake and red cabbage, two dishes that had become her specialty under her mother-in-law's tutelage. After they found place to squeeze them in, Anna pulled open the oven door to check on the steaming *Helstegt svine kam*, or roast pork. The aromas that wafted through house set up a grumble of anticipation in Julie's stomach.

It was shortly before noon when they arrived, and Julie, Dan's sisters, and the older girls needed no urging to help Anna get dinner on the table. All of them valued the time they spent working together in the kitchen at these family gatherings, sharing their concerns with laughter or tears.

As usual, while they worked Anna and her daughters confided stories of Dan's youthful escapades that sent Julie into fits of laughter and provided ammunition for months to come. Posted at the counter beside the stove, where he could sample the savory meat under the guise of slicing it,

Dan endured their teasing with wry good humor and unwavering denial.

He was the youngest of Niels and Anna's six children, all born on the mission field in Sierra Leone. His mother had been forty, his father forty-five when he had made his appearance. Perhaps because of his parents' age, Dan had been more intense than most children in his love of study and early, passionate faith. At the same time he inherited from Anna a fun-loving nature and a streak of mischief that had needed tempering.

Like each of his siblings, he attended the elementary grades at the mission school in Freetown before being sent to live with an aunt and uncle in Minnesota to complete his education. The pain of separation from his parents had been reflected in rebellious behavior that gave his aunt and uncle many anxious hours.

During those years Dan had been determined to have nothing to do with the ministry or even with God. But the Lord had other plans. Gently, but firmly, he broke down Dan's resistance and wooed his child back to himself. By the time Dan graduated from high school he had come not only to understanding the commitment his parents had made to serving God, but also to affirming that commitment in his own heart.

Not long after the grandfather clock in the living room tolled the noon hour, everyone gathered around the graceful, ornately carved dining room table. With a feeling of deep contentment Julie took in her surroundings: the pale ivory walls with their delicate tracery of stenciled vines and flowers just below the ceiling, the gleaming mahogany table and chairs, the matching sideboard, now groaning under an array of dishes that sent a heavenly fragrance into the air.

Her gaze returned to the faces gathered there, lingering finally on Dan's. Silently she thanked the Lord that she had been adopted into this family by marriage and by love. For a few hours it would be possible to lay aside the burdens of her heart. More than ever she needed the peace she found there.

Niels wasted no time offering the noontime grace, then plates were eagerly passed and piled high. After complimenting Anna on her cooking as he had at every meal since their marriage, Niels sent an inquiring look in Dan's direction.

"What are you preaching on tomorrow?"

Julie smiled to herself. This was always their first topic of conversation.

"I'm finishing up that series on the power of the Holy Spirit I told you about," Dan responded.

Julie finished buttering Amy's roll and handed it to her. "Since Dan began this series, five new families have joined church."

Niels nodded in approval. "And your friend Terry? You said he has been accepted at seminary. He is adjusting well to being home and to the work he's undertaken, then?"

Dan swallowed a generous bite of cabbage before answering. "He's still having extremely traumatic nightmares—when he can sleep at all. He's also finding it more difficult to adjust to life outside the military than he expected. He's in counseling, and that's helping a great deal, but please keep praying for him and for Angie and the children, too, as they deal with all the changes in their lives."

For a while longer each of them shared about their individual ministries. After dessert had been served and everyone was comfortably full, the children escaped outside to play under the supervision of their older cousins. The men helped clear the table, then gravitated to the living room while the women made short work of clearing away leftovers and washing the dishes. Finished, they rejoined the men.

Smiling to hear the children's laughter from outside, Julie curled up in a deep, upholstered armchair. The house was furnished with antiques handed down from Anna's and Niels' parents and grandparents, some of which had been brought over from Denmark by their forebears. Interspersed among them were pieces they had brought home from Sierra Leone.

African masks, carvings, and pottery mingled with Danish furniture and folk art in a cheerful mixture of colors and styles. Cushions and curtains stitched from African cloth dyed in a rainbow of brilliant hues contrasted with fabrics in a more muted Scandinavian palette. It was an unexpectedly whimsical and delightful mixture that reflected Anna's personality as perfectly as Julie's mother's was reflected in her home.

Listening to the lazy conversation of the others, Julie felt herself drifting off into a relaxing haze. A few minutes after she sat down, Amy came inside, trailing the frayed baby blanket she cuddled up with each night. Ignoring her parents, she crossed the room to Niels, who occupied the large old oak rocker, and held up her arms. Without slowing the rhythm of his rocking or pausing in what he was saying, he lifted her onto his lap and snuggled her against his chest. Julie exchanged a smile with Dan.

The conversation turned to concerns for Julie's mother and for Mike. All of them talked on the phone at least once a week, sharing joys and struggles, so Julie gave only a brief update. Anna and Niels promised to stop by to visit Julie's parents the following week, then they spent some time praying for Mike's and Thi Nhuong's safety, asking that the Lord would keep Mike from anger and bitterness at his father's rejection, that he would allow God to work in his life, and that Frank would have a change of heart. While they shared and prayed, Amy drifted off to sleep on her grandpa's lap.

The shadows beneath the trees were long by the time the rest of the children came inside, happily tired out from their play. Anna immediately collected Amy, whose head nodded sleepily over her shoulder, as she led the children off to the kitchen for a snack. A few at a time, the adults wandered after them to find seats around the kitchen table in front of plates of leftovers.

Finally Dan glanced down at his watch. "Yikes! It's six o'clock already. I have a sermon to finish. We'd better head home."

The others took this as a signal to leave as well. Waving and honking their horns good-bye, one by one they drove off into the twilight.

With Amy dozing in happy contentment in the back seat, Julie and Dan drove in companionable silence along the winding road home. As the miles passed, Julie's thoughts drifted to the genuine enjoyment Dan's family found in one another's company and to the concerns and prayers that had been shared.

In contrast, the tension between her own father and brother, beginning when Mike had entered teenage and intensifying into open conflict by the time he graduated from high school, stood out with painful clarity. She felt an ache deep in her breast thinking about it. If only her family would be blessed with the unity that existed among Dan's parents and siblings.

Into her thoughts crept the memory of the first time she had met Dan's family, opening the door to a flood of other memories: of how she and Dan had met, of the painful confusion of those early months, and of how he had so quickly captured her heart.

IN AUGUST 1960 Julie's family had taken a vacation before the school year began and Julie entered nursing school. While they were out of town, Dan preached a candidate sermon for the small new congregation that called itself Bethlehem Christian Church, where Julie and Maggie attended regularly, and Frank and Mike whenever they could be persuaded.

Meeting in the high school cafeteria for the previous two years, the congregation had grown to an average of seventy people at Sunday worship when their pastor accepted a call to a large church in Anoka. An extensive search that spring and summer produced no acceptable candidates to take his place. As the months passed, it became increasingly difficult to find guest preachers to fill the pulpit each Sunday, and attendance began steadily to dwindle.

The congregation was on the verge of disbanding when Dan, who was then pastoring a larger church in Mankato, accepted an invitation to preach. On the strength of one sermon he was immediately called as pastor, and to the search committee's delighted surprise, accepted. It wasn't until his first Sunday in the pulpit a month later that he and Julie met.

A few minutes before the service was due to begin, the choir members gathered in the high school choir room a short distance down the hall. Joking and laughing with friends on either side of her, Julie had just finished zipping up her robe and was finding her place in line.

"That's him—Daniel Christensen," the lady beside her whispered loudly, her hand cupping her mouth.

Julie swung around to see a stranger conferring with the choir director, Kathy Franklin, across the room by the door. "He looks younger than I thought he'd be," she whispered back.

She studied him with curiosity. He was in his mid or late twenties, she guessed. Sandy-haired and blue-eyed, he wore gold wire-rimmed glasses. His expression reflected an openness and good nature that instantly attracted her.

She was still staring at him when he glanced unexpectedly in her direction. She could feel the blood warming her cheeks as their eyes met. For seconds that seemed to Julie like hours, he held her gaze with a penetrating one before turning away to respond to someone else.

He didn't leave the room, but remained just inside the door. Julie's blush deepened as she realized he intended to greet each of the choir members as they filed out.

There was no other way out of the room and nowhere to hide. Asking herself why she felt as if she needed an escape route, Julie followed the line in front of her to the door. For no apparent reason, her heart was beating ridiculously fast. She felt as awkward and tongue-tied as she had the first time she'd presented a report in front of her class back in junior high, and she had no idea why.

When she reached Dan, he took her hand between both of his and smiled down at her. "I don't think we've met."

It felt as though champagne bubbled through her veins. "No—we weren't here when you came before . . . that is . . . we're members, but my family was on vacation . . . " Feeling as though she was babbling, she stopped abruptly.

"And your name is . . . ?"

"Julie," she blurted out. "Julia McRae. My friends call me Julie."

Was it possible for her to sound any more like an idiot?

His eyes were a clear, bright blue like her father's. The light in them as he smiled down at her left her feeling as if there was no ventilation in the room.

"I hope we'll be friends, then."

Was this really the first time she had heard his voice? The timbre of it affected the pulse of her heart in a way she had never experienced before.

"Y-yes. Of course, Reverend Christensen. Please call me Julie."

As though becoming aware that he'd delayed her too long, he let go of her hand. "My friends call me Dan." His smile widened.

"Dan," she repeated, feeling even more incomparably stupid. "I'd better go."

Her cheeks blazing, she ducked out the door, hoping no one else had noticed. To her humiliation, as they took their places at the front of the lunchroom, several of the other choir members directed amused or questioning glances in her direction.

"Are you all right?" the lady beside her asked.

"Yes, I'm fine!" Julie fanned herself with the bulletin.

The young woman on her other side gave her an arch look. "Well, I guess you are," she drawled meaningfully.

The first part of the service passed by in a blur. Julie was entirely too aware of Dan sitting across from them, then moving to the pulpit to read the scripture passage, to be conscious of what hymns they sang. Twice she found herself on the wrong verse.

The sound of his voice, neither too deep nor too high, captured her, she discovered. When he took his guitar and led them in several choruses, his voice was the only one she heard.

She quickly forgot everything else when he began to preach, however, found herself totally absorbed in the message he brought. She had committed her life to Christ a couple of years earlier, but something in his words touched an unknown well deep inside her. Unexpectedly she was filled with a hunger to know her Lord as well as this new preacher appeared to.

As they were leaving, she managed to introduce her parents and brother to Dan with acceptable self-possession, taking the precaution of keeping her hands behind her back with her fingers laced together. She was certain he noticed her odd behavior even though he appeared to give most of his attention to her family.

What had come over her anyway? Whatever had caused her to act like an infatuated eighth-grader certainly wasn't going to happen again, she scolded herself.

The following week, the demanding schedule of her first-year classes at nursing school quickly pushed the encounter out of her mind. When she walked into the high school choir room on Wednesday night, however, her heart sank. Dan was also there, though to her relief he barely gave her a glance. Throughout the hour, as they practiced the hymns for Sunday, he interacted with the other choir members with easy good humor and paid scant attention to her.

Even so, the feelings of confusion and awkward self-consciousness possessed Julie once more. Worst was the disappointment that nagged at her when he kept his distance.

What's the matter with me? she chided. *He's my pastor, for goodness sake! He couldn't possibly have any interest in me, and I certainly don't have any interest in him at all.*

Somehow she got through the hour, convinced she was off key on every hymn. When they finally finished, as the others were slipping on coats and jackets and preparing to leave, Dan picked up his guitar and sat down on one of the chairs in the front row. Julie grabbed her coat and swung around, intending to escape outside.

"Julie, do you know 'Sweet, Sweet Spirit?' "

Teetering between a feeling of doom and an unaccustomed, but strangely heady, excitement, she stopped on the threshold. She sent up a hasty prayer that her emotions didn't show on her face before forcing herself to turn around slowly.

To her relief, Dan's head was bent over his guitar. She watched him with apprehension as his fingers found the chords and deftly coaxed the melody from the strings. He seemed to be oblivious to her.

"I've heard it a few times. I don't think I know it well enough to sing it." The words came out in a croak, and she rolled her eyes, praying he hadn't noticed.

"It's easy to learn, and your voice is perfect for it." He looked up, his gaze barely brushing over her before transferring to the choir director, who stood in the doorway ready to turn out the lights.

"Kathy, can you play 'Sweet, Sweet Spirit' on the piano?"

"Sure!" To Julie's dismay, Kathy crossed to the piano without hesitation and found the page in the hymn book. "I don't believe we've sung this one before."

Reluctantly Julie joined her. Kathy opened another hymnal to the correct page and handed it over.

"I think this would be a good one to introduce the call to worship, don't you?"

"Absolutely," Kathy agreed.

"Julie, would you mind coming over here and singing it with me?"

Her heart was beating so hard she was afraid Dan would be able to hear it. Her feet dragging, certain she would not be able to hit a single note, she went over to him. When she didn't immediately sit down, he patted the chair beside him. There was no choice but to sit next to him.

Kathy launched into the introduction. Bravely Julie followed Dan's lead, amazed that her voice sounded relatively normal. They sang it through several times, and with each repetition Julie felt more confident.

At last Dan approved, "I think we have it. We'll sing it this Sunday. Thank you Kathy."

Waving to them, Kathy headed out the door. Julie squirmed into her coat while Dan tucked his guitar into its case. He reached the door before her and waited, his hand on the light switch. Head high, cheeks burning, she walked past him into the hall.

"Thanks, Julie. You have a beautiful voice. I hope I didn't keep you too long."

She swung around long enough to throw him a quick smile. "Not at all. I've got to run now."

Hurrying down the hall to the exit, she escaped with relief into the cool evening air.

It had been several more weeks before Dan finally asked her out, much later still before he confessed how he had agonized over the propriety of dating a member of his own congregation. And the fact that she was not quite nineteen, that there was almost nine years difference in their ages, added to his dilemma.

He was determined never to compromise his reputation or bring disgrace on the gospel he preached. But in spite of every argument he could muster to convince himself that he must keep his distance from her, she occupied his thoughts to the point of distraction until he began to worry for his ministry.

Fervent prayer brought no relief. Every inclination of his heart was to believe that she was the companion God had prepared for him. Still he distrusted himself, fearful that he was heeding merely his own sinful desires.

At last he sought his parents' advice. They cautioned him to continue to seek God's guidance and to take no action until he was assured that he had it. The difficulty he faced was not in agreeing with their counsel, but in adhering to it.

For her part, Julie did nothing to relieve Dan's misery. All she knew was that whenever they were in the same room she could hardly feel the floor beneath her feet. Frustrated by the confusing rush of emotions that would not go away and by a troubling tension she felt between them every time they were together, she finally took matters into her own hands.

One blustery Wednesday night in late October she deliberately walked the ten blocks to the high school wearing only a thin jacket. As luck would have it, she ran into Dan at the school entrance.

"Good evening, Julie." He held the door open for her to enter.

By now she was shivering in the cold wind. "Good evening, Dan," she repeated, blowing on her hands to warm them as she walked ahead of him into the foyer.

He followed her inside. "That wind's too cold for such a thin jacket."

She gave a rueful laugh. "It didn't seem that bad when I left the house. I was halfway here before I began to think I should have driven over."

Alarmed, he demanded, "You walked all this way?"

She lifted her shoulders in a shrug. "It's a nice evening—just a little breezy."

He reached out to take her hands. She gave them to him willingly, trembling at the feel of his warm fingers massaging her cold ones.

"Your hands are like ice," he murmured. "Didn't you wear gloves?"

She shook her head. "I forgot. Pretty dumb, huh?"

She could tell from the look in his eyes that dumb was the last thing he was thinking.

"By the time practice is over, it's going to be way too cold for you to walk all the way home."

They were standing very close together, his head bent over hers. As she looked up into his eyes, the breath caught in her throat at the emotion she read there.

For an instant his glance lingered on her lips. Abruptly he released her hands and shoved his deep into his pockets.

"I'd better drive you home when we're finished."

"Please don't go to any trouble. It's not that far really. I can walk."

"I go past your house on my way home anyway," he insisted. "It's no trouble at all."

THINKING OF THAT RIDE HOME, Julie glanced over at Dan and smiled. A week later he had taken her to a Ramsey Lewis concert in Minneapolis on a double date with Terry and Angie just before Terry had left for his first tour of Viet Nam. The following week Carl and Hannah had picked them up and taken them to the first of many Christensen family gatherings that she would attend.

That evening before they had gone home, at the urging of their children Anna and Niels had sung "Children of the Heavenly Father" for them, as they had often on the mission field. Julie had not been familiar with the hymn, but in the years since that day it had become precious to her.

Without realizing it, she began to hum the tune. Smiling, Dan reached out for her hand, and they began to sing the hymn together. And as his clear tenor blended with her sweet alto, the tender words warmed them both, as it had that other night years earlier, like a glowing fire blazing on a sheltered hearth.

Chapter 9

When Dan sorted through the mail the following Tuesday, he saw the airmail envelope they had been waiting for and hastily dialed the McRaes' number. As soon as Julie and Maggie learned that Mike's letter had finally arrived, they hurried over and gathered anxiously around the kitchen table while Dan tore open the envelope.

May 18, 1967

Dear Mom, Jules, and Dan,

I apologize that it's taken so long for me to write. We've been involved in a lot of heavy action, and I only have a few minutes now before we move out again, so this will have to be short.

Thanks for all the support you're giving us. Even though I tried to prepare myself for the worst, it was still a shock to get Dad's letter. I was hoping he wouldn't react that strongly, and the reality of being disowned pretty much left me with a hole in the pit of my stomach. I'd tried to prepare Thi Nhuong just in case, but she was already convinced that my family wouldn't accept her, and the confirmation was really devastating.

After I got over the worst of being hurt and mad, I realized that at this point we don't have any choice except to respect Dad's refusal to communicate with us. So I'll take your advice and write to all of you at this address. I love you all a lot—and I love Dad too, though he doesn't want to hear that.

I do have some of the best news, though, that helps to ease the disappointment. Guess what—we're pregnant! Can you believe it? I'm going to be a daddy! Thi Nhuong saw the doctor at the base, and as far as he can tell she's about six weeks along. That puts her due date around the middle or end of December. I'm hoping and praying that it'll be at the end of the month, because if she is too far along, she may not be able to fly when I'm due to come home. If that happens, I'm going to stay until the baby comes and both of them can travel.

Just so you're aware, I've taken care of all the necessary paperwork and made arrangements to get Thi Nhuong out of this country and home to Shepherdsville if anything should happen to me. I'm sure praying it won't because I want to see my child grow up more than anything I've ever wanted in this life. But just in case, I'm counting on the three of you, and hopefully someday Dad too, to be there for this little family of mine if I can't be.

Julie stopped reading, the scrawled words on the page blurring through the tears that flooded her eyes. Fear for their future tempered her joy at the news of Mike's safety and Thi Nhuong's pregnancy. Without needing to speak, the three of them reached for one another, their hearts too full even for prayer.

THE LAST WEEK OF MAY it occurred to Julie that Mike's twenty-first birthday was the thirtieth of June, barely a month away. It would be hard for all of them to face the day with him so far from home. So, in a flash of inspiration, she decided to arrange sending his gifts far enough in advance that he would receive them as close as possible to the thirtieth. Then she and Dan would throw a birthday party in his honor and let Mike know the exact time the celebration would be taking place.

To Julie's gratification, the idea excited her mother and took her mind off the unpleasant side effects of the chemo. She spent hours planning the menu, and Julie consulted with Terry about what gifts Mike might want and what items could safely be sent overseas. To keep her mother from becoming overtired, Julie decided to invite only Olivia, Terry, Angie, and their children.

Over the next two weeks, she and Dan shopped for suitable presents, then packed and delivered them to the post office in plenty of time for them to reach Mike by his birthday. In the package they included a large construction-paper birthday card Amy designed. Without any prompting, Amy also drew a card for Thi Nhuong with a large red heart in the center, and with Julie's help, printed on it in crooked letters how much all of them loved her.

FRIDAY, JUNE 16, was Julie and Dan's anniversary. They made plans for Amy to spend the night with Dan's parents so they could go to dinner that evening.

Dan met Julie at the door when she came home shortly after five o'clock. In the center of the dining room table sat a stunningly beautiful flower arrangement. At sight of it, Julie caught her breath.

"It's from your folks," Dan told her. "Livy did the arrangement herself. It came just after I got home."

"That's so sweet of them!" Julie went over to the table to admire the bouquet, then turned to throw her arms around Dan's neck. "Six years. Can you believe it?"

He engulfed her in a hug, gazing down at her with a warmth in his eyes that always sent a shiver down her back. "And many more ahead of us, I hope."

For some moments they kissed. At length he released her to check his watch. "We'd better get ready to go, babe. Our reservation is for six-thirty."

He followed her up the stairs. When she stepped into their bedroom, a flash of color drew her attention to the bed. Against the white chenille bedspread lay six red roses tied in creamy satin ribbon.

"Oh, Dan!" She turned to find him smiling at her.

"I thought you might like them."

This time it took a while longer before Julie would let him go. Humming, she hurried to find a vase for the roses before showering and dressing. She pinned her hair on top of her head and put on a dress she had bought just for that night. The supple moss-green fabric of the bodice fitted her slim figure snugly, and the full skirt swirled around her legs as she twirled in front of Dan.

"What do you think?"

He shook his head in admiration. "That I'm a very lucky man." The expression in his eyes left no doubt that he meant it.

They drove six miles out into the country to the Captain's Table, a local restaurant specializing in fresh seafood that had a reputation throughout the area. The rustic log building hugged the shore of Crescent Lake. The dining room had been built out over the water, with its three outer walls lined with windows that rose from floor to ceiling, providing a romantic view of the heavily wooded shoreline and the crystal water that lapped against the massive pilings supporting the floor.

When Julie and Dan arrived, the sun hung low in the sky, its rays sparkling and dancing across the waves. On the opposite shore the firs and pines, cast into shadow, rose in a deep green-black silhouette against the gleaming light.

Inside, high above their heads, intricate chandeliers constructed of intertwined elk antlers hung at intervals from the massive oak beams that crossed the dining room's vaulted ceiling. They cast a honeyed glow across the golden logs that formed the building's outer walls.

Julie took an appreciative breath of the delicious aromas that mingled on the air with the soothing music. On each table an old-fashioned oil lamp flickered in the middle of a deep red tablecloth. Underfoot, thick, brilliantly hued rugs woven in Native American designs covered the broad plank floors, cushioning their steps and muting the sounds of conversation and the clatter of dishes.

The hostess ushered them to a table by the windows overlooking the lake. As Dan held her chair, it suddenly dawned on Julie that they had sat at the same table the night he had proposed. His smile told her that it was no coincidence.

After they ordered, they held hands across the table, dreamily watching the rhythmic slap of the waves on the shingle below them. A line of flaring torches extended for some distance along the water's edge on either side of the building, adding their multiplied reflections to the lengthening rays of sunlight shimmering on the water.

"I knew you were going to ask me to marry you that night," Julie confessed. "And at the same time I was so afraid you wouldn't. I had butterflies in my stomach."

"So did I," he admitted. "And I wasn't at all certain you'd say yes."

She smiled. "You knew I loved you."

"Well . . . yes. But there are a lot of obligations that come with being a preacher's wife. I wasn't sure you'd be willing to take them on."

Julie gave a soft laugh. "I haven't done so badly, have I?"

His fingers tightened over hers. "Not badly at all."

Reaching into her purse, Julie brought out a small package wrapped in paper printed to look like birch bark. She laid it in front of him.

Dan looked questioningly from the package to her.

"It's for you. Go ahead and open it."

He tore open the wrapping to reveal a compact, streamlined fly box. When he opened the lid he drew in his breath and looked up at her in delight. Inside were several subtly colored, hand-tied flies.

"How did you know I wanted these?"

She giggled. "I have my ways. Actually, your dad helped me pick them out."

One at a time he lifted the flies out of the box to scrutinize them. "Wow! These are great! Now I really don't have any excuse not to get out on the river."

"I thought I overheard you and Carl plotting a fishing trip over the phone."

He reached to take her hand again. "What more could a man ask for? A beautiful wife and daughter and now these flies. Life is good."

They laughed heartily together. For that moment, life seemed very good indeed.

IT WAS LATE WHEN THEY GOT HOME. The night was warm, hazy with moonlight, and a summery breeze fluttered the sheer curtains at the open windows. Outside they could hear the crickets and see the starpoints of fireflies blinking on and off in their mysterious rituals.

Julie clicked on the dim light over the television while Dan put one of her favorite records on the changer. After a moment the mellow harmony of The Association's "Never My Love" filled the darkened room.

Embracing, they sang along with the words, swaying to the music. Then "Cherish" came on.

"Julie, I cherish you," Dan whispered, his lips moving against the feathery curls at her temple. "I am so grateful the Lord brought you into my life."

Blinking back tears, she wound her arms around his neck and pressed her forehead against his. "You are God's gift to me. You are my shelter and my safe haven, and every day I thank the Lord for you. I love you more than words could ever say."

His fingers found the pins that held her hair up, and he dropped them one by one onto the floor. The bright flood cascaded loose over her shoulders. Burying his hands in the shining red-gold curls, he tipped back her head to kiss her throat, his lips following the curve of her neck to the hollow at its base.

Then he swept her up into his arms. And carrying her up the stairs, he brought her to their room and to their bed.

ALTHOUGH FRANK TRIED, he could not block out of his consciousness the preparations for Mike's birthday party. When both Maggie and Julie brought up the subject, however, he told them in no uncertain terms that he had no interest in discussing it or even in listening to any of the details—now or ever.

He could tell they were hurt, but at least they dropped the issue. He hoped they would never bring it up again. Each time they talked about Mike, his chest constricted so painfully it scared him.

On the thirtieth he found it all but impossible to focus on his work. Finally he headed for home uncharacteristically early. Maggie was busy getting ready for the party, so he decided to do some yard work.

He was pruning the bushes when Julie stepped out the back door carrying Maggie's best tablecloth. He pretended he didn't see her, but she detoured over to join him. Forcing a smile, he turned to greet her.

Before he could speak, she cut him off. "Daddy, you know today is Mike's birthday. We're going to celebrate it whether you join us or not. But can't you see how much your attitude hurts Mom—not to mention me? We keep tip-toeing around this issue, and it never gets settled. I love you, and I love Mike. And so does Mom. We don't want to be forced to choose between you."

Frank set his jaw. "Nobody's asking you to do that. You can do whatever you want. Just don't ask me to welcome one of those gooks into my home." Hastily he returned his attention to the bush he was trimming so he wouldn't see the tears well into her eyes.

"Do you really think we can go on like this forever?" she demanded, her tone incredulous. "It's tearing us apart! How can you be so bitter toward all Asians that you'd refuse to give even one of them a chance, and even worse, disown your own son?"

Frank turned his back on her and walked over to the fence where crimson roses spilled across the creamy white pickets. His movements jerky, he balanced the pruning shears on the top rail before rounding on her. Folding his arms across his chest, he leaned against the fence.

"Okay, if you want to know the whole story, I'll tell you. Are you sure you want to hear it?"

She lifted her chin. "Yes, I am. I don't care how painful it is. You need to get it out, and I need to know why you feel the way you do."

Frank narrowed his eyes. "All right, then. You know Bobby ended up on Bataan. After MacArthur left it finally fell, though our men held on with everything they had.

When the war ended I met one of the survivors who'd known Bobby. He told me what our boys went through on the Death March. It isn't fit for a woman to hear. But somehow some of them survived. They spent more than two years being brutalized in a prison camp before they were shipped to Japan on what they called hell ships, packed together like sardines, their survival depending mainly on their buddies dying first.

He took a ragged breath and the long pent-up words poured out of him. "In Japan Bobby was put in a POW camp in Nagoya and assigned to forced labor in a factory. At that time my unit was fighting its way across the South Pacific as fast as we could. I was determined to get to wherever Bobby was and get him out, bring him home if I had to crawl through hell to do it. After all, that's what he was enduring.

"When Japan finally surrendered, I found out that Bobby died in October 1944, less than a year before the Japanese surrendered. His buddy told me he'd been bayoneted to death because he tried to stop a guard from beating one of the men who was too weak to obey an order. Bobby weighed eighty-three pounds at the time. He was six feet tall, and he weighed eighty-three pounds!

"I can only imagine what he must have gone through, Julie. And I couldn't save him. I couldn't get to him in time. A Japanese soldier killed him just like you'd step on a roach.

"I'm not just taking somebody else's word for what went on either," he went on, cutting her off before she could speak. "While I was in the Philippines, an old Philippine man with horribly twisted hands came into our camp. He could only speak Spanish, but he had a little kid with him who could speak enough English to translate what he said.

"He cried while he told us the Japanese tried to force him to give them military intelligence even though the old guy didn't know anything. He didn't know anything! But those soldiers tied his hands to a table so he couldn't move them, and then beat them with rods until all the bones were broken. His hands healed all broken up so that he was crippled and in constant pain, and he had to beg for food because he could never work anymore.

"And that's just one of the things I personally was a witness to out there. I saw things that would make you sick to your stomach if I described them to you. I understand Terry having nightmares because I still have nightmares about things that happened more than twenty years ago. Now you tell me how I'm supposed to forgive those people."

With cold satisfaction, he watched Julie look down at the ground. The color had drained out of her face, and she was unable to meet his accusing gaze.

"I know, Daddy," she murmured. "Horrible things happen in war—on all sides. I don't know how any human being can do things like that to another human being. Maybe we'll never know the answer until we get to heaven."

After a moment, she looked up, pleading, "But I do know that every one of us does evil things and thinks evil thoughts, not just certain individuals or one group of people. In God's eyes sin is sin, no matter how big or how small it may seem to us. Under the right circumstances, every one of us could commit some unthinkable act that other people would find unforgivable.

"The Bible says that not one of us is righteous, that we've all gone our own way. That's why God's own Son had to die for us, because there's no way we could pay the price for what we've done. If we're not willing to forgive those who wrong us, then how can God possibly forgive us for the wrongs we've committed?"

Frank pressed his lips into a hard line and turned abruptly away. "Well, you know your own heart better than I can, but I've never done anything nearly as bad as what I saw out there on the battlefield. I'm not capable of doing things like that, and no matter what situation I ever find myself in, I can guarantee I never will. I'll never forgive those people for what they did or the Vietnamese for what they're doing now. And I'll never accept one of them as a member of my family."

FOR SOME MOMENTS Julie stared at her father's back. Ever since learning that he had disowned Mike, she had suffered a deep ache inside that wouldn't go away no matter how fervently she prayed or how resolutely she tried to push it aside. Every attempt over the past weeks to broach the subject with him had only resulted in his becoming angry.

Bitter tears pricked her eyes. At last, without speaking, she left him, her heart heavy with the anguish he had carried inside him for so many years.

She was so troubled that she couldn't conceal her distress from the others at the party that evening. When they gathered in the kitchen after the meal, refilling their drinks and nibbling on chips and the last remnants of cake, she broke down and told them what had happened.

Terry listened intently to her recital. "Don't be too hard on your dad," he said when she finished. "I couldn't begin to tell you some of the things I saw in battle—like my men getting blown apart by booby traps set by the Viet Cong or the NVA. It messes with your mind, and you can learn to hate real quick. You've got to realize that in Frank's mind Thi Nhuong's people are responsible for Mike's being out there and in danger."

"You know, Frank lost his brother and father during the war, then his mother in a car accident three years ago," Maggie mused. "Now I have cancer and Mike's so far away fighting a war. It's fear that's driving him. He must feel that everything is being taken away from him and he can't protect the ones he loves."

Terry nodded, his expression sober. "If you ask me, he wrote Mike that letter because he loves him and wants to protect him from what he believes are real threats. He genuinely believes the Vietnamese, like the Japanese during WWII, are out to destroy this country and everything he holds dear, including his son."

Dan put his arm around Julie's waist and drew her into the crook of his arm. "I suspect," he said, "that if we knew the real reason for why others do the things they do, we'd find it much harder to judge them harshly. So often we act out of the deep pain of our souls when what we really need is for someone to understand and to love us unconditionally."

CHAPTER TEN

AS THE WEEKS WORE BY, it became apparent that Olivia was gradually adjusting to the fact of her divorce. In filing for a quick dissolution of the marriage in Nevada, Rob had given up rights to their property. Olivia consulted with a lawyer and had the house and the flower shop transferred to her sole ownership.

Maggie was pleased at the realization that Olivia found much comfort in visits with her and Frank and with Julie and Dan. Olivia doted on Amy, and when she wasn't occupied with the flower shop, she fussed over Maggie as much as Julie did. On Maggie's worst days the three of them spent hours together, which helped the time to pass more quickly, and Maggie came more and more to depend on her neighbor's presence.

Looking for activities that wouldn't tire her on the days when the effects of the chemo diminished, Maggie began to crochet a rainbow-colored baby afghan for her new grandchild. Whenever she felt well enough to shop, she went in search of supplies and gifts for the baby. After carefully wrapping each item in pretty paper and ribbons, she added it to the growing pile in the large white wicker trunk she had found at her favorite antiques shop.

She made a point of talking about Mike, Thi Nhuong, and the baby in Frank's hearing to friends and acquaintances who came to call. More than once when she mentioned

Mike's name while talking on the phone, she noticed that he found an excuse to wander into the room. Although he invariably pretended not to hear, she was beginning to believe that her words, and perhaps even the confrontation with Julie, were getting through to him.

JULY DAWNED HOT AND HUMID. Tests showed that her mother's tumor was continuing to shrink, though more slowly. Relieved at her progress, Julie decided it was time for her to act on an idea she had been mulling over.

She was involved in the children's ministry at the church, but for some time the idea of starting a women's ministry had returned often to her thoughts. After some prayer and discussion with Dan, she announced that she would host a weekly women's Bible study at her home on Tuesday evenings. They would begin with a study of the book of Ephesians.

Lily Chou, along with Olivia, Maggie, and several women from the church immediately joined, and a couple of them invited neighbors. Ten women attended the first meeting.

Just before their second meeting an urgent letter arrived from Mike. After an extended operation Mike had gotten back to base in a state of exhaustion only to discover that Thi Nhuong had begun experiencing irregular bleeding and strong cramps and had been taken to the base hospital. The doctor feared that she might lose the baby.

Finding Thi Nhuong distraught and inconsolable, Mike had immediately sent for Father Tranh, the old priest from the mission who had married them. Father Tranh had arrived within the hour to anoint Thi Nhuong with oil and pray for her health and the baby's.

As he prayed, Thi Nhuong stopped crying and became very quiet and calm. At the same time my fear and exhaustion just drained away. I felt a sensation so strong it raised the hair on the back of my neck as if a bolt of electricity had gone through the room.

When he finished praying, Father Tranh took both our hands in his. He said God has a special plan for this baby, and that we need to continue to pray because there are evil forces working against him. I felt a chill go through me, but it's strange—at the same time I felt this deep sense of peace.

I've been really skeptical about anything to do with religion for a long time. There's a lot I don't understand, a lot that doesn't make any sense to me. But I do want you to pray for us. We're grateful beyond words for your prayers.

The letter thrilled them with its witness to the Lord's working in Mike and Thi Nhuong's lives, but left them as well with increased concern for their safety. It was a concern Julie brought to her study group, and the women committed themselves to keep Mike, Thi Nhuong, and their baby in prayer daily.

THAT FRIDAY, JULY 14, was the first day of Shepherdsville's third annual Christmas in July Flea Market and Craft Fair. The town's quaint, turn-of-the-century feel was one reason the annual December Christmas festival had become so popular in the region, and the July fair was rapidly gaining in popularity. The festivities encompassed most of Shepherdsville, from the fairgrounds, to downtown, to Shepherdsville City Park where a host of activities enticed fair-goers who had gotten their fill of shopping and eating.

Downtown, the four-story late-Victorian courthouse with its high Mansard roof dominated the center of the square. Built around the turn of the century, the majority of the tidy, two- and three-story red brick buildings that bordered the square remained untouched by extensive modernization. Colorful awnings covered many doorways, and wide, tall shop windows, glinting in the sunlight, displayed an enticing array of home furnishings, clothing, gifts, cards, souvenirs, and the like. The old-fashioned wrought-iron street lamps, originally gas lit before being electrified, gave the finishing touch to the picturesque scene.

Outside town, acres of booths stretched across the fairgrounds, bursting with a staggering assortment of Christmas ornaments and decorations, folk art, paintings, crafts, pottery, new and used books, and antiques. One entire section was devoted to the flea market, and at the fairground's opposite end, midway games and rides filled the sky with flashing lights, rainbows of neon, and lilting music.

Friday turned out to be a warm, cloudless day with a cooling breeze from the west. Julie had arranged for Amy to spend the day with Dan's parents, knowing her little daughter would have scant interest in the wares available for sale and would soon grow tired and cranky. Since both and Dan and Frank were taking the day off, they all agreed to meet at the Bethlehem Christian Church Youth Fellowship's booth.

When Dan and Julie arrived at the fairgrounds, their senses were assaulted by the oily scents of frying funnel cake and elephant ears mingled with the pungent aromas of Polish sausages, barbecue, and Italian, Scandinavian, and Chinese dishes. Other booths offered a choice of desserts that included everything from homemade ice cream in every flavor imaginable to a staggering variety of baked goods.

They found Angie and Terry supervising the booth, where a contingent of teens—dressed like hippies, Julie thought wryly—was enthusiastically, and successfully, hawking psychedelic tie-dyed T-shirts, intricately airbrushed denims, and handmade jewelry. While they were sorting through the wares, Julie's parents joined them.

After her father and Dan headed off together, Julie and her mother drifted next door to Olivia's booth. Easily the most creatively decorated of the festival, the Angel Florist booth consisted of an ivy-entwined bower draped with angel motif fabric in rich hues, against which lush plants and exotic arrangements of brilliantly colored flowers ran riot.

They admired the booth and made several small purchases, then headed for the green, purple, and gold striped archway over the Three Kings Card and Gift Shoppe's booth to see the shop's proprietor, Elena Hernandez. While Maggie lintered at the displays of Christmas cards, ornaments, and decorative items, determined to get a head start on Christmas purchases, Julie crossed to the booth belonging to the Wise Man Bookstore.

Above it hung the store's sign, which depicted a bearded, saintly looking old gentleman peering genially over his spectacles. The tables were generously stocked with gift books with colorful dust covers, histories of the Shepherdsville area and its Scandinavian heritage, cookbooks, and children's storybooks.

"Have you seen Emma Winthrop's booth yet?"

Completely absorbed in selecting a storybook to give Amy for Christmas, Julie almost jumped at the sound of her mother's voice.

"Oh—not yet." Absently she wiped a trickle of perspiration from her cheek with the back of her hand. "Whew! It's hot out here."

"She has the most beautiful *scherenschnitte*!" Maggie urged. "You've got to come see them."

Emma Winthrop, wife of Ed Winthrop, the young publisher of *The Shepherdsville Evening Star*, was an accomplished artist, and they spent some time admiring the exquisite, hand-cut pictures that lined the walls of her booth. A delightfully whimsical piece caught Julie's eye.

"Look at this one!" She pulled her mother over to look at it more closely.

The picture was simply, but beautifully, framed in weathered driftwood. Against an ocean-blue background, the bottom section of a single piece of sand-colored paper depicted a lighthouse at one end of a beach. Above it a series of dolphins leaped among ocean waves, and above them, on the side opposite the lighthouse, danced a clipper ship. The piece was not large, but so skillfully and cleverly done, that Julie knew she had to have it.

Holding her breath, she turned it over to look at the price tag. Forty dollars. She let out her breath, deflated. The piece was well worth it, but far beyond her budget.

Maggie peered over Julie's shoulder. "It's charming! Are you going to buy it?"

"I can't afford it," Julie mourned.

Emma came over to them, pushing a wayward strand of her sun-streaked blonde hair behind her ear. "That's one of my favorites. I had so much fun designing and cutting it that I almost hope it doesn't sell."

"Unfortunately, it's safe from me." Julie set the picture down, her expression rueful. "I'm afraid my budget doesn't include art right now."

When Julie moved to the far side of the booth to rummage through the unframed pieces, Maggie winked at Emma. "Save it until I can get back. It'll make a wonderful birthday present for Julie."

Emma laughed and nodded. When Julie's back was turned, she whisked the picture behind her table.

After a few minutes Maggie directed Julie's attention to a booth across the way that displayed pottery and drew her off to investigate. With some maneuvering Maggie managed to slip back to Emma's booth alone.

"Julie's occupied for the time being," she told Emma. "Let me write you a check before she wanders back in this direction."

While Emma deftly wrapped the picture, Maggie eyed the slender young woman and her five-year-old son, Jamie, who was happily playing with his toy cars in one corner of the booth behind her. For months Maggie had been meaning to witness to Emma and invite her to church, but she hadn't felt comfortable sharing her faith with someone she didn't know well. She was afraid she would come across as judgmental or pushy.

But today she felt an urgency about talking to her. Sudden concern that the opportunity might not present itself again tugged at Maggie's heart.

The verses from Second Timothy drifted into her thoughts: *For God has not given us a spirit of timidity, but of power and love and discipline. Therefore do not be ashamed of the testimony of our Lord.*

No, I won't be ashamed of witnessing for my Lord anymore, she told herself. *The Holy Spirit will give me the right words. After all, it's the Spirit's responsibility to save people, not mine. My responsibility is to be a vessel the Lord can use.*

"You know, we'd love to have you visit our church," she ventured. "Our children's Sunday school department is developing some innovative programs that I think Jamie would really enjoy. You and Ed would fit right into the young marrieds' class too."

"Oh, heavens!" Emma exclaimed as she handed the wrapped package to Maggie. "Thank you for the invitation, but I'm afraid I'm already overcommitted. I simply don't have time to get involved in another organization. Besides, Ed doesn't believe in God and has no use for religion."

Maggie gave Emma the check and tucked the package into her bag with her other purchases. "Do you believe in God?"

"Well, sure," Emma said brightly. "It makes sense that something had to create all this. But I guess I see God as more of an impersonal force. I grew up in a church and used to attend, and pray and all that, but I dropped out when I was in college because it was just one more obligation, and it never seemed to change anything. To be honest, church was . . . well, it was boring. We always sang the same old hymns and listened to the pastor drone on for half an hour. Then we went home. I didn't get anything out of it."

"Do you know Jesus as your Savior?" Maggie persisted.

"Now, Maggie, I don't believe in all that 'savior' stuff," Emma scoffed. "I mean, it's not as if I'm a bad person. Sure, I make mistakes just like everybody else does. But I don't lie or steal or cheat people. I've never killed anybody. And Ed and I are totally committed to our relationship. Our moral standards are as good as anyone's who goes to church—and better than some.

"I know you're sincere," she concluded, "and I don't mean this the wrong way, but you have to admit a lot of people who attend church and act holier-than-thou on Sundays are real hypocrites during the week."

"Mmmm . . . of course, I've never known any nonbelievers who were hypocrites," Maggie responded, her tone thoughtful.

Emma stared at her with uncertainty. "Look, I take care of my family, work hard, and try to do what's right. Do you honestly believe that a loving God would condemn a person like me to hell?"

"That's not for me to judge. But I don't believe anyone, including myself, can ever be good enough to earn their way into heaven," Maggie countered softly. "The Bible says that everyone has sinned and come short of God's glory. And because God is holy and can have nothing to do with sin, the penalty for sin is death. That's why there had to be a perfect sacrifice for the wrong things all of us have done. Only Jesus was able to pay that penalty by dying on the cross so we wouldn't be separated from God forever. But we have to repent of our sins and accept Jesus as our personal Savior."

Emma busied herself straightening the framed pictures hung on the wall beside her. "I just can't believe that there's only one way to heaven. Honestly, there are so many different religions, not to mention so many different Christian denominations. How can anyone know which one is right? Christians are so intolerant. Your Jesus is only one path to the truth. If that works for you, fine, but I'm taking a different route."

Maggie reached out to give her a hug. "Oh, Emma, all I can say is that I know Jesus personally, and that has made all the difference in my life, especially now that I have cancer. It's terrifying and painful going through all this, not knowing whether I'm going to live or die. But I do know one thing. I know where I'm going when I die. I hope you can say the same thing."

WHEN JULIE RETURNED to the booth, Emma was still standing there, staring after Maggie's retreating back, a frown of puzzlement and doubt creasing her forehead. Julie glanced over the pictures hung on the walls of the booth.

"Oh, no! You sold it."

"Yes . . . I'm afraid I did," Emma answered.

Noting that her friend appeared distracted, Julie said, "I just wanted to look at it one more time, but I'm glad you sold it."

Forcing a smile, she waved and went to look for Dan.

SATURDAY MORNING Dan's parents brought Amy home and joined him and Julie, along with Maggie and Frank, at the park, where a variety of groups offered every musical style from jazz to rock and roll. In an open area on the far side of the pavilion, a stage and seating in the round had been set up. Hourly, Scandinavian folk dancers and singers gave way to polka bands, square dancing, Irish step dancing, and country or pop music groups.

Every half hour horse drawn carriages bound for downtown drove out through the park gates, their seats brimming with passengers who waved and called to passers-by. A line of people snaked along the shore of the creek beyond the bridge, waiting to rent canoes and paddle down the tree-shaded, winding creek as far as the fairgrounds at the other end of town.

After a carriage ride, they stopped at a hamburger and hot dog stand to grab lunch. By now it was getting close to Amy's usual nap time, so with her riding on Frank's shoulders, they went to find seats at the rear of the stage area where they could rest while watching a troupe of country cloggers.

Dan finished off the last bite of his hot dog. "Anybody want anything? I'm going back for a burger."

Given orders for chips and a refill on cola, he took off for the hamburger stand. While he was paying for his purchases, Ed Winthrop stepped into line behind him.

"Covering the fair, Ed?" Dan asked.

Ed nodded. "I'm going to do a full page spread. This year looks like the best one yet. Attendance is up over last year, and the vendors are raking in the dough."

He ordered a hot dog and lemonade, and then fell into step with Dan on his way back to the stage. "You been following the news on the war? Things are really heating up over there. Looks like we're finally going to bomb those commies back to the stone age."

Since moving to Shepherdsville, Dan had made no secret that he was a pacifist. Knowing that Ed was familiar with his stance, he settled for a peaceable answer.

"With Mike over there, we sure appreciate the great job *The Star* is doing reporting on everything that's going on—including the political situation here in the States."

"Oh, yeah, you're a pacifist, aren't you," Ed noted through a mouthful of hot dog.

Dan kept his tone bland. "I'm not aware of any instances in history where a conflict between two parties was brought to a just resolution by violence. The Bible says vengeance belongs to God, not to man. And Jesus told us to turn the other cheek."

Ed washed down his lunch with a swallow of lemonade. "Dan, I've always wondered how someone as smart as you could believe all those old myths in the Bible."

Dan cocked an eyebrow and regarded him with amusement. "And I've always wondered how someone as smart as you could to simply dismiss a subject you don't know anything about."

Ed frowned. "I've read the Bible."

"So—what do you know?"

"Come on," Ed scoffed. "The Garden of Eden? A world-wide flood? Jonah being swallowed by a whale? You surely don't believe all that stuff."

"You have proof it isn't true?"

Ed considered Dan with skepticism. "Can you prove that it is?"

"Archaeology is substantiating more of it all the time."

"It stands to reason the Bible contains some facts, but there's no scientific evidence for the existence of God," Ed persisted. "In fact, science disproves it. The theory of evolution even disproves the necessity for a God. All religions, Christianity included, are based on ancient legends and myths that primitive peoples developed to explain natural phenomena they couldn't understand or control."

Dan laughed, unmoved. "Ed, the theory of evolution is just that—a theory—even though our schools teach it as fact. It's never been proven, and the scientists who support it cover up all the evidence against it."

"I'd say trained scientists know more about the subject than I do. If they believe it, they must have good reason to do so."

Dan snorted. "Not all scientists believe in evolution, but even if they did, the fact remains that no one has yet come up with a satisfactory explanation of how the universe came into existence. They've devised all sorts of scenarios, but no matter how they try to squirm out of it, there had to be a force that created the first particle of matter that everything supposedly evolved from. And that force had to have intelligence. There's no other way to explain the extreme diversity that we see all around us.

"But that doesn't convince you, does it?" he guessed shrewdly. "It isn't reason, but faith you need, my friend. Jesus said unless you come as a little child, you'll never enter the kingdom of God. Without a relationship with him, none of it will ever make sense."

"I'm afraid I can't just 'have faith'—whatever that means," Ed countered stiffly. "Excuse me, but even if there is some sort of supernatural power out there, which I see no evidence of, I simply can't believe in the sort of God reflected in the Bible."

"So what?" Dan shot back. "What difference does it make what you believe—or what I believe, for that matter? Our belief or lack of it doesn't change the truth. Our job on this earth isn't to *define* what truth is—it's to *discover* it, and then live according to it."

Ed rolled his eyes. "How can you be so sure there is such a thing as absolute truth?"

Dan allowed a faint smile. "Because the universe in all its ordered complexity couldn't possibly rest on shifting sand. It has to have fixed foundations. Science will tell you it couldn't function otherwise."

He put his hand on Ed's shoulder. "At least think about it, study it, give it a fair trial, Ed. Don't just assume that you already have all the answers, or that if *you* don't understand something, it can't be true. Life has a way of knocking out from under us all the props we base our confidence on. And that's when we discover that, after all, we need to depend on a Being greater than ourselves.

"And that Being is there. All you have to do is seek him with an open heart, and he'll reveal himself to you."

CHAPTER 11

JULIE RETURNED HER MOTHER'S WAVE as Maggie went down the porch steps. "Bye, Mom! I'll see you tomorrow." Going back inside, she closed the front door behind her.

"She's definitely looking better." Bending, she scratched behind Judge's ears. "Those new meds Dr. Radnor prescribed are a lot more effective against the nausea than the others were."

"She looks stronger than she has for a long time," Dan agreed. "How many more courses of chemo does she have left?"

"Four, and then she's done. She was so sick at the beginning I was afraid it was going to be a real struggle. But I'm encouraged. The latest tests all show that the tumor has shrunk a lot."

"*Mommieee*! Can I get up yet?"

Judge gave a deep woof and headed for the stairs. Rolling her eyes, Julie caught him by the collar.

"Sweetie, we just put you down ten minutes ago."

"But I can't go to sleep!"

"Of course you can't. You're talking, and I bet you're not lying down either. Now lie down and be quiet."

"It's not fair!" Amy wailed. "You don't have to take a nap."

"I take naps when I need them, but I'm not three years old. Now hush!"

"Listen to your mother." Dan's voice was stern. "Believe me, you don't want me to come up there."

"Oh, yes she does." Julie mouthed the words, giggling. "You're such a pushover."

"Daddy, can you read me a story?" inquired Amy meekly.

Dan struggled to choke back his laughter. Managing suitable firmness, he responded, "I already read you a story, Amy. If you don't go to sleep now, you'll have to go to bed right after dinner, and you know you hate that."

There was a moment of silence. Finally a small voice said, "Okay. I love you, Daddy."

"I love you too, Sweetheart. Sleep tight."

Quiet reigned upstairs.

"Well, apparently she doesn't love *me*." Julie grimaced as they tiptoed through the dining room.

Giving her a smug grin, Dan shut the kitchen door behind them. "She's Daddy's little girl."

Going over to the kitchen table, Julie picked up the letter from Mike that had been delivered that morning. Maggie had come over right away, and they had rejoiced together over its contents. Scanning it again now, Julie couldn't help smiling once more.

July 7, 1967

Dear Mom, Jules, Dan, and Amy,

You guys are the best! Thank you so much for the birthday presents! Thi Nhuong and I especially love the nifty little record player and the Beatles and Beach Boys albums. I'm finally able to treat my little surfer girl to a taste of what's in store for her on the beautiful beaches of Minnesota. Er, well—can you surf on snowdrifts?

As you can tell, things are getting crazy around here! I'm Waiting for the Day when I'll be home, but God Only Knows when that'll be. I Just Wasn't Made for These Days, but I Know There's an Answer! Wouldn't It Be Nice if we could just sail away on the Sloop John B, or better yet, take a Magical Mystery Tour on a Yellow Submarine with Sergeant Pepper's Lonely Hearts Club Band? Talk about Good Vibrations!

Even reading the letter the second time, Julie was laughing so hard she had to wipe away tears. With Dan chuckling as he read over her shoulder, she skimmed through the rest.

The camera and film are just great too! I can finally take decent pictures of my bride and our cozy little place so you can see what they look like. There hasn't been any let-up in the fighting in our sector since I got here, which is why I haven't had the chance to answer your questions about my home away from home yet. I've been gone more than I've been here. That doesn't leave much time to write, but I promise I'll try to do better. Next time I'll have some pictures to send, and I promise I'll finally try to give you a description of Nha Trang, though I can't tell you much about the base because of security issues.

Luckily, my unit got back to base the 29th, so I was able to go into town the next morning. When I got to our pad, Thi Nhuong had baked a cake and laid out all the loot for me to open. I couldn't believe it! You really took me by surprise. Not only was I able to spend the day with my wife, which is a blessing I never get enough of, I also spent it with all of you in spite of the miles between us.

And hey, I hope your party was a swingin' one! We figured out what time it would be starting local time, and we did some celebrating too. After all, it isn't every day a man turns 21!

By the way, Thi Nhuong is doing much better. She got a good report from the doctor, and everything seems to be just fine with the baby. He—or she—has a strong heart-beat and is kicking now! What fun it is to feel that!!

Feeling your love directed at us keeps us strong. You don't know how much the card you made for Thi Nhuong meant to her. I bless you for your kindness to my wife. She was so touched, and she keeps it beside the bed to look at every night. She said to tell you she loves you all too and can't wait to come home.

Gotta go. We're moving out again. Dear ones, pray for us.

Love,
Mike

Slowly Julie ran her finger over the last line. "Pray for us." Could God really be changing Mike's heart—and Thi Nhuong's?

She put the letter down, happy memories of her little brother flooding over her. One memory in particular stood out with vivid clarity.

"Do you remember the first time you drove me home from choir practice?"

Dan threw her a questioning look, then chuckled in understanding. "I'll never forget. What possessed you to walk so far with only a thin jacket on when it was so cold outside?"

Julie gave him an enigmatic smile. "Never underestimate the wiles and the determination of a woman."

He caught her in his arms. Giggling, she pretended to struggle to break free.

"So you were plotting against me!"

"And if it hadn't been for Mike, it might all have been for nothing," she confessed relaxing against his chest. "I could have killed him, and at the same time I wanted to kiss him."

"Bless Mike," Dan agreed. "Sometimes he's painfully direct, but that night I was thanking the Lord that he was."

Gazing into each other's eyes, they both smiled, remembering that night not quite seven years earlier.

DAN INSISTED THAT JULIE call her parents to let them know he was driving her home because of the cold. Before they left the high school, he also made a point of mentioning it to the choir director.

To Julie, driving those ten blocks seemed to take an hour. The tension between them had returned, and everything felt even more strained than before. It had been a mistake for her to put Dan into a position where he had to offer to drive her home, she scolded herself.

No matter how hard she tried, she couldn't think of anything to say to him. And when he asked about her nursing classes, every answer she gave made her feel like an idiot. She was certain this would be the last time he would ever bother to pay any attention to her.

When they turned into the driveway, she heard a suspiciously familiar sound and glanced at Dan. "Is your stomach growling?" she blurted before thinking.

He put his hand over his stomach, and she saw the color come into his face. Oddly enough, seeing him blush bolstered her confidence.

"Excuse me!" he apologized, embarrassed.

"Didn't you have dinner?"

"I had a lot of calls to make this afternoon. I didn't finish until time for choir practice."

"Mom made a roast this evening, and there are plenty of leftovers. Come on in, and I'll fix you a plate."

He hesitated, obviously tempted. "It's very kind of you to offer, but I can't impose on you and your parents this late and at such short notice. I can grab a bite on my way home."

"But it's almost nine," Julie protested. "Most places close in a few minutes. Besides, it's no imposition at all. My folks will definitely be upset if I let you go home hungry."

"Well . . ." Still he hesitated.

"Nobody makes better pot roast than Mom does. Plus there's gravy. And mashed potatoes."

He laughed and threw up his hands. "You win. I'm a sucker for mashed potatoes and gravy."

They went into the house. "Mom, Dad!" Julie called. "Dan's here."

Her mother was in the living room reading, and at her call her father came out of the den to join them. As he shook hands with Dan, Julie explained why she had invited Dan inside.

"Julie insisted," Dan broke in. "Really, I don't want to impose—"

Maggie brushed Dan's embarrassed protestations off. "Julie knows perfectly well I'd be furious if she sent you away hungry. I just wish I had more to serve you than leftovers."

"I lured him with promises of your roast." Julie directed a smug smile at Dan. "He admitted he's a sucker for mashed potatoes and gravy."

They all laughed, Dan ruefully. Patting the slight paunch he was developing, he said, "As you can see, I'm not overly supplied with willpower when it comes to food."

"We've been intending to invite you for dinner," Frank put in, "but you seem to have a pretty full schedule."

Dan gave him a sheepish grin. "Since moving here, I've received so many invitations from church members to share a meal that if I didn't starve rigorously between visits, I'd have gained fifty pounds by now."

After Frank excused himself to return to the den where he had been plowing through a pile of paperwork needed the next day, Maggie led the way to the kitchen. "Then you've starved enough for one day," she teased. "Let's add a little to that poundage. You can work it off tomorrow."

"The trouble is that tomorrow never seems to come," Dan grumbled as he moved to follow her and Julie.

After helping Julie heat the food and prepare a plate for Dan, Maggie discreetly disappeared before Julie could stop her.

Her shyness returning, Julie fixed a sandwich for herself. As she carried her plate to the table, she heard footsteps thundering down the stairs, then Mike skidded around the corner and through the doorway into the kitchen. Annoyed, Julie took in her gangling fourteen-year-old brother with a disapproving frown.

"Do you always have to be so noisy?" she asked, trying mightily to keep the irritation out of her voice.

"I thought I heard voices down here. Hey, Rev!"

Dan grinned. "Hey, Mike. How's it going?"

"Good." On stockinged feet, Mike skated across the smooth floor tiles to the stove. He plucked a morsel of roast out of the pan with his fingers, dipped it into the gravy, and deposited it in his mouth, dripping gravy down the front of the stove and his shirt in the process.

"Michael!" Her cheeks burning, Julie went to wipe up the spilled gravy with a dishrag. "What happened to your manners?"

When Dan laughed, Julie directed her frown at him. "Don't encourage him!"

"Are you guys dating?" His expression angelically innocent, Mike fished another piece of roast out of the pan.

An awkward silence descended on the room. Too shocked to come up with a scathing putdown, Julie stared at Mike in astonishment. She couldn't bring herself to look at Dan.

"That depends entirely on your sister."

Dan's voice held a strange softness. When Julie found the courage to glance over at him, she saw that he was leaning back in his chair, arms folded across his chest, watching her with an unreadable emotion in his eyes.

"Yes!" she snapped.

Horrified at her boldness, she grabbed Mike by the shoulders and spun him around, marched him out of the kitchen and through the living room to the stairs. Maggie looked up in surprise from her magazine. Seeing Julie's face, she sprang to her feet and came to intercede.

"What's he done now?"

Ignoring her, Julie shoved Mike up the first couple of steps. "Go to your room! I bet you don't even have your homework done.

"*What is the matter with you, anyway?*"

"Aw, Jules—"

Mouthing the words so Dan wouldn't hear, Julie raged, "How could you?"

In a reversal so typical of her little brother, he wrapped his arm around her shoulders and laid a wet kiss on her cheek. "I like him," he whispered in her ear. "He's a good guy. Don't let this one get away."

Openmouthed, Julie watched him bound up the stairs, her anger evaporating. *How did he know?*

She became aware that her mother stood beside her, her expression wavering between amusement and concern. "It's nothing, Mom. Just Mike being Mike."

Leaving her mother staring after her, puzzled, Julie forced herself to go back into the kitchen. She felt as though she was going to her execution.

Dan had pushed back his chair and was staring out the window, his food untouched. When she came through the doorway he shifted his steady gaze to her. Julie couldn't bring herself to meet it.

She sat down across from him and stared down at her plate, appetite gone. "I apologize for my little brother."

"He reminds me a lot of myself at that age." There was a smile in his voice.

Taking a deep breath, she looked up. "You'd better eat your dinner while it's still warm."

He sampled the roast, savoring it. "You were right. This is really good."

"Things always taste wonderful when you're starved," she observed tartly.

He chuckled and helped himself to a bite of mashed potatoes and gravy. When he met her eyes again, what she read in them caused her to quickly drop hers.

He put down his knife and fork. "Do you have any idea what you're letting yourself in for, getting involved with a preacher?"

The question was so unexpected and so gently spoken that the breath knotted in her throat. It was a moment before she could speak.

"Probably not. But from what I can see, it looks pretty good to me."

His glance caressed her. He reached out his hand to her then, and without hesitation she laid her hand in his palm.

He laced his fingers through hers and held her. "It looks *very* good to me."

The light in his clear, blue eyes ignited the bubbles swirling in her veins. She clung to his hand for dear life.

After a moment he sobered. "A couple of years ago I was engaged. She broke it off because she couldn't take the scrutiny, the church's involvement—and at times interference—in our relationship. It hurt for a long time, and I almost gave up the thought of ever getting married. I don't look forward to going through an ordeal like that again. I definitely don't want to put you through it."

She took a shaky breath. "All we can do is live one day at a time and trust the Lord to lead us. If you're willing to take the risk, I am too."

His fingers tightened over hers. "I'm willing."

"I DON'T THINK THE PASSAGE you assigned was long enough." Sherrie Martin's grin was wry. "I like the next part best—the one about husbands having to love their wives as Christ loved the church."

The women gathered around Julie's dining room table giggled guiltily. It was obvious they all agreed.

Julie returned Sherrie's grin. "I suspect we all feel that way. We'll get to that, but first we're going to take a look at our part."

Julie turned to Ephesians 5:21-33 and began to read. "And be subject to one another in the fear of Christ. Wives, be subject to your own husbands, as to the Lord. For the husband is the head of the wife, as Christ also is the head of the church, He Himself being the Savior of the body. But as the church is subject to Christ, so also the wives ought to be to their husbands in everything."

She looked up from her Bible. "So what do you think about what Paul is telling us in these verses?"

The women exchanged glances around the table. "I thought it was interesting that you chose verse 21 to begin the lesson," Olivia said.

"I thought so too," Maggie chimed in. "That makes it sound as if each of us is supposed to be subject to all other believers."

"That would include husbands as well as wives, wouldn't it?" demanded Hazel Jorgenson, a friend Olivia had invited to the study group. A seeker, she had quickly endeared herself to the rest of the members with her probing questions and perceptive responses.

"What do the rest of you think?" Julie asked again.

Lily looked up from scrutinizing the passage. "What exactly does Paul mean by 'be subject to'?"

"My translation says 'submit to,'" Sherrie offered.

Maggie absently smoothed the page of her Bible. "If a husband and wife are both believers, then both of them are called to be subject to—or to submit to—each other in the fear of Christ. But it's more complicated when one partner isn't a believer. For most of our marriage, Frank wasn't a Christian. Oh, he believed in God on an intellectual level, but he didn't have a personal relationship with Jesus. So there were stress points in our marriage because serving God was more important to me than even our relationship."

"That's what finally broke my marriage apart." Olivia stared down at the table, pain shadowing her features.

The others nodded and murmured sympathetic responses. Sitting beside her, Hazel put her arm around Olivia's shoulders.

Angie broke the short silence. "Even when you're both believers, it's hard to be subject to your husband. Part of it is just human nature, pride, determination to have our own way. Plus all of us have personal issues to deal with."

She hesitated, then rushed on, "Terry's doing a lot better since he's been seeing a counselor, but he's carrying around so much emotional baggage from his experiences in Viet Nam. Things get better, then they get worse again. I keep reminding myself that he hasn't been home all that long, but there are times when I wish he would just get over it, even though I know it isn't something he can control. So I struggle with submission. I feel like his mother—like he's the child, and I'm trying to control his behavior."

"Look at verse 33," Julie prodded. "There Paul changes it to say that a wife must respect her husband. Does that make things a little clearer?"

Angie thought for a moment. "It makes sense to me. If you respect someone, you don't try to control them. You allow them the freedom to think for themselves and make their own decisions."

"Angie, it sounds like you've been trying to take responsibility for Terry's life, trying to do God's work." Lily laid her hand on Angie's arm. "It's the Lord's job to heal Terry's wounds and change him into the man God designed him to be, not yours. When we try to take over God's job, there's no way we're going to succeed. We just frustrate ourselves."

She stopped herself with a muffled laugh. "It's taken me a while, but I've finally learned that the only person you can control is yourself. You're only responsible for your own thoughts, feelings, and actions, not anyone else's."

For several moments they all shared personal struggles they had encountered in their marriages. Maggie recounted some of her experiences with Frank, concluding that she had finally realized she had to accept and respect him as he was, faults along with strengths.

"I used to try to 'fix' Sam too," Lily admitted, "but I found out pretty quickly that it doesn't work. The harder I tried, the more he kept on doing the things that irritated me. You remember the talk we had at the Vikings' Lair back in the winter?" she asked Julie and Angie. "That's when I realized that if what I was doing wasn't working, then I should stop doing it! Just doing more of the same thing or trying to somehow do it more perfectly was only going to make things worse.

"So I decided to try the opposite, to concentrate on being the wife Sam needs instead of trying to make him into the husband I thought I needed. I told myself that God made me, so he surely must know my needs. And he promised he'd give us the desires of our hearts. At that point I made a conscious decision to trust God to give me my heart's desire and to do what this verse says: to submit in love to my husband. I began to pray for Sam instead of criticizing him, to encourage him instead of nagging. I began to thank God for him just as he was—and sometimes that was really hard!"

They all laughed in embarrassed agreement.

Sobering, Lily looked around the table at her friends. "And things began to change. I almost didn't believe they would. But one night a couple of months ago when we got home from work, we were both tired. We'd both had a difficult day. Sam was really touchy, and he made a remark to me that really stung. Ordinarily I'd have snapped back at him, but this time I bit my tongue and didn't say anything.

"He was quiet for a minute as if he was waiting for me to answer back, and when I didn't, he changed the subject. I made myself answer him cheerfully, without that resentful attitude that had been taking over. I just acted as if nothing had happened and my feelings hadn't been hurt, even though they had been.

"Sam went into the bedroom to change his clothes while I began dinner, and then all of a sudden he came back and put his arms around me. He apologized and said he hadn't meant what he'd said. He asked me to forgive him for being so hard to get along with. He's never done that before."

She stopped, her eyes moist with tears. "I'm not perfect at this yet, and neither is Sam, but I can see real growth in both of us. It all started when I decided to submit to the Lord and to my husband and to really accept and respect him. Sam has begun to love me in the way I need to be loved.

"Demanding my rights and my 'respect' didn't work. This way does. I think that's what Paul is trying to tell us."

CHAPTER TWELVE

STANDING WATCH AT NIGHT *has to be the loneliest job in the world. At every sound the hairs on the back of your neck stand up, and you just know you're in somebody's sights. It's pretty creepy, though the long-timers tell me you learn how to cope with it after a while. But I've been here for eight months now, and that feeling still puts a chill in my bones.*

Our base camp is just outside the city of Nha Trang, which is right on the coast in the Central Lowlands. The climate is tropical, the beaches are beautiful—what little I've seen of them!—and growing rice and fishing are the main businesses.

Base is pretty much just a tent city bisected by dirt roads. Home consists of a tent with cots for several men to sleep on and a footlocker to stow your gear. For air conditioning we keep the sides of the tents rolled up. It's a nice thought, but with sandbags stacked 4 or 5 feet high under the flaps just in case the Viet Cong start shooting, it doesn't do a whole lot of good.

Another one of my buddies took a hit while we were out on our last operation. Webb accidentally triggered a trip wire and set off a mine. He was still alive when they helicoptered him off, but he was in a bad way. The tough part is when somebody you're close to is just suddenly gone. The last you see him is when he's being carried off on a stretcher, and you never find out what happened or if he survived.

What little news we get from the real world makes me wonder how much is true. We hear reports about peace demonstrations and student protests that make it sound like the demonstrators are all supporting North Viet Nam. That's pretty discouraging when you spend days slogging your way through the jungle only to take a bullet yourself or see your buddy blown up right beside you. Especially since we're supposed to be going through all this to defend the good old US of A.

Believe me, there's no way I can describe what really goes on here or what it's like to feel like just one insignificant pawn in a giant chess match. We aren't given any choices—we're just expected to follow orders and not ask questions, even if it's obvious that the guy in charge doesn't have a clue what he's doing. And that happens a lot more often than you'd think.

Most of the time we see only our own small part of it, and the broader strategy behind what we're ordered to do is just as much a mystery to us as it probably is to you folks back home. Maybe more so. From what I've seen so far, there aren't too many of us over here who believe this is a good thing we're doing fighting this war. We just want to get home alive.

Truth is, I keep asking myself why I went ahead and joined up instead of taking a student deferment so I could finish my studies at Minnesota State. At the time I thought, hey, I'm nobody special. A lot of good men are putting their lives on the line for our country, like Dad did in WWII.

Some of my buddies from school were going, and Terry was on his second tour. I felt like I'd be abandoning people I cared about, being a coward, making our old man ashamed.

I guess I just assumed that I'd disappoint Dad if I didn't sign up, and I'd done that often enough already. I've never felt like I really measure up to his standards, but then we've never been able to talk about things like that either. Anyhow, now I wonder if he would have been disappointed if I'd told him I don't believe this war is either moral or winnable or that I'm just not cut out to kill people. Maybe instead of arguing, we could have talked it out for a change. Or maybe I should just have headed for the Canadian border like a couple of my classmates did and kept on going.

What is all this suffering for anyway, Jules? You have any idea? Right now I'm not sure about anything. Each one of us sees things in a different way, and maybe there's right on both sides—and wrong on both sides. After all, if there is a God, then he made us the way we are. And he'd deal with us as individuals, wouldn't he? If that's true, then maybe what God means for us to do is to follow the light he reveals to each of us at the point we are in our journey with him.

I know it sounds crazy considering that she's Buddhist, but maybe there's a reason why Thi Nhuong and I found each other. Maybe she's the real reason why I'm here. She needed me, and I needed her. I know that now, though I don't know why.

Do you think all our questions will be answered some day, Jules?

Julie, Dan, and Maggie pored hungrily over the color pictures enclosed in the envelope. In clear, vivid images, scenes of the city of Nha Trang, Mike's tent and buddies at the base, and Mike and Thi Nhuong's apartment leaped out at them, distilling into reality for the first time. They laughed over the photo of Mike and Thi Nhuong showing off her pregnant belly.

Then, growing serious, they discussed the issues Mike had raised in his letter. The questions he posed were profound ones, though the answers remained elusive. Yet the clear evidence that Mike had begun to seriously seek for spiritual answers filled them with hope.

How hard it was for Julie to think of them so far away—this dear younger brother of hers and his new wife, whom none of them had met but whom they already loved and longed for. It seemed so long until December's homecoming.

Looking over at her mother, without warning Julie felt the cold fingers of fear close over her heart. How healthy and happy Mike looked in the pictures. How much improved her mother was now that the chemo was almost done. And with the passage of only a few more months, they would all be together again.

Wouldn't they?

Why did she suddenly feel so afraid?

MAGGIE'S LAST COURSE OF CHEMO was on Wednesday, August 30. She felt better than she had for two years and had even begun to put on a little weight. Her complexion glowed with vitality, and except for the bright scarves she wore wound around her head to conceal the loss of her hair, there was no outward sign of the desperate battle she had waged for so long.

Frank's birthday was on September 5, and he decided that a romantic two-week holiday in New York City was what they both needed. Julie, Dan, and Amy saw them off at Minneapolis airport Sunday afternoon, the 3rd, smiling and waving as they watched the two of them walk arm-in-arm down the ramp to the plane.

DAN WAS ON HIS WAY out of the house Thursday morning when Terry's car pulled up at the end of the driveway. As Dan came down the walk, Terry leaned out the window.

"You going over to the church?"

"I'm on my way right now," Dan replied.

"I'd like to pick up that youth resources catalog you were telling me about."

"It's in my office. Come on—I'll get it for you."

Terry got out of the car and joined him. Absorbed in conversation about how Terry's seminary classes were working out, Dan neglected to walk around to the church's rear entrance off the parking lot as he usually did. Instead they entered through the main door. Their voices echoing from the high, vaulted ceiling, they walked the length of the sanctuary, the kaleidoscope of jewel tones that shimmered through the stained-glass windows radiating a soothing rainbow around them.

Near the front and to the left, just inside the hall leading to the classrooms and the fellowship hall, they stepped through the doorway into the office where Rose Jamison, Dan's secretary, reigned. A grandmotherly type with a tendency to being overly emotional, Rose only worked three days a week.

Generally several hours on Mondays, Wednesdays, and Fridays were all she needed to take care of paperwork, run copies on the mimeograph machine, and keep Dan's schedule organized while answering the telephone. When she wasn't in and he had no appointments, Dan tried to spend at least part of the morning in the church office in case someone called to ask about the times of the services or needed a minister.

The office was dark that morning. Flipping on the light, Dan turned toward the door of his own office, then hesitated, frowning.

It was closed. He made a point of always keeping it open.

Throwing Terry a warning glance, he crossed to the door with Terry close on his heels and pulled it open. He stopped instantly in the doorway.

In the chair in front of his desk sat Jayne Webster, a woman who had been attending worship fairly regularly for the past three months, always alone. Mr. Webster never set foot in the church. Dan had called on the Websters soon after Jayne's first visit. Even that brief call had made it clear to him that the couple's relationship was anything but amicable.

Dan guessed Jayne to be a year or two younger than he was. She was quite attractive, and she knew it. Her lustrous black hair was carefully curled, her large, dark eyes highlighted with copious amounts of mascara and eye shadow.

Right now, her long, shapely legs were crossed to expose the maximum amount of thigh. The provocative cut of the dress that molded to her body's ripe curves like the draperies on a Greek statue advertised the full range of her charms without leaving any essential detail to the imagination.

She had propped one nicely turned elbow on his desk, her hand supporting her head. She looked as if she had been crying. The effect was very dramatic.

Stiffly Dan ventured, "Are you all right, Mrs. Webster? Can I help you with something?"

She dabbed her eyes with a handkerchief. Her wide-eyed gaze wandered to Terry, then imploringly back to him.

"Oh, Reverend Christensen, I just learned that my husband has been having an affair." She struggled to stifle a sob, but failed. "We had a horrible argument and he . . . he wants . . . a divorce."

Her glance drifted back to Terry, shifted away. "Would it be possible for us to meet . . . in private? I desperately need your counsel."

Dan heard her out. "I'm sorry, Mrs. Webster. You'll need to call my secretary to schedule an appointment when my wife can be present. Mrs. Norman is here three days a week from nine to two, as you know. She'll be here tomorrow."

Amazingly, the tears dried up, and offended astonishment took its place. "But I need to talk to someone right away! I assumed since you're a pastor I could turn to you for spiritual advice and comfort."

Dan became aware that Terry had stepped back out of Mrs. Webster's view and was regarding him with a peculiar expression that mainly reflected amused perplexity.

Keeping a firm grip on his annoyance, Dan repeated, "I'm not the one who should be comforting you. If you and your husband would like to meet with me to try to work out your relationship, then you'll need to schedule an appointment."

"I refuse to live with that man any longer!"

"Then what you need is a lawyer. Now if you'll excuse us."

Dan stepped back out of the doorway, pointedly indicating that he expected her to leave.

"Well! I never—!"

She jumped up and flounced to the door. Dan stepped back quickly, but not quite fast enough. Deliberately she brushed against him on her way past, leaving the trace of her perfume on his shirtsleeve.

At the outer door into the hallway, she stopped to direct a resentful gaze from him to Terry. "If this is all the help I can expect from the pastor of this church after all the money I've put in the offering, I won't be coming back!" She disappeared into the hall.

Jaw clenched, Dan stood motionless, ramrod straight, his back against the wall beside the door, arms folded across his chest, listening to the staccato tattoo of her high heels across the tiles of the floor. After a moment the church's rear door creaked open, then slammed shut.

Looking Dan up and down with a bemused air, Terry approved, "Excellent defensive posture. All you need is an M-16."

Dan threw him a disgusted look. Shoving away from the wall, he marched into his office, ripped the youth resources catalog off the shelf above his desk, and sliced it through the air toward Terry, who had followed him inside.

Deftly catching the catalog in midair, Terry folded his tall form into the chair Mrs. Webster had recently vacated. They could hear the screech of tires spinning out of the parking lot.

"What was that all about?"

Dan grimaced. "You wouldn't believe it."

"Try me. All week I've been telling myself that I was imagining it, or that maybe I'm to blame for what happened last Wednesday night."

At Dan's inquiring look, Terry explained, "At the youth group meeting when we were cleaning things up, I somehow ended up alone in the kitchen with this cute little blond chick. I wouldn't call what she was wearing a miniskirt. It was more like a micro skirt. Anyway, she came on to me!

"Now, I've had plenty of women hit on me, so I know how to handle it. But I'm a married man with two kids, I'm working toward becoming a youth minister, and most of all, I'm black. She's all of maybe fifteen and white. I could be lynched!"

Dan massaged the back of his neck. "Well, this is Minnesota, not Mississippi, so I doubt they'd get out the ropes. It would be a bad scene, though. As far as the age thing is concerned, fifteen's not too young. The rest of it doesn't make any difference."

"Maybe I'm naïve, but . . . do you have to deal with this a lot?"

Dan snorted. "Brother, I'm afraid you're in for a revelation."

Going to the window, he jerked it open to let the fresh air dissipate the lingering scent of perfume, then sat down in the chair behind his desk. "Don't get me wrong. It's not as if incidents as obvious as this one happen every day—just often enough to make you wonder." He gave a short laugh. "I've run into this kind of thing maybe half a dozen times since I've been in the ministry. I try to keep my guard up, but every time it happens, it still shocks me.

"The great majority of the time though, it's like what happened to you the other night. Someone comes on to you. Thankfully, the solution for that is almost always to pretend you're oblivious to it."

"That's basically what I did."

"Young girls that age are exploring their sexuality. They naturally want to find out how attractive they are to men. Be careful you don't get sucked into a response that could be taken the wrong way."

Terry nodded. "I understand all that. Thankfully, I'm not attracted to little girls."

"Don't assume you're invulnerable in any area, my friend. We're all human beings, and we all fail. I can't tell you how many times I've come very close to falling. If there's any chink in your armor, trust me, Satan will find it."

Terry expelled his breath and gave him a wry look. "Amen to that."

Dan gave a short laugh. "Guard your reputation the way you guarded your life on the battlefield because once you lose it, it'll take a long time and a lot of work to get it back—if you even can. Sure, there's forgiveness for mistakes, but the consequences will follow you wherever you go. And if you ever get into the wrong situation with one of those young kids from the youth group, I guarantee it'll level your life like a nuclear meltdown."

Chastened, Terry said, "From now on Angie sticks to my side like glue. And I'm sure going to have a no-holds-barred discussion with all our volunteers before the next meeting."

He studied Dan. "But that doesn't explain what just happened. How did Mrs. Webster know you'd be coming over here just now?"

"How did you know?"

"Oh . . . right."

"My schedule isn't exactly a secret." Sighing, Dan added, "I know better than to come in here without first checking to see if there are any cars in the parking lot. But then, it's easy enough for someone to park down the street and walk over."

"Maybe you should consider keeping the church locked," Terry suggested.

"You know why I don't want to do that. But believe me, from now on I'm keeping this door locked."

Swiveling his chair, Dan stared out the window. At length he said softly, "The hardest part of it is that for the past three months she sat under my preaching and teaching. I feel like I failed. I must not have presented the gospel in a way that touched her life."

Terry cocked his head. "Is that your failure—or hers?"

"Maybe both. But I can't help wondering if I'm the one who's more responsible."

"I felt the same way when it happened to me," Terry admitted with a shrug. "I guess I always assumed women would consider a minister to be off limits."

Dan ran his hand through his hair in a gesture of frustration. "Maybe it's a challenge—I don't know. It was bad enough when I was single, but it seems like it's gotten worse since I've been married."

"You don't think it's because you're such a sexy guy?"

Dan grinned. "Well, that too."

Slowly he sobered. "Modern society is so steeped in sex that it's really not surprising it's become a major weapon in the arsenal of the Evil One. Plus, it's been my experience that sharing with another person spiritually is so intimate that it leaves both of you in an extremely vulnerable emotional state. When that person is the opposite sex, it can be very hard to distinguish the tenderness of soul you feel in that moment from physical desire. And if you're not careful the Adversary will carry you in the wrong direction.

Before we were married there were times after Julie and I studied the Bible and prayed together that I just had to get away from her."

Terry raised his eyebrows. "How did you handle it?"

"At the beginning of my ministry I made a decision that I was never going to be alone with any woman, except my wife or my mother, under any circumstances. I keep the door and the curtains of this office open and the lights on at all times. And even though Rose is old enough to be my mother, I limit the time I spend over here when she's the only one in the building. I've seen too many fruitful ministries wrecked simply because a pastor allowed himself to be put into a compromising position, whether he actually gave in to temptation or not."

There was a new respect in Terry's gaze. "Man, you've got a lot of angles covered that I never thought about. I don't think I could have handled Mrs. Webster the way you did. My first thought was we ought to pray with her. I mean, this time I was here to back you up."

Dan considered him skeptically. "Two men with one woman? I don't think so."

Terry winced. "You have a point. Yeah—bad idea."

"You have to look at it from all angles. My father had a heart-to-heart talk with me when I went into seminary. If he hadn't set me straight, I would have been completely blindsided the first time it happened. And I wouldn't have known enough to be on guard against a lot of things he warned me about. That's why I'm having this conversation with you."

"My dad's never said anything about this to me—though, come to think of it, I remember overhearing a conversation or two between him and Mom when I was a kid. And he never went anywhere without her. I think I'm going to have a long talk with him."

"What did you do when you were dating Julie?"

"I made sure we spent as little time alone as possible. The longest drive we ever took in the car was to my folks' place, and my sister and brother-in-law drove us. I always had Julie home before the sun went down unless we double-dated with friends. We only went to public places. I never took her to my apartment unless someone, preferably her mother or mine, was with us. And whenever we were together, I kept daylight between us."

"Hey, man, I don't know if I have that much willpower."

Dan's laugh was rueful. "It was torture. All I wanted to do was scoop her up and carry her off someplace where we could be alone."

Terry chuckled. "And what was Julie's reaction?"

"We talked about it and prayed about it. There were times when it was really hard, and there were times when neither of us was happy about it. But the Lord kept us on the straight road—and we got married as soon as we could," Dan concluded with a mischievous grin.

"Angie and I waited just long enough for her to get through high school before we got married. But I've never regretted marrying so young. I sure hope she hasn't. I know I wouldn't make it without her."

"I don't see any evidence that she regrets it," Dan said. "I know how much she loves you. But you both need to keep your eyes on the Lord and trust him to make the bad times better.

"Watch and pray that you don't yield to temptation," he added. "None of us knows the day or the hour of our Lord's return. We need to be ready."

CHAPTER 13

STANDING BY THE KITCHEN COUNTER near the back door, Julie slipped into her running shoes. The sun was just above the horizon, and as every morning, Judge had his massive, velvety muzzle pressed against the back door screen, fringed tail waving, eager for his morning run.

"Now that Mom's through the chemo, there's practically nothing for me to do as far as taking care of her or helping her out. If she keeps on doing as well as she has been these past few weeks, there's no reason why I shouldn't be back at work by the end of the month."

Dan set the dirty dishes into the hot sudsy water in the sink and scrubbed the counter with the dishrag. "Do whatever seems best, babe. If you feel like it's better to wait a while, that's fine with me too. You know how much I like having you at home, but you need to follow your own ministry and calling."

Julie finished tying her shoes and straightened. "I love to be home too, close to you and Amy. But you're right. It is my calling, and as soon as it's confirmed that Mom's out of danger, I need to get back to it."

Hesitating, she added, "I don't tell you often enough how it comforts me to know you're taking care of Amy when I have to be at work."

Dan took his hands out of the dishwater long enough to pull her to him and give her a quick kiss. "You know how much I love to be with my girls," he said, gazing down at her with the warmth in his eyes that had won her heart from the beginning.

Amy took a last sip of orange juice, then slipped out of her chair at the table and ran over to crowd between them and share in their kiss. After giving both of them a hug, Julie went to pull Judge's leash down from the hook near the back door. The huge dog gave an eager woof and pressed impatiently against her legs, almost knocking her down. Before Julie could clip the leash onto his collar, the phone on the wall beside her rang.

It was Olivia. Julie could hear the panic in her voice as she asked whether she could talk to her and Dan right away. Concerned, Julie glanced at the clock. It was five minutes to seven.

"Yes, of course. Come on over."

Dan threw her a questioning glance as she hung up the phone.

"It's Livy. She sounded awfully upset, and she wants to talk to us right away."

Dan hurriedly set the last of the clean dishes in the drainer and let the water out of the sink. "I have a bad feeling this has something to do with Rob."

"Their divorce was final months ago. What could he do to upset her now?"

Hanging up the leash, Julie released Judge into the fenced backyard. She had just gone into the living room when Olivia pulled up in front of the house. Slamming the car door, she ran for the porch, obviously distraught, tears streaming down her cheeks.

Dan sent Amy to play upstairs, and he and Julie met Olivia at the front door. Through convulsive sobs, Olivia explained that Rob's parents had called her a couple of hours earlier. She had talked to them for some time, then, struggling alone with grief and anguish, had waited to call Dan and Julie until she was sure they must be awake.

"Rob and Diane—the woman he's living with—overdosed on heroin yesterday. Apparently they'd been mainlining for a couple of days, and by the time someone called an ambulance, they were both close to dying.

"They managed to revive Diane in the emergency room. She lost the baby. Rob's heart stopped, and he wasn't breathing for almost ten minutes before they were able to get it started again. He's in a coma and unresponsive. The doctors say there's little brain function, and they're not holding out any hope that he'll regain consciousness."

Dan shook his head, incredulous. "Why did Rob's parents call you? You're not married anymore."

Olivia bit her lip, fighting to keep her voice steady. "They said they still consider me to be Rob's real wife. They think he made a big mistake—that it's all because of the drugs—and they said how sorry they are for what he's done. Rob never married Diane, and they think I'm the only one who has the right to decide whether to turn off . . . "

She stopped, her hand pressed over her mouth. "Turn off the life support systems," she managed at last. "They want me to fly out there as soon as possible."

Horrified, Dan squatted down in front of the sofa where she sat. "Livy, it's unfair for them to put you in this position after all you've gone through!"

Enfolding Olivia in her arms, Julie agreed. "To see Rob again after all that's happened—and to see him this way—then to have to make the decision whether to remove life support—" She stopped, shaking her head. "It's going to tear you apart. You've just started to put this all behind you and move forward. This is going to be even worse than when you found out Rob was living with that woman and that she was pregnant."

Olivia made an attempt to get control of her emotions. "I feel as if I have to do it. In God's eyes, we are still husband and wife. This is the last thing I can do for Rob. And his parents aren't believers. They must be in terrible pain because they have no hope. If the Lord prompted them to call me, then I feel I have to minister to them in any way I can, even though to see Rob like this . . ."

Again her voice trailed away, and she made a quick, painful gesture as though brushing away the words. "I have to trust that the Lord will show me what to do."

"I don't know how to counsel you on this," Dan admitted. "I agree with Julie that seeing Rob under these circumstances and making a life-and-death decision for him can't help but take a terrible emotional toll on you."

Letting out a sigh, he studied her for a moment. "But you have to follow the Lord's leading. If you feel his prompting to do this, then he'll give you the strength to see it through."

"I wish one of us could go with you," Julie said. "How can you go out there and face this alone?"

Olivia was trembling all over, but when she spoke, her voice remained steady. "I'll call Tony. I know he'll go to the hospital with me in spite of how he feels about Rob. And my parents are in Santa Rosa. I can stay with either Tony or Mom and Dad for a while if I don't feel like I can handle it."

The question of who would manage the shop in her absence was more difficult to settle. One employee, Miriam, took orders and handled payments, while Steve, who ordinarily worked with Olivia on the floral designs, could fill the orders. Together they could handle most of the daily business. However, if Rob died, as seemed certain, then Olivia might have to stay for an indefinite time to help his parents settle Rob's affairs. In that case, it would be necessary for someone to supervise her employees and make the decisions they could not.

Dan and Julie looked at each other. "If it's just a matter of checking in at the shop every day and being available to help out with whatever is needed, then I can do it," Julie volunteered. "Mom and Dad are going to be back from New York in a couple of days, and as well as Mom has been feeling, I know she'd be delighted to help out too. In fact, if I know her, we won't be able to keep her away. She just loves your shop."

"And Frank and I will be available to give any help that's needed," Dan offered. "Whenever you check in to let us know how things are going, then we can discuss any details we need your input on."

Olivia sighed with relief. "Yes. That's the best solution. But are you sure it won't be too much trouble?"

Both insisted that they would feel better helping out than sitting by and doing nothing. Dan suggested that Julie accompany Olivia home to help her get organized and pack for a possibly lengthy stay. As soon as they left he got on the phone and made arrangements for her flight to San Francisco that afternoon.

While Julie and Dan, with Amy's eager help, packed her luggage into their van, Olivia made a hurried visit to the shop to explain the situation to her employees and to give them Julie and Dan's phone number. By the time Olivia got back, it was almost eleven. They made a quick stop for lunch, then headed for Minneapolis.

This time there were no happy smiles and gay waves as the three of them saw the departing passenger off. Instead, tears and hugs, whispers of encouragement and prayers accompanied Olivia as she walked down the ramp toward the plane. To Julie she looked so achingly alone with her shoulders bowed under a burden of love and anguish.

WHEN OLIVIA CALLED shortly before noon the next day, Julie took the kitchen phone while Dan got on the one in his office. Olivia told them she would stay with her brother and his family for the time being and gave them the phone number.

"Have you been at the hospital yet?" Dan prodded. When Olivia answered in the affirmative, he asked, "How did it go?"

"Well, in spite of all the tubes and wires he was hooked up to, Rob didn't look as bad as I was afraid he would," Olivia told them, her tone wistful. "He looked almost like he did when I first met him in college. His face was peaceful.

"Tony and I and Rob's parents met with the doctor. She said there was no hope he would recover. The life support could keep him technically alive for a while longer, but in the end infection or pneumonia would set in."

"I'm so sorry," Julie murmured.

She could hear Olivia sigh. "I asked Rob's parents if they wanted to pray with us. They seemed eager to. So Tony and I prayed, and after talking about it, all of us agreed that it wasn't doing Rob any good to prolong his suffering. So we had them take him off the respirator. He didn't move or make any sound. He just slipped away very peacefully."

Julie's hand tightened over the receiver. "Are you all right?"

There was a short silence on the other end of the receiver. "I will be all right," Olivia said then. "It's been a hard day, and the hardest part is knowing that Rob died lost. But I know now I was meant to come. Rob's parents are devastated. He was their only child, and his death has made a deep impression on them. They asked to hear more about my faith, so while we're making the funeral arrangements, I'm going to make time to talk to them, and afterward, too, if they want to."

"Don't forget to take care of yourself too," Dan reminded her.

"I will. Tony and my parents are being so supportive, and they're making sure I get enough rest and food. Thank you for all you are doing, and especially for your prayers. I can feel them undergirding me."

"As soon as you've made the funeral arrangements, please let us know so we can be praying for the Lord's comfort for you and the family and especially that he will be very real to Rob's parents," Dan said. "Are you still thinking about going to see Diane?"

"I feel I have to, though I'm afraid that's going to be the hardest of all. She's lost not only Rob, but also her baby, and on top of it, she's struggling with addiction. I want to bring her some hope, even though I know she may refuse to listen to me."

"You'll be planting a seed," Julie responded. "If she isn't able to accept it now, down the road somewhere your kindness may still bear fruit. All you can do is to be faithful, and leave the result to the Holy Spirit."

LATE FRIDAY AFTERNOON Dan and Julie met her parents at the airport on their return from New York. To Julie's relief, her mother looked rested and as well as when she had left. There was no shadow on her features or in her eyes to make Julie uneasy.

On the ride home, their conversation focused on Broadway plays, visits to museums and art galleries, restaurants and shops. It wasn't until they arrived home that Dan and Julie filled them in on Olivia's situation. Their initial concern quickly gave way to insistence on helping in any way they could.

Julie had been right about not being able to keep her mother out of the flower shop. She and Julie quickly settled into a routine of spending a part of each day running errands, making deliveries, handling any minor crises or questions that arose, often with Amy happily in tow. Within days, they were fast friends with Miriam and Steve, who adopted Amy as their own.

In phone calls over the next few days, Olivia shared funeral arrangements and details of the service. When she confided her discussions with Rob's parents, they rejoiced to learn of the couple's decision to begin attending a local church and to seriously seek the Lord.

Olivia also told them about visiting Diane, who was still in the hospital and very weak. "She was propped up in the bed with pillows, and she looked as if a breath would blow her over. I brought her a vase of flowers, and she just lay there staring at me as if she couldn't believe I'd come, much less that I brought her a gift. I think we were both scared, but I told her how sorry I was that she had lost her baby and asked how she felt.

"She just shrugged, but finally she asked if I had come to gloat. I reached over and took her hand and said no, that I was really sorry and wanted to tell her so. She kept staring at me as though I was a space alien or something."

Chuckling, Julie heard Dan do the same on the other phone. "I guess that's what the world really thinks of us Christians," she said.

"It must seem very strange for a nonbeliever to experience the Lord's mercy and grace," Olivia said. "I asked her if she had any family. Right away she dropped her eyes and wouldn't look at me. She shook her head no, but she had tears in her eyes, so I suspect she doesn't have a relationship with her family anymore because of the way she's been living."

"I'd say you're probably right," Dan agreed.

"Anyway, I asked if she would mind if I came to see her again. She didn't answer at first, then she said she didn't care, that I didn't need to bother, she was doing all right. I told her I wanted to come, and I went back yesterday. She was sitting up in a chair, and she looked almost grateful to see me, as if she hadn't really expected me to show up.

After a brief hesitation, Olivia added, "I brought her a small New Testament, and I read to her in the gospels where Jesus said he is the way, the truth, and the life. Then I read in Revelation where he says, 'Behold, I stand at the door and knock; if anyone hears My voice and opens the door, I will come in to him and will dine with him, and he with Me.' She seemed to listen, but when I finished reading she said that she didn't believe all that stuff. I just smiled and set the Testament on her bedside table. I told her it was hers and she could read it or give it to someone else if she didn't want it. She said she was tired, so I left. I'm planning to go back tomorrow."

"Good for you," Dan approved. "When we hit our lowest point, we generally grab for a lifeline. If she sees that you're genuine, over time she may come to want the relationship with the Lord that you have."

WEDNESDAY AFTERNOON, while they were outside the shop's back door, loading the shop's van for a couple of deliveries, Julie turned to pick up a basket brimming with the brilliant colors of autumn mums in time to see her mother press her hand to her abdomen and bite her lip. Alarmed, Julie rushed to her side.

"What is it? Are you all right?"

"Oh, it's nothing. I ate something last night that didn't agree with me, that's all."

Julie studied her anxiously, thinking that she seemed unusually pale. How long had she had those dark circles under her eyes? Why hadn't Julie noticed them earlier?

"We've been so occupied with Livy's situation that I forgot you were supposed to make an appointment with Dr. Radnor as soon as you and Dad got back from New York. It's been almost a week. Did you remember to call?"

Maggie shrugged off her concern. "Now, Julie, you're overreacting. It's only indigestion. I'll make an appointment for a check-up next month. I've seen enough of doctors to last me a good long while, and I need a break."

"Mom, you can't just ignore this! The tumor isn't completely gone, and Dr. Radnor said he needed to evaluate your condition as soon as you got back so he could decide the best course of treatment to get rid of it once and for all."

"Just let me put this behind me for a little while," Maggie snapped. "I can't face any more chemo or radiation or surgery right now. I need to think about something other than my health. I need to feel like I have a life. It won't make any difference if I wait a few weeks to see the doctor."

"Have you discussed it with Dad?"

"Yes, I have. He agrees that I'm doing so well that there's no rush to go back. I need to trust God for healing . . . then maybe when I see the doctor again the tumor will be gone."

Hearing the longing in her voice, Julie studied her earnestly. How well she understood the fear of what the doctor might find during a check-up and the longing for a miracle that would eliminate further pain and worry, seemingly endless visits to the doctor, and additional hospitalizations.

"Most of the time the Lord uses human agents to heal people," she said, searching for words of encouragement. "The sooner you find out what the next stage of treatment is, the sooner you'll be finished with it for good."

Maggie balked at discussing the subject any further, however, and reluctantly Julie let the issue drop for the time being. Privately, she decided to keep a careful eye on her mother. If any further sign of trouble surfaced, she would take matters into her own hands and personally arrange an appointment with the doctor.

THE NEXT TO THE LAST WEEK of September, Olivia returned home. At the airport, thinner, her expression weary but at peace, she walked into Julie and Dan's welcoming arms.

On the drive back to Shepherdsville, Olivia told them she had divided the extra week in California between her family, Rob's parents, and Diane. On her last visit the day before leaving for Minneapolis, she had met Diane's mother at the hospital.

"She flew in from Seattle to take Diane home with her. We talked for a while, and she thanked me for being so kind to her daughter."

"I'm glad you followed your heart in going out there," Dan said. "You were right after all."

In the backseat, a smile lighted Olivia's face. "When we said goodbye, Diane hugged me and told me how grateful she was that I didn't give up on her. We exchanged phone numbers, and she said she has applied to a drug rehab center and hopes to turn her life around."

Julie twisted around to look back at her. "That's nothing less than a miracle!"

"You know the best part?" Olivia gave a soft laugh. "After she was released, when the orderly took her downstairs in a wheelchair, I walked along with her and her mother. And I saw the New Testament I gave her sticking out of the bag of things she was taking home."

CHAPTER 14

MAGGIE'S PAIN DID NOT GO AWAY. She alternated between denying it to herself and rationalizing the cause, as gradually, over the next couple of weeks, the discomfort intensified. She became constipated, and at the same time it became difficult for her to hold food down. By the end of September, when she began to vomit every time she tried to eat, she had no choice but to admit to Julie that something was seriously wrong.

"Oh, Julie, I just know it's come back," she cried, distraught. "I can't face going through all this again. I just can't!"

Embracing, both of them broke down.

"Mom, we'll do whatever is best for you," Julie assured her. "Let's talk to the doctor and find out what the situation is. I promise you'll be the one to decide what to do. Dan and I will talk to Dad, and we'll support you no matter what."

Shaking, Maggie clung to her and whispered, "Thank you. Make him understand I *have* to give up this fight, but I can't until he does. Please."

"We will," Julie promised. But Maggie saw the doubt in her expression.

A HARD, TIGHT KNOT OF FEAR had taken possession of Julie's chest. Her hands clenched in her lap, she stared in bleak dismay at the X-rays, the doctor's words echoing in her ears.

Metastasized.

Kidneys. Liver. Stomach. A spot on the lungs.

And worse.

Research was just beginning to confirm that, although the experimental drug that had been administered to her mother initially caused almost miraculous improvement, it lost effectiveness rapidly, opening the door for the cancer to spread with even greater virulence.

In the month since she had finished the last course of chemo, the cancer had blossomed inside her abdominal cavity like an evil, malignant flower. The mass on her small intestine had grown even larger than before and had thrown out tentacles that were now creeping rapidly throughout her body.

Feeling sick, Julie glanced at her mother, not wanting to see what she read in her face. Ashen, she was staring into space, her eyes gone blank, while on her other side, Julie's father leaned back in his chair, frowning at the doctor.

"If surgery is out of the question, what treatment do you recommend?" Frank asked.

For a tense moment the doctor made no reply. Finally he cleared his throat.

"We could try further chemotherapy. Promising new drugs are always coming onto the market, and there are newer experimental drugs under research. We might be able to get Maggie into another study."

"I'm not doing any more chemo. Or radiation. Or surgery." Maggie's voice sounded flat. "All the treatments have done is make my condition worse. I'm not going through any more of this."

Frank put his arm protectively around her shoulders. "What's the prognosis if we go ahead with the chemo?"

"Dad," Julie interrupted, her voice trembling, "there is no 'we.' Mom is the one who has to undergo any treatments. She has the right to decide how much she can handle."

Frank frowned at her, but before he could answer, Dr. Radnor said, "I'm afraid the prognosis isn't good, Maggie. As I said, we could try some different drugs, but that would probably only prolong your life by a few weeks, if you could even bear the treatment. More likely any further chemo would do more damage than good. I'm sorry, but my recommendation is to make arrangements with the hospice for home care. I'll prescribe whatever medication is necessary to keep you comfortable."

Frank took a deep breath and let it slowly out. "Let's go home and talk about it."

He drove them home, feeling almost cheerful. The others talked little until they were all seated around the kitchen table.

Shaking, Maggie said, "I've gone through all this suffering for nothing. The only thing the treatments did was raise my hopes—which makes it all the worse now that I have to face the fact that it's been a losing battle from the beginning."

Again Frank enclosed her in his embrace, willing his confidence to calm her. "This is my fault," he said soothingly. "I shouldn't have insisted that you go through this ordeal. But I guess it's taken this for us to understand that we have to trust God completely for your healing.

"Nothing is impossible for the Lord, and he's promised that he's going to heal you. I'm just sorry we followed the doctors' recommendations instead of relying on our faith from the beginning."

When Maggie looked up at him, the lines of exhaustion, pain, and hopelessness that etched her features cut him to the core. In her eyes he read her longing to give up the struggle, to finally lay it all down and find peace. But to let her go was worse than unthinkable.

All Julie's and Dan's efforts to gently reason with him were to no avail. What he desired so passionately he knew with unshakable certainty also to be the Lord's will, and he doggedly brushed off any arguments to the contrary.

BY THE SECOND WEEK OF OCTOBER, Maggie's level of pain from the intestinal obstruction had become so severe that she gave up her objections and allowed them admit her to the hospital. Since she had been unable able to eat anything solid for three weeks, she was immediately hooked up to an IV to restore her fluids and to provide minimal nutrition.

A tube also had to be inserted through her nose into her stomach to drain off the bile that collected, causing her continually to retch. Inserting the tube was an ordeal Julie had assisted with many times, but she had never grown hardened to the sight of a patient gagging, retching, and choking during the process. Being witness to her own mother's suffering aroused emotions that were all but intolerable.

She wanted to scream at the nurses to leave her mother alone so she could die in peace. At the same time, Julie knew that without draining off the accumulated bile, her misery would only continue to worsen.

The tube rubbed a sore spot in Maggie's throat that added to her discomfort. It seemed to Julie that her weakness and pain increased hourly in spite of the medication administered in hopes of keeping her comfortable. Mercifully, she spent much time in a state of drug-induced insensibility.

Their lives now revolved around vigils at the hospital. Among them there was tacit agreement that her mother never be left alone.

Julie's Bible study group began to pray earnestly for God's will to be accomplished in her mother's life and for her suffering to be shortened. The entire church joined in prayer for her, while her father continued to insist that a miracle was right around the corner.

SEVERAL TIMES, OUT ON THE BATTLEFIELD, *with bullets and rockets flying by overhead, I've had the experience of being the last person they see. I was really afraid of that—watching a buddy die. You know, it's strange, but as hard as it is to watch someone die, it gives me a sense of purpose that I didn't have before, a sense that my life is of some use.*

I try to shield them with my body while the medic works on them or while they're being rushed to the rear lines on a stretcher. Sometimes I have time to pray with them or tell them I'll let their family know. Sometimes all I can do is hold their hand while life ebbs away and reassure them that they're not alone. Just to be there in a buddy's final moments is, oddly enough, as much a comfort to me as I hope it is to him.

Over here the guys who don't have some kind of anchor wind up dead—physically or emotionally. I'm finding that I want something to cling to when the going is rough. When Dad gave me that old army hymnal of his, I thought it was going to be just so much dead weight. This will probably shock you, Sis, since you know how I've felt better than anyone, but lately I've been singing those old hymns to myself at night till I go to sleep. "Rock of Ages" has become my favorite.

Dad must have gotten a lot of comfort out of those words when he was crossing the Pacific, not knowing whether there was a torpedo out there with his ship's name on it, or when he was in the chaos of battle. They've come to mean a lot to me when the bullets are flying just inches over our heads.

Wrestling with the certainty that her mother was going to lose her long fight, Julie was increasingly overcome by grief and dread. But rereading Mike's words alone late at night, she found comfort in his words, in the knowledge that the two of them, though separated by thousands of miles, were engaged in the same battle of faith.

All she could do was what Mike also was doing. Be there. Hold her mother's hand. Reassure her that she was not alone while her life ebbed away. Cling to the anchor. Find shelter in the Rock.

Throughout October, the rapid buildup of men and materiel in Viet Nam had continued to accelerate. There were now 463,000 U.S. troops in South Viet Nam, and reports of heavy fighting around Song Be monopolized news reports. On October 21 a march on the Pentagon drew fifty thousand protesters against the war.

It seemed to Julie that the nation was in as much upheaval over that distant war as she was over the one her mother fought in her hospital bed.

THE LAST FULL WEEK OF OCTOBER, in desperation, Maggie brought up the possibility of surgery to relieve the intestinal blockage. If she could only eat solid food again, she told them, then she might be able to regain some strength.

Dr. Radnor was reluctant to operate, pointing out that the cancerous tissue at the site of the incisions was unlikely to heal. Julie agreed with him and tried to persuade her mother of the futility of such a procedure. By now, however, Maggie was almost too weak to raise her head off the pillow, and her pain was so great that she insisted that something be done even if it provided only temporary relief. Against his better judgment, the doctor finally agreed to exploratory surgery.

The morning before the operation Maggie asked to speak to Dan privately. When the others had left the room, she said, "I need you to do a favor for me."

Leaning over the bed, Dan took her hand between his. "You know I'll do anything I can."

"I have Christmas presents for Frank, you, Julie, and Amy, and for Mike and Thi Nhuong too," she said, struggling to speak, but barely able to raise her voice above a whisper. "There are also presents for the baby and for Julie's birthday. I didn't have time to buy presents for your birthday and Amy's."

When he made a dismissive gesture, she rushed on. "Everything is packed in the white wicker trunk in my sewing room. You have a key to the house, and I want you to take the trunk to your house when Frank and Julie aren't around. Make sure each of them receives their present at the right time. They're all clearly marked. I'm afraid I won't be there to do it, and it will be too hard for Frank and Julie to handle it."

His fingers tightened over hers. "Of course I'll take care of it, Maggie," he said hoarsely. "Please don't worry."

THEY CROWDED THE WAITING ROOM, silently staring at the clock or at the floor, occasional exchanging terse words of encouragement and hope. Along with Maggie's parents—Dottie and Ed Clayton—Dan's sisters and their families, Terry, Angie, and Olivia kept anxious vigil while Dan's parents took Amy home.

Late in the afternoon the doctor came in, still in his scrubs. Wordlessly they gathered around him in a somber circle.

The cancer had advanced throughout Maggie's intestines and colon, he told them. Her stomach was also riddled with cancer. He had done what he could to relieve the blockage. The tissue, however, was so cancerous that it was doubtful the site of the surgery could heal enough to allow solid food to pass through or for the intestines to absorb any nutrition.

She had at most three, perhaps four, weeks to live.

Unable to find any comforting words, Dan glanced over at Frank. To his surprise, he appeared unmoved.

Terry frowned down at the floor. "I'm going to see what I can do to have Mike brought home."

"That won't be necessary," Frank broke in. "He'll be home before Christmas anyway, and by then Maggie will be over this."

Julie gave an audible gasp. "Dad, surely you can't—"

Before she could continue, Dan pulled her and Terry aside. "Ordinarily I'd agree with you," he told Terry, "but if we ask to have Mike sent home and Thi Nhuong is unable to travel or can't get clearance, he'll be forced to leave her behind."

Terry's face fell. "You're right. He'd have to choose between his mother and his pregnant wife. We can't do that to him."

The three of them agreed to let the matter drop for the time being and pray that Maggie's condition would stabilize.

Frank refused to even consider making funeral arrangements. It fell to Julie and Dan, along with Maggie's parents, to talk to the funeral director the next day. They arranged for Maggie's body to be picked up after her death and chose a couple of different caskets for Frank to decide between when the time came.

Dottie and Ed paid for two burial plots, for both Maggie and Frank, side-by-side in the same cemetery where Frank's parents were buried and where they also had their own plot. They went together to see them.

Standing in the cold wind beneath the leafless branches of an ancient, spreading oak tree, they held hands and prayed for Maggie and for Frank. When they finished, Dan waited with Julie while her grandparents wandered a short distance along the snow-covered expanse of lawn dotted with grave markers.

"It's going to be beautiful when spring comes," Dottie murmured when they rejoined them.

"Yes, Grandma," Julie said, her voice choked. "It's so peaceful. Mom will be pleased that you chose this place."

Dan fumbled in his pocket to retrieve a tissue. He handed it to Julie, and she dabbed away the tears that trickled down her cheeks. Giving him a grateful look, she took her grandmother's arm to help her back to the car.

ON NOVEMBER 7 they were able to bring Maggie home from the hospital. They moved the sofa out of the way and placed a hospital bed, along with an IV stand, in the living room by the side windows where she could see a corner of her garden. It was a great relief to all of them to be spared the stressful drive into Minneapolis.

By now the flowers were all dead, and in the mornings a heavy crust of frost glittered like molten silver on the brown grass and along the bare limbs of the trees. Even so, when she was awake Maggie found great pleasure in seeing something other than drab hospital walls outside her window. She took special joy in watching the blue jays and cardinals and chickadees that gathered at the bird feeder.

She spent much time dozing, dreaming of her childhood, only intermittently aware of family and friends who came to sit with her. Floating in and out of a drugged haze, she lost consciousness of the passage of time. It was late afternoon when she forced her eyes open. Sitting beside her, Dan stared out the window, his face shadowed in the unlighted room.

She felt so weary and weak she could hardly turn her head to look at him. When she did, searing waves of pain radiated through her body, and it was a moment before she could catch her breath. He leaned over her, his face tense with concern.

"Is the pain worse? Can I get you anything?"

She slowly shook her head. Through dry, cracked lips, her words halting, she said, "I was so hoping . . . I'd get to see Mike again . . . his wife and baby. I'm not going to make it, am I?"

"I don't think so, Maggie. But only God knows our ends for sure."

"No. I can't hold on much longer. And that's all right. I'm ready to go. I told Julie too. I'm at peace with dying. I just wish Frank could be."

Dan took her hand. "I do too. But he'll find peace in time."

She hesitated, then with wistful longing in her voice said, "Do you think Frank really is saved? Do you think he'll go to heaven?"

Dan's response was firm. "Yes, I believe he will. He'll be with you again, Maggie—we all will be. This separation is only temporary."

She was silent for several minutes, gathering strength. At last she whispered, "I'll miss all of you so much."

"Remember what John says in Revelation? All tears will be wiped from our eyes. There will be no sorrow in heaven, so I think you won't be sad. It will seem like a very short time until we're all there with you."

A faint smile touched Maggie's lips. When she spoke, she could barely make her voice audible in the quiet room.

"You've watched people die. What is it like?"

For a moment Dan didn't move, and she thought he hadn't heard her. But at length he said thoughtfully, "I think it's like walking from a dark room into the light. You're afraid while you're in the darkness, the way a child is afraid of monsters in the night. But Jesus will be there with you, and he'll lead you from that darkness into bright light. You won't be afraid then, and there'll be no pain. You'll feel great joy and peace."

Maggie gave a soft sigh. "I had a dream just before I woke up. I was standing on the shore of a beautiful, wide river as blue as the sky. There were willows growing along the water on either side, with branches that reached down to dip into the stream, and on the other side a wide valley stretched out between high, snow-topped mountain peaks. The grass was so green and the air was so cool and pure that I just wanted to stand there looking at it."

She stopped to regain breath before continuing. "Then all of a sudden, down the valley, I saw a flock of sheep coming toward the river. There were so many they filled the valley floor. Their wool was as white as the snow on top of the mountains. But when they came closer I saw they weren't sheep at all. They were people dressed in white robes, and Jesus was leading them, carrying a little girl in his arms.

"They came right up to the bank across from me, and Jesus reached out his hand as if he wanted me to come to him. I wasn't afraid of the water at all. I stepped right into it, without even thinking about how deep it might be. I wanted to go to him so badly. But I woke up.

"You'll stay with me?" she whispered then. "I don't want to die alone."

"We'll be right here," he answered, his fingers tightening around hers. "And when you feel Jesus take your hand, then you'll let go of ours and go with him across that peaceful river."

THEY HAD NOT RECEIVED any letters from Mike in several weeks. While November dragged by, Terry kept them updated on reports from Viet Nam and as much as possible stayed in contact with army buddies about the bloody battles involving Mike's unit that were spreading like an evil wildfire, raging with ever increasing viciousness through the region surrounding Dak To.

In one of her more lucid moments Maggie pleaded with him to try to have Mike brought home so she could see him one last time before she died. Speaking privately to Dan, Terry told him that the chances of anyone making contact with Mike and having him removed from the arena of war were slender at best and dwindling rapidly. Nevertheless, he agreed to try to get a message through.

Toward the end of the month, his efforts to get information finally solicited the terse confirmation from army headquarters that Mike's unit was involved in the heaviest part of the action and could not be reached.

CHAPTER 15

JULIE PADDED INTO THE DARK KITCHEN on silent slippers. Without turning on the light, her movements automatic, she filled the percolator with water at the sink, spooned coffee into the basket, and clicked the on button.

While the percolator quietly bubbled, she sat at the table. Wearily she ran her fingers through her tangled hair, then propped her chin in her hands and sat motionless, staring out the windows. As the cozy room filled with the welcoming scent of brewing coffee, night gradually gave way to the first flush of dawn.

First the oaks and maples nearer at hand came into tentative focus. Their vivid hues of russet, scarlet, and gold that had flamed into brilliant life earlier in the autumn had by now settled into soggy, brown drifts around the faded starpoints of ruby, amethyst, and topaz chrysanthemums at their feet.

So slowly that it was almost unnoticeable, the tall pines behind the garage, beyond the spectral maples and oaks in the backyard, began to emerge shyly out of the darkness, at first only ghostly black shadows wreathed in smoky streamers of mist. As the sky brightened, revealing pastel shades of pink, blue violet, and yellow, with each moment they assumed more substantial definition until she could make out individual branches, first darkly green-tinged, then emerald in the shadows, touched with amber at the outer edges.

Realizing an hour had passed, she sighed and rose to pour a cup of coffee. As she returned to the table, Dan came quietly into the room. She went to lay her head on his shoulder, and he wrapped her in his arms.

He glanced at the steaming percolator. "Have you been up long?"

"An hour or so. I keep thinking about Dad. Mom's holding on just because of him, because he refuses to let go."

When Julie went to bring him a cup of coffee, Dan joined her at the table. "I know. It's just making it harder on her—and on him too. Do you think it would do any good if I talked to him?"

"I'd better do it," Julie decided after a brief hesitation. "I don't think he's going to listen to either of us, but coming from me, it might make more of an impression."

Dan studied her unhappily. "This has been such a burden on you. I wonder if it was such a good idea for you to take over all of Mom's home care."

"You know I'd never have felt right if I hadn't done it. The only thing I feel bad about is neglecting you and Amy."

"Amy's doing fine, really. You'd be surprised how much she understands about what's going on. And I support you one hundred percent. So don't worry about us—we're all right. I'm just worried about the toll it's taking on you."

"Honestly, I don't think it can be much longer." Resignation and grief mingled in her tone. "Physically she can't take another crisis like this last one, and she's so down emotionally that if it weren't for Dad, I know she'd give up the struggle."

Dan pushed aside his coffee cup and stood up. "I know you need to get ready to go over to your folks. Are you going to talk to Dad today?"

Julie let out a sigh, finally nodded. "As long as it looks like he'll listen to me without getting mad. He can't stay in this state of denial much longer."

WHEN JULIE CAME INTO THE HOUSE, Frank was sitting beside Maggie's bed in the living room, reading the morning paper to her with determined cheerfulness. He could feel Julie surreptitiously studying him while she checked Maggie's vital signs.

"Please excuse us for a minute, Mom," she said finally. "I need to talk to Dad about some things."

Maggie smiled groggily and waved them off. Her eyes were closed before they reached the door into the hall.

Strangely unsettled, Frank followed Julie to his study. He went to sit on the sofa. She closed the door and came to sit down beside him.

"So, what's up, Jules?" He lightly tugged one of the curls that fell across her shoulder, cloaking his wariness with a smile.

She smiled at his use of Mike's nickname for her but after a moment sobered. "Dad," she said tentatively, "Dan and I were talking this morning. We're both concerned about you as much as about Mom. It's time for you to face the fact that she isn't going to get well."

He could feel a flush heating his face, but before he could stop her, she rushed on. "You've faced a lot of tough decisions in your life. You faced battle and made it through.

You built a business from scratch. You've always been the strong one in our family, the one we all leaned on. I know this is probably the hardest thing you've ever had to face, but you have to let Mom go. She's in so much pain, and she's so tired. She wants to go. But she's holding on because you won't accept it. She has to know that you have some peace about this so she can give up the fight. For her sake, you have to let her go."

He jumped to his feet, unable to keep his movements from reflecting the panic that seized him every time he let himself think about Maggie dying. In a strained voice he said, "She's going to be healed—"

"It is possible the Lord might still perform a miracle, but there's no sign he's going to. We're going to have to accept God's sovereign purpose even in this."

"I can't, Julie! I can't let her go! If she dies, how can I go on?"

The words came tumbling out against his will. For a tense moment Julie stared at him, clearly shaken by his vehemence.

He gave a strangled laugh. "I never thought there wouldn't be forever after. I always thought after I retired your mother and I would spend every day together. We'd travel to all the places we'd only dreamed about, do all the things she'd ever wanted to do. That's why I worked so hard all these years—to provide a nice house, clothes, food on the table, some security for your mother and for you kids. I told myself the time away from you was worth it because we'd have years together to enjoy the good life.

"But it was all a lie, wasn't it? It's come down to weeks, maybe only days, and all we had together is going to be ripped away. And I keep asking myself, what will I have left to live for?"

He took a restless turn around the room, unable to stand still. "Your mother is the first person I remember outside of my mom and dad and Bobby. She lived right next door to us, and we were best buddies from the time we could walk. I remember running out to the playground at recess holding her hand. There was never anyone else but her.

"I don't remember when I first knew I was going to marry her. I couldn't have been more than eleven or twelve. But I knew. And so did she. We didn't need to talk about it—it was just right. I kept thinking God made us for each other.

"Then I got drafted right out of high school, and I thought—it's only one year, that's all, and when I get back, we'll get married. But, of course, after Pearl Harbor it ended up being four years instead of just one."

He was talking automatically now, hardly aware of Julie's presence. "Some of my buddies and I managed to get a week's leave in March before we shipped out for the South Pacific. We called our girls and they came out and met us in San Francisco. We all got married and we had one week together. That was the hardest goodbye I ever said. Until now."

He sucked in a shuddering breath. "You were born and dad died while I was out there. I hung onto every letter and picture your mother sent. I didn't know if Bobby was alive or dead, and the two of you were all I had to cling to. I knew I couldn't die because I had to get back to you.

"When I got off the plane, the two of you were there waiting for me, and except for you, it was as if all those years had never happened. Your mother was so beautiful standing there, I couldn't believe I was that lucky. We looked at each other, and it all fell away. We'd grown up, gotten older, wiser, stronger, but what we felt for each other was as solid as the day I shipped out."

Abruptly, he turned away, speaking to himself more than to her. "You know, we've been married twenty-five years, and I can't remember a bad day. I know there must have been some, but I can't remember a single one."

Stiffening, Julie stared at him, feeling as though a knife stabbed through her chest. *How can he say that? Maybe he can't remember a single bad day, but what about Mom? How does she feel about the terrible argument they had over his disowning Mike, about him refusing to change his mind even now?*

She opened her mouth to protest. But as quickly as it had come, the anger drained away, and her shoulders slumped.

No, he really can't think about that right now. He's just hurting too much.

Suddenly deep gratitude flooded through her that she and her mother had heeded Dan's advice and had not allowed their relationship to be broken even by such a hurtful action. God had known how much her father was going to need their love.

Tears welled into her eyes. After a moment her gaze was drawn to the small photograph he had kept on his desk for as long as she could remember. It was yellowed and faded now, but the glow of joy that surrounded the young man holding the laughing two-year-old and shined on the upturned face of his beautiful young wife was as clear as on that day twenty-two years ago.

She looked up, saw he had followed her glance. "You were so handsome, Daddy," she faltered. "I was so scared and so excited all at the same time. Then I saw you coming toward us with your red curls just like mine, and I knew my daddy had finally come home."

For an instant he grinned at her, the same smile that had tugged at her heart on that bright day when her father had stepped out of the picture on her mother's dresser and had become flesh and blood. But quickly his smile faded.

"Holding you for the first time was the proudest moment of my life up until then. I hated it that I'd missed your first baby years. But after Mike came along, I used to hold him and think that's how it would have felt to hold you at that age. And it helped make up for that. I thought I had everything a man could ever expect to have in life. Oh, your mother and I have had our disagreements, but neither of us ever considered pulling out for one minute. We've always known we're exactly where we're meant to be."

He returned to the sofa and sat down as though he could no longer stand erect. When he spoke again, the panic had crept back into his voice. And anger.

"So how can I just sit here and watch it all being stripped away from me? What kind of God would let this happen? Your mother's only forty-five years old—that's too young to die! How can I watch her suffer like this in spite of all the prayers that have been said for her? What am I supposed to do without her? How can I let her go away to someplace where I can't see her or talk to her or hold her or love her? How can I go on alone?"

The words were punctuated by the sound of his fist pounding on the arm of the sofa. He was fighting back tears, and his breath came in harsh gulps.

She had never seen her father cry out with agony like that. He had always held his deepest emotions inside.

"Daddy," she said finally, her throat so tight she could hardly force the words out, "how do you think I feel? Or Dan—or Amy? I want to hold onto her as long as I can too, but it's costing her too much now. We can't change this! We just have to find some way to help her get through these last days."

"I don't want to go on without her, Julie."

His voice was level and cold now. She knew he meant it as he had never meant anything in his life.

She pressed her fist hard against her lips, searching desperately for words that could ease his pain. "But you have to," was all she could come up with.

"Why?"

The bitterness in that single word cut through her. "There's still Mike. And me and Dan and Amy. We couldn't bear to lose you both."

His face softened slightly. "But all of you have lives of your own. And Amy will grow up and go off to live her own life. That's the way it should be. You can't be there for me like your mother always has been."

Tears pricked her eyes. "I know, Daddy, but we'll always stay close. We need you. We love you."

He made no response. Motionless, he stared blankly straight ahead, withdrawn to a place she could not reach.

CHAPTER 16

THIS TRIP TO THE HOSPITAL, Julie told herself, was going to be the last one. The last crisis, from which her mother would not recover unless the Lord chose to do a miracle. And Julie had given up that hope some time ago.

Snow was falling thickly as they wove through the dark, icy streets of Minneapolis, following the blinking lights of the ambulance. When they reached University Hospital, she accompanied her mother's gurney up to her room while Dan and her father took care of the necessary paperwork.

Gently, as though she handled an infant, Julie helped the technician slide Maggie onto the bed, got her settled and wrapped in soft blankets, held her hand while the nurse found a vein and inserted the IV that would drip the pain medication into her body. Just as she had for so many other women. Dying patients.

This time her mother.

Icy fingers closed over Julie's heart. Maggie had become so thin, her skin so fragile and papery dry that the angular bones beneath looked as if they were going to tear through.

"I'm not going home again. I know that," she said suddenly, the words clear and unslurred.

"No, Mama. You *are* going home."

Maggie considered her words, then nodded, so weak she was barely able to move her head. "Yes, you're right," she whispered. "Home."

She was silent for several moments, finally licked her dry lips and said, "I keep thinking that dying is like labor. When I was waiting for you and Mike to be born, I watched the clock and counted the pains. It's like that now too. It makes it a little easier when I think about it that way."

Julie forced a wavering smile. "I've never thought of it like that, but you're right. The physical body is struggling to give birth to the spiritual. There's pain involved in both births."

Her mother took a shallow, painful breath and let it out with a sigh. "I don't want any of you to grieve too much. I'm glad I'm going now. I'm ready to go home."

"I know you are, Mama. It's just that we'll miss you so until we can see you again." Julie stopped, at last went on, fumbling for the words. "You're the first woman I ever knew. You taught me how to be a woman, a wife, a mother. You taught me to know the Lord. You were the Lord for me until I could know him for myself. It's so hard to lose you."

With a trembling hand, Maggie reached out to her, and Julie gathered her into her arms and buried her head against her neck, weeping. She felt her mother gently stroking her hair.

"Take care of your father. We've been together so long. He's taking this so hard."

"You know I'll always be there for him," Julie said through her tears. "I promise he'll be all right."

THE NEXT DAY, November 22, was Julie's birthday. In the emotional stress of the past few days, she had almost forgotten it and assumed everyone else had also.

Dan's parents stopped by the hospital that evening to say their goodbyes to Maggie. They took Amy home with them to keep her as long as was needed.

Julie and Dan didn't get home until almost midnight. The house seemed unbearably dark and empty and chilly when they walked in. Dan turned up the heat, then exhausted, they went upstairs to prepare for bed, planning get up early in the morning to return to the hospital.

Numb from physical weariness and emotional exhaustion, Julie went through the motions of brushing her teeth and washing, shedding her wrinkled clothing for a fresh nightgown. When she came into the bedroom, Dan was sitting on the side of the bed.

He held out a flat, gaily wrapped package. "This is from Mom. She got it at the festival last summer and she asked me to give it to you because she was afraid she wouldn't be able to."

With fumbling fingers, Julie slipped off the ribbons and tore open the paper. It was the *scherenschnitte* she had so admired at the Christmas in July festival. She caressed the frame as she read the whimsical note Maggie had written on the card tucked inside.

Lovey,
Whenever you look at this, think of me. I'll be the lighthouse lighting your way. I'll be the dolphins, leaping

and laughing in the sea. I'll be the clipper ship skimming over the waves.

And I'll always love you.

Mommy

It was her mother's long-forgotten nickname for her when she had been tiny that brought the wrenching sobs welling up. For a long time Dan held her tightly in his arms, their tears mingling.

"She asked me to make sure all of us got the Christmas presents she bought for us," he explained when her sobs subsided. "I thought I'd better tell you now so you won't be so overwhelmed when Christmas comes and her presents are with the others under the tree."

Julie nodded, dabbing at her tears. "I knew she was buying things. This just makes it real . . . " Her voice trailed off.

Picking up a small package that lay beside him on the bed, he pressed it into her hand. "This one's from me. Happy birthday, Brown Eyes."

Smiling through her tears, she tore open the wrapping and opened the small box. Inside was a delicate gold chain from which hung a tiny, gracefully wrought gold angel.

"Thought you might need a guardian angel."

She threw her arms around his neck, tears flowing freely once more. "I love you."

"I love you," he said, his voice breaking. "I wish so much I could take this hurt away or at least make it better somehow."

"I couldn't get through it if you weren't here with me. You help me to be strong. You don't know how much I appreciate just having you near."

In the darkness of that night, they clung to each other, each dreading the dawning of the coming day.

FRANK SLUMPED ON A CHAIR drawn close to Maggie's bedside. He held her hand, thinking numbly that if he held it tightly enough, she could not be taken from him. He couldn't take his eyes from her face.

Wife. Mother of his children. His better self. The great love of his life.

Julie was right. He had to let her go. The burden of clinging to life out of concern for him was too heavy for her to carry any longer.

So he leaned over the bed, holding her hand between his, trying to memorize the feel of her skin, the color of her hair, the curve of her cheek, so thin now.

"It's okay," he whispered brokenly. "I know you need to go home. I want you to go. I don't want you to hurt anymore."

His voice choked, and he stopped. Finally, he forced out the words he knew she needed to hear.

"I'll make it right with Mike . . . somehow . . . I swear to you. And don't worry about me. I'll be all right. Maggie, I'll always love you."

Even though she did not open her eyes or give any indication that she had heard him, it seemed to him the strained lines of her face eased and her expression became more peaceful. Behind him, Julie slipped softly into the room and came to bend over her mother. At Frank's nod, she turned and went to call the others in.

Still holding her hand, Frank rested his other arm on the pillow beside her cheek and buried his face in the crook of his elbow. Hardly aware of when the others came in, he neither raised his head nor looked up.

In mute sorrow Julie joined those gathered around that stark hospital bed where her mother lay motionless in the center of the white sheets. Her breathing raspy and shallow, her skin thin and yellowed like parchment, she lay curled up on her side, appearing to Julie painfully shrunken and fragile, as delicate and ethereal as a child in slumber.

Julie's heart contracted at the thought that she could easily lift her in her arms without effort. So fearfully had the disease wasted her mother's body.

At her side, her small face somber, Amy held up her arms in a wordless plea. Wondering if Amy really understood that her adored grandmother was dying or even what that meant, Julie lifted her onto the bed. The little girl cuddled into the crook of her grandmother's arm with the calm confidence of childhood and laid her head on her breast. For just an instant Julie was certain her mother shifted slightly, instinctively making place for the child.

Careful not to make any noise that would disturb what seemed to her a most holy moment, Julie sank onto a chair opposite her father. Their movements tentative, Julie's grandparents moved around him to stand by the window at the head of the bed. There they leaned on one another to watch their daughter die. Julie's grief was so intense she could not even imagine what her grandparents felt, they who had borne and reared her mother and loved her all her life.

And her father. He had cherished his wife for so many years with a love faithful and passionate and tender.

Her eyes stinging, Julie took her mother's other hand between her own and gently stroked the unresponsive flesh. She was overwhelmed by the realization that this would be the last time she would ever touch the one who had given her birth.

She felt Dan squeeze her shoulder, then he bent over the bed, curving his arm onto the pillow and placing his hand on Maggie's head as though in reassurance and blessing. An unearthly stillness gathered in that darkened hospital room lit only by the faint shaft of light from the shaded bedside lamp. By degrees the rasping sound of Maggie's labored breathing muted.

Without conscious thought, knowing that hearing is the last sensation to leave before death, Julie began softly to sing "Be Still My Soul," hardly even aware that she sang the words aloud, yet knowing surely in that moment that her mother needed to hear the words of her most cherished hymn, and that she herself needed to sing it to her as a mother sings a lullaby to a suffering child.

After the first few lines, the painful tightness of her throat made it almost impossible to go on. When she came to the final verse, her voice faltered, yet she continued to the end.

Be still my soul, the hour is hastening on
When we shall be forever with the Lord.

When disappointment, grief, and fears are gone,
Sorrow forgot, love's purest joys restored,
Be still my soul, when change and tears are past,
All safe and blessed we shall meet at last.

Dan reached out his other hand to take Julie's. Slowly, tenderly, he recited the Twenty-third Psalm.

When he finished, in the silent waiting of the room, Julie heard her mother sigh, and then her eyes flickered open. Her father lifted his head, sudden hope lighting his features. But it was clear to Julie that her mother did not see anyone in the room, that she looked beyond them.

A faint, welcoming smile touched her pale lips. "Michael . . . " she murmured, her voice barely audible.

Her eyes drifted shut, and Julie heard the catch of her final breath. As gently as a dove rises into the air, she felt her mother's soul depart from her body to be gathered at last into the loving arms of the Father who had first breathed into her the fragile breath of life.

Wearily, through eyes blurred with tears, Julie glanced toward the uncompromising black rectangle of the window, then down at her watch. It was five minutes past midnight.

Thanksgiving Day.

CHAPTER 17

IF I CAN JUST KEEP MY EYES ON JESUS, Julie thought, *I can get through this.*

Frowning, she concentrated on the majestic depiction of Mary holding the infant Savior that soared behind and above the altar. Each hue stood out in vivid relief, brilliantly illuminated by the morning sunshine that streamed through the stained glass. The Christ child's chubby face was suffused with such serene joy that Julie clung to the vision, vainly willing the tight knot that choked her throat to loosen.

Inevitably her eyes were drawn again to the gleaming white casket that stood in front of the altar covered in drifts of coral-pink roses—her mother's favorite. The front of the sanctuary overflowed with flowers and plants, their fragrance so heavy in the sanctuary's heated, unmoving air that Julie felt nauseated.

The hardest moment had been when they closed the lid of the casket. It was so final. Until then it had been easier to pretend that her mother was still somehow present with them, that she would awaken and rise from that narrow, unnatural bed.

When the funeral director lowered the lid, Julie had wanted to cry out, to stop him. She had clung to Dan's arm, unable to look over at her father, her grief too raw for her to find the strength to comfort anyone else.

Against her will the tears welled up in her eyes again now, muting the brilliant autumn colors of the flowers, blurring her mother's casket and the pulpit above it where Dan stood, the faltering of his normally steady voice at last melting the hard knot of her tears.

"Do not let your heart be troubled; believe in God, believe also in Me. In My Father's house are many dwelling places; if it were not so, I would have told you; for I go to prepare a place for you. If I go and prepare a place for you, I will come again and receive you to Myself, that where I am, there you may be also. . . . Peace I leave with you; My peace I give to you; not as the world gives do I give to you. Do not let your heart be troubled, nor let it be fearful."

Amy snuggled under Julie's arm. "Don't cry, Mommy," she pleaded in a whisper. "It's okay. Grandma's with Jesus. Me and Daddy will take care of you and Grandpa."

Dabbing her eyes, Julie looked down into her daughter's anxious, flushed face, her brow creased with the un-self-conscious love and concern only a child can give. Hugging her fiercely, Julie nodded her head, her throat too choked for her to answer.

Again she became aware of her father sitting motionless between her and her grandparents. His body was there, but she sensed that he had withdrawn far into himself. She longed to reach out to him, to comfort him, and to be comforted by him. But at the moment she needed him the most, it seemed as though there was a wall around him. His expression blank, he remained remote, as unreachable as he had since the hour of Maggie's death.

Somehow they got through the service and the drive to the cemetery. The sky had become overcast, and the icy wind sliced through even their warm coats. An inch-thick layer of snow covered the frozen ground, crunching under their boots as they walked to the gravesite.

Surrounded by their family and friends, they huddled together under the tent, trying not to let their eyes wander to the mound of earth piled up at one side or to the gaping trench beneath the rails that supported the casket. When she glanced at her father, Julie thought with a shock that he had aged ten years in the four days since her mother's death.

Her heart aching, she reached out to take his hand. But although his gloved fingers curved around hers in response, the movement was automatic. There was no answering pressure when she squeezed his hand.

After the short graveside service, they returned to the church, where a noon meal had been prepared in the fellowship hall. Julie found, to her surprise, that she was hungry. She had been able to eat little during the past few days while they were occupied with plans for the funeral. Preparing a plate for herself and Amy and chatting with the women in the kitchen about ordinary, everyday things helped to ease her pain for a little while.

Frank ate almost nothing. When someone spoke to him, he forced a brief response. It was obvious he felt stifled in the crowded room and was anxious to get away.

After all the dishes had been cleared and most of the mourners had gone, Olivia and the Bringelands, then Julie's grandparents, and finally Dan's parents, sisters, and brother and their families came to hug and kiss each of them before leaving to go home. Terry and Angie lagged behind to walk outside with Dan and Julie, Frank, and the children.

Not wanting her father to return home alone to an empty house, Julie volunteered to make hot chocolate for everyone. To her surprise and relief, Frank insisted they come to his house, so they drove around the corner and pulled into the driveway.

Climbing out of the Beetle, Julie at first didn't notice the dark green sedan across the street in front of the park or the two uniformed army officers who got out of it when they drove up. It wasn't until Terry got out of his car and turned sharply to stare hard at the two men that she became aware of them.

When they came closer she saw the insignia on their uniforms, with a shock realized that one of them was a chaplain. A sudden tightness closed over her chest. From behind her, she felt Dan's hands close around her upper arms as he pulled her against him.

The two officers came over to Frank, who by now was also staring at them, eyes narrowed.

"Frank McRae?" The chaplain reached out his hand. "I'm Major Kidd, and this is Lieutenant Colonel Reynolds."

No. Not this. Not now, Julie thought in dull disbelief. *This can't be happening.*

His face contorted with rage, Terry blocked their way, leaning over the chaplain, fists clenched. "What you doin' here, man? Don't you see we just came from burying this man's wife? And you gotta come here and mess—!"

"Baby, don't!" Angie grabbed hold of the bulging muscles of her husband's arm, trying desperately to pull him away. "You'll just make things worse!"

The officers looked uncertainly from Terry to Frank.

"You're going to tell me my son is dead, aren't you?" he said, his voice thick.

Julie sagged back against Dan, her knees suddenly losing the strength to hold her up.

The colonel indicated the shivering women and children. "Sir, could we step inside?"

His movements mechanical, her father led them into the house. He went straight to the living room sofa, pushed hurriedly back into its place after the hospital bed had been removed, and sat down without bothering to offer the two officers a seat. In her distraction, Julie noted the afghan and pillow bunched up next to him and realized with a stab of pain that he had been sleeping there instead of in the bed he had shared with her mother for so many years.

The late afternoon sun slanting between the drapes laid wide bars of light and shadow across the flowered Aubusson rug, giving the familiar room an unaccustomed aura of melancholy unreality. Feeling numb, Julie perched on the edge of her father's recliner while Dan pulled a chair next to hers and the others found seats.

Staring at the colonel, she willed him to say, "Mike's been hurt. We're bringing him home."

Because the words he was saying were incomprehensible.

"You knew Mike's unit was pulled into the fighting around Dak To at the beginning of the month?"

"Yes," Frank said stiffly.

As though the officers were speaking a language she barely knew, Julie had to force herself to concentrate on each word. Their voices faded in and out, dreamlike, but it was all horrifyingly real.

"Mike's platoon was pinned down by the North Vietnamese," Colonel Reynolds was saying. "Their radio was hit, and the relief units didn't know any of our men were still on the hill when they called for an air strike. They couldn't get out, and no one was able to get to them in time."

"You're telling me Mike was killed by our own bombs." Her father's voice registered disbelief.

Major Kidd looked down. "Unfortunately, yes. In the kind of war we're fighting—"

"That's your excuse?" Terry jumped to his feet to pace up and down the length of the room. "We called an air strike on our own men, and—"

"They didn't know—"

"They didn't know because they didn't take the time to check it out! They didn't care that our own soldiers were dying down there! Grind up as many of our men as we need to while we're bombing the whole snake pit back to the stone age. What does it matter, just as long as we win?"

Julie had never seen Terry out of control like this, teetering between panic, rage, and anguish. Even Angie's description of his nightmares hadn't prepared her for the violence of his emotion.

"How many of them are dead?" he demanded.

The major hesitated, cleared his throat. "None survived."

Terry staggered as though he had taken a vicious blow in the abdomen. He swung away, his hands covering his face.

"The whole platoon? All my men? I should have been there! If only I'd been there—"

"Baby, if you'd been there, you'd be dead too!" Angie protested.

"My God—I wish I were! They were my men and I should have been there to get them out!"

The children huddled together in the corner of the sofa, terrified at the scene that was playing out before them, unable to understand the distress of the grownups. Shawna began to whimper, then Amy to wail. Even Terrence was sobbing convulsively, his head buried in his arms.

Feeling disconnected as though she watched from a distance, Julie noted absently that Dan had pulled off his glasses and covered his face with his hands, that tears were seeping between his fingers.

Before she could move, her father got to his feet, strode over to Terry, and grabbed him by the arm, dragging him around to face him. "It's not your fault!" he barked, like a drill sergeant. "Don't let me ever hear you blame yourself for this. It wasn't your responsibility, and there's nothing you could have done about it even if you'd been there. The ones who are really responsible for this are the officers who ordered the strike."

Terry stared at him, his face gone blank. His expression made it clear to Julie that her father's words couldn't penetrate

the fog of agony that overwhelmed him, obscuring everything else.

The children's sobs had quieted. Releasing Terry's
arm, Frank swung around to face Dan, his body tense with
accusation.

"So," he sneered into the silence of the room, "where's
your God now?"

CHAPTER 18

GROWING MORE BITTER AND ANGRY as December waned toward Christmas, increasingly tortured by the overwhelming loss of Maggie and the now irrevocable separation from Mike, Frank buried himself in his work. Each day he rose early from a fitful sleep, made a pot of strong coffee, then got ready and headed into Minneapolis to his office. It became his regular routine to work until eight, nine, ten o'clock at night.

His moods became so volatile and unpredictable that even Larry Bringeland had finally had enough. Confronting Frank in his office, he offered what help he could give as a friend and advised Frank to seek counseling before he alienated himself completely from his co-workers and his family.

Frank's response was to tell him to mind his own business. Storming out of the office, he slammed the door violently behind him. He drove around town for hours, his agony and loneliness so deep he couldn't face returning to his empty house.

Home. What a joke.

He went to the house when he became too exhausted to continue working and then only because he had nowhere else to go. Nights were the worst. That was when the panic took over. At those times he found it difficult to breathe, and when he did sleep, he often woke up gasping.

His dreams were chaotic, filled with bloody images of battle in the South Pacific, then of Maggie as a young girl and Mike as a chubby, gurgling baby, both always just out of reach of his hungry arms.

He could find no rest. Waking up was a relief until the accusing thoughts began to worry over him like lean vultures, driving him back to work in the attempt to crowd the desperate emotions out of his consciousness.

In spite of all his efforts, the last words he'd written to Mike and his refusal to answer Mike's letter pleading for understanding and acceptance haunted him. He could keep insisting to himself that he'd been right, that Mike had disobeyed him and had acted foolishly and unwisely. That it was God's fault. That it was the war's fault. That it was Thi Nhuong's fault.

None of it erased the gnawing guilt that caused him to lash out at anyone who came too close.

Brusquely he shrugged off Olivia's offers of a home-cooked dinner or help with the laundry or housework. Dan and Julie got no further. Their attempts to get him to return to church were also futile. He refused to allow Julie to put up the Christmas decorations Maggie had always filled the house with. She had made Christmas a celebration for the whole family, but now it was too painful to remember the fun and happiness they had taken so for granted.

When Julie proposed that Frank join her and Dan and Amy for Christmas, he growled, "No thanks. From now on, Christmas is just another day as far as I'm concerned."

"Is that what I'm supposed to tell Amy?" she demanded, her voice shaking. "Daddy, she can't understand why you don't come over anymore and why she can't come over here. She misses her grandma so much, and it seems as if she's lost her grandpa too. It feels as if I've lost my father.

"You're the only one I have left of my own family, and I can't reach you. Everything I do and say is wrong. You've pulled back behind a thick, high wall that no one can break through, and it's hurting you as much as it's hurting us. No one can help you get through this if you shut everyone out."

"Look, Julie, I did everything you're supposed to do!" he exploded. "I started going to church every Sunday. I prayed. You and Dan and Amy prayed. The people from church prayed. I asked God to forgive my sins, and I promised that if he healed your mother I'd serve him for the rest of my life.

"But nothing happened. God didn't heal her, and he didn't let the doctors heal her either. And in spite of everybody praying for Mike, he was killed far away and all alone by our own men in some godforsaken country clear on the other side of the globe. So what good was any of it?"

Julie stared at him, stricken. "Daddy, God isn't some white-haired old man sitting up in the clouds like Santa Claus that you can bribe or threaten or cajole to do anything you want him to. Even if you were the best man who ever lived, he wouldn't jump when you snapped your fingers.

"God is sovereign. He knows what we don't know, and he works according to his own plan—"

"What good is a God who won't answer your prayers?" he flung back.

For a long moment, she stared at him. "He has answered them," she said at last. "He said it was time for Mom and Mike to come home. All of us die. They were going to die sooner or later. Their time was now, and we couldn't change that no matter how much we prayed."

"You mean it was God's will for your mother to suffer and die like . . . like a tortured animal and for Mike to get blown apart by American bombs in a pointless war we have no business being involved in? What kind of monster would take pleasure in that kind of suffering?"

Julie shook her head. "It's never God's will for us to suffer, and he takes no pleasure in it. We suffer because we're human beings who are subject to all the evils of a dying world. God's own Son was tortured to death at the hands of evil men, but he rose again to show us that the separation of death doesn't have to be final."

His face contorted with rage, Frank turned away, his back rigid. "I refuse to believe in a God who would allow his people to be tormented like this. As far as I'm concerned, God doesn't exist."

He focused on the muted ticking of the clock in the still room. He wanted her to go away, to leave him alone.

"You can shake your fist in God's face all you like," she countered softly. "But his existence doesn't depend on what you or I or anyone else believes."

He refused to turn back to face her or to speak. As far as he was concerned, there was nothing more to be said. And finally he heard her retreating footfalls and the quiet click of the door as she left.

With Dan's help, Terry continued attempts to contact Thi Nhuong and to find out when Mike's body would be flown home. Retrieving all the bodies from Dak To had been difficult, and then identification was taking additional time. While they were forced to wait there was no possibility of closure, just a raw, constant heartache.

Attempts to learn Thi Nhuong's whereabouts were equally unsuccessful. The first chaotic aftermath of the battle made it impossible to contact anyone who could provide information, and there was no phone in her apartment in Nha Trang. But two weeks before Christmas Terry finally got hold of one of Mike's buddies, who assured him that Mike had made arrangements for Thi Nhuong to go to the States in case anything happened to him. He thought Thi Nhuong had left for Saigon with Father Tranh and one of the nuns from the mission the week before. To Terry's frustration, he couldn't tell him anything further.

Although grateful for Terry and Dan's efforts to locate her, Julie felt emotionally paralyzed, unable to focus on Thi Nhuong's situation. Even worse than grief at her mother's death were the questions about Mike's salvation that haunted her. She read his last few letters over and over again, futilely searching for a solid assurance she could not find that he had accepted the Lord before the end. If her little brother was not going to be there, she told Dan, then as far as she was concerned, there would always be an empty place in heaven.

In their mourning, she and Dan drew closer. They found it harder than usual to be away from each other for any length of time and often spent hours talking. At night, alone in their room, they clung to each other in the darkness and wept.

Sharing her grief with her Bible study group helped. Angie and Terry visited often, as did other members of the church, and phone calls and visits with her grandparents and Dan's family also brought much comfort. The consciousness of the prayers that surrounded them daily made it possible for them to endure the anguish that never seemed to entirely ease its grip on their hearts.

Dan had put her mother's white wicker chest in their extra bedroom. He told Julie so that she wouldn't come upon it unexpectedly.

Several days later she forced herself to go into the room. Kneeling in front of the chest, she slowly opened the lid. For a long moment, she could only look at the treasures inside enclosed in delicate tissues and colorful Christmas wrapping paper. But at last she reached out to touch them as her mother must have touched them, to run her fingers over them hungrily, one by one. The sensation of her mother's closeness flooded through her like an electrical charge, filling her with the warmth of a tangible embrace.

It was when she saw the presents for Mike, Thi Nhuong, and the baby that the pain of separation from her little brother rose up once more, raw and unresolved. He had died so far away and alone.

But, no, not alone, she reminded herself. He had been with his buddies, doing what he could to take care of them. With the realization, the constriction of her heart eased a little.

That night she dreamed she entered the shadowed dining room of her parents home, and Mike and her mother were waiting there for her, their faces alight with a radiant joy. To see them, to savor their embrace, brought her an overwhelming sense of peace.

Don't cry, Lovey. It's so beautiful here. Oh, you should see the flowers!

C'mon, Jules, it's okay. We're all going to be together again before you know it . . .

The voices were so clear, the vision of them so sweetly vivid that when it dissolved into consciousness she didn't realize at first that she had been dreaming.

Overcome with gratitude and joy, she could only whisper, "Thank you. Thank you. Oh, thank you . . . "

"WHEN CAN I SEE GRANDMA?"

The question took Julie by surprise. Amy had not asked about her grandmother since the funeral.

"Grandma is in heaven with Jesus, Sweetie."

"Then let's to go to heaven to visit her—and Uncle Mike too," Amy responded with innocent confidence, standing on the stairs above her.

For a moment Julie was at a loss as to what to say. "We can't go to heaven until Jesus has everything ready for us," she explained. "For now you have to stay here with Daddy and Grandpa and me. You have to go to school and get married and have babies of your own and watch them grow up before you'll be ready to go to heaven."

"But Grandma misses me, Mommy!" Amy protested, her plaintive voice urgent. Tugging at the sleeve of Julie's sweater, she insisted, "I need to go see her. Grandma will cry if I don't come to visit."

Julie sat down on the stair beside her daughter, her heart aching, wondering how she could explain the separation of death to a four-year-old. "You know, when we're in heaven with Jesus, there are so many wonderful things to do and see that the time flies by very fast. Grandma knows that you and me and Daddy and Grandpa are going to come to be with her and Uncle Mike when the time is right. So she isn't sad. She's happy."

Amy stared down at her doll, her forehead creased in a frown. "But we're sad, aren't we?" she said in a small voice.

Julie caught the child to her in a fierce hug. "We're sad because we miss Grandma and Uncle Mike. It's natural to feel that way when someone who's close to us goes to heaven. It's hard even for grown-ups to understand why the people we love have to go away. We want them to be here with us like they used to be."

Smiling, she tipped Amy's face up to hers. "But you know what? If we keep remembering that Jesus is taking care of them just like he's taking care of us, after a while we'll stop being so sad. And we're going to be with them again. That's a promise as sure as the sun coming up to-morrow."

A smile curved Amy's lips. She wound her arms around Julie's neck in a tight hug before happily skipping off to play.

As much as possible Julie avoided Shepherdsville's Christmas festival, which took over the town the entire second week of December. She forced herself to decorate the house for Christmas as usual, however, and to finish shopping for Amy's presents. Knowing how badly Amy wanted to see Disney's *The Jungle Book* but unable to face sitting through a movie, Julie gratefully accepted Hannah's offer to take Amy along with her own children.

To Julie's relief, Dan agreed that they forgo buying presents for each other. Neither of them had the energy or interest to even think about shopping for gifts neither of them wanted. But although their heartache at the absence of her mother and Mike was at times overwhelming, both were determined to keep the season as normal and cheerful as possible for their daughter's sake.

With Maggie's surgery the last week of October, Amy's fourth birthday had barely been acknowledged, and they had all lost Thanksgiving. They didn't want Amy to lose Christmas too.

Julie chaired the committee to decorate the church, and she doggedly went through the motions of preparing the sanctuary for the children's pageant, the choir program, and the Christmas Eve candlelighting service. She tried to ignore the sympathetic glances the other committee members directed her way, but each loving hug and pat on the shoulder brought stinging tears to her eyes. She couldn't keep them from spilling over when they set up the large crèche with its life-sized manger in front of the altar.

That week Frank received a box containing Mike's effects. He refused to open it. Instead, he called Dan and Julie to come get it, and they took it back home with them.

They made no attempt to discuss it with him. Both of them could see in his face the devastation impossible for him to conceal.

Dan helped Julie sort quickly through the items inside the box. There was only clothing—uniforms, fatigues, underwear, boots —nothing else.

"Thi Nhuong must have all his personal things," Dan said.

They looked at each other, neither able to conceal the anguish they felt. Staring bleakly at the small remnant of Mike's earthly possessions, Julie wondered if she would ever stop crying.

In a choked voice, she said, "Put this up in the attic until I can think what to do with it."

Without a word Dan picked up the box and carried it out of the room.

THE FOLLOWING WEEK Frank received a telephone call from Major Kidd, telling him that Mike's body was being brought home and that the casket would arrive at the airport two days later. Coldly he informed Julie and Dan that he had arranged for the funeral home to take the coffin directly to the cemetery, where Mike would be buried in a plot beside Maggie's.

Julie stared at him, her eyes wide, the color draining out of her face. "But what about the funeral? We need to have at least a memorial service for the family and our friends."

"Mike is dead, and I'm not going to go through another religious charade when I don't believe any of it," he snapped.

"How can you do this?" she cried. "And what about Mike's wife? She's the only one who can make that decision. We don't know where she is yet. How can we bury Mike without her being here?"

"Frank, this is a big mistake," Dan agreed. "You're going to regret this later, and the rest of the family and all of Mike's friends will have a hard time understanding it. You'll make it look as though you have no respect for your own son."

Frank clenched his teeth and swung away, trying without success to blot their arguments, and their pain, out of his consciousness. Finally Julie came to stand in front of him, her face ashen, her fists clenched at her side.

"I won't let you do this, Daddy. Mike is my brother. I have a right to see his body laid to rest with proper respect. If you refuse to listen to us in this, I swear I'll never speak to you again."

He could tell she was deadly serious. And for a moment, in spite of his determination to remain unmoved, the intensity of her grief got through to him.

He only shrugged, however, pretending none of it meant anything to him. "If anyone wants to come to the cemetery when he's buried, it makes no difference to me."

"We'll need an army honor guard."

Dan's tone was uncharacteristically stiff, and when Frank met his gaze, he read the steely challenge reflected in Dan's eyes. "Fine, then," he agreed gruffly.

IT WAS A COLD, WINDY DAY of unclouded blue skies and thin, silvery sunshine the week before Christmas when they gathered with a small group of family and friends around yet another coffin, this one a couple of paces from Maggie's grave. Her gravestone wouldn't be placed until the spring, and the earth, mounded over at her burial, had sunk slightly and was achingly bare.

Frank's heart contracted as his gaze skipped over the small puddle of solidly frozen water near the head. It was the first time he had come there since her burial.

Lily and Sam Chou came too, he noted with resentment. He made a point of not standing near them and in a voice loud enough for them to hear asked Julie why they were there. He could tell Julie was humiliated by his attitude, but she only reminded him in an undertone that Lily had graduated with Mike.

Unwillingly Frank returned his attention to Mike's coffin. It was covered with a U.S. flag. His heart as cold and hard as the day, he stared at the draped fabric, feeling as though it were his bitter adversary. He flexed his fingers, aching to rip it to shreds with his bare hands.

He jumped slightly when the uniformed honor guard began firing a twenty-one gun salute, shattering the cemetery's stillness. As the sound of the shots drifted away on the wind, the bugler began to blow the haunting notes of "Taps."

Against his will Frank glanced over at Julie, who was fighting back tears without success. But it was Maggie's face he saw, joyfully expectant as in that instant when she had called Mike's name seconds before her spirit had left him.

It took all his strength not to break down, not to throw himself across the iron-hard box that held his boy, not to rip it open, clasp that broken body to his breast, and fall to his knees on the frozen, unyielding earth that had claimed his wife, that yawned before him darkly now to claim the body of his only son.

With bleak despair he watched as two of the soldiers removed the flag and folded it deftly into a tight triangle. One stepped forward briskly to present to him.

He took it from the soldier's hand without a word, and turned, his movements stiff, to shove it into Julie's hands, letting go of it as though the cloth burned his flesh.

For a moment, Julie stared at him in numb disbelief. Before she could speak, he turned on his heel and stalked off between the gravestones to the car, leaving them all standing there.

His expression reflecting sad concern, Dan watched him go before turning back to the others. "Let's all take the hand of the person on each side." Glancing over at Terry, he said, "Terry, would you pray? I'll close."

Terry nodded, and they all bowed their heads.

"Our loving Father, we give this boy back to you today, gone from us too early, lying here beside his mother."

His voice was hoarse with emotion, tentative, as though he searched for the words, as though he stood alone there, talking to his God.

"Lord, we don't understand why you took Mike from us so young when he had so much to give to this world. We don't understand why you took his mother at such an early age. We believe they're with you, and that's good. We believe they're safe with you, they're well now, they're happy. But we miss them both, Father. We want them back here where we can see them, where we can enjoy the fellowship that gave us joy.

"And so we stand here with many questions in our minds, overcome with grief, with sorrow, with pain. All we have to cling to is the faith that your purposes are righteous, that you bear our sorrow in this moment, that you won't leave us, that you're able to bring what is good even out of the hurt we feel right now.

"We cling to you, Jesus, knowing that you won't fail us even when we reach out and can't seem to touch you. We cling to you in the faith that you won't leave us forever without hope. Give us courage and strength to go on, knowing that the day will come when the joyous light of morning will break from this deep darkness, when there will be the balm of comfort for our grief, and healing for our pain. Help us to remember that when we return to your eternal kingdom, Lord, we'll find again sweet fellowship with those who have gone before us."

His voice broke, and he fell silent. After a brief hesitation, Dan began to pray, his quiet, sure voice falling sweetly after the rough pain of Terry's.

"Father, today we commit into your eternal arms our son, our brother, our friend. We thank you with full hearts for all Mike was to each of us and to those we will never know. Thank you for the life you shared with us and with others through him. We release him to you now, Lord, trusting that as you knew his heart, you have gathered him home. In so doing we ask comfort, not only for ourselves, but also for his wife and his baby. We entreat your protection over them, wherever they may be. We ask that you would bring them to us so that our arms may embrace them and that we may care for them with the love you have shown us.

"As we go forward from this day, walk with us, Lord. Take us by the hand and guide us, soften our hearts with forgiveness and reconciliation and love. This we ask in the name of the Father, and of the Son, and of the Holy Ghost. Amen."

Blindly Julie reached out to embrace him, then her grandparents and Dan's family, and the others, her tears mingling with theirs. At last she turned to Lily and Sam, and they put their arms around her in silent sympathy.

"I'm so sorry—no, so ashamed—of Daddy for what he said."

Lily stopped her quickly. "You don't need to apologize. Your dad's hurting. He's lost his wife and son, and the pain is too fresh for him to think rationally right now."

"Let God work on his heart," Sam agreed. "There's nothing anyone else can do. He has to work through this on his own."

"Thank you for understanding. I know you're right. It's just so hard to see him this way."

"Give him time—and space," Lily said. "I feel in my heart it will be all right."

Tears blurred Julie's eyes. For a long moment she and Lily embraced. Then, with Dan's arm around her shoulders, leading Amy with his other hand, they followed the others back to the cars.

CHAPTER 19

SLUMPED IN HIS EASY CHAIR in the darkened living room, his expression blank, Frank stared at the television screen, raw images of war exploding in his head long after the news had finally ended, replaced by an inane sitcom. The grainy black-and-white video of battle-weary troops slogging through the sodden rice paddies and shadowy jungles of Viet Nam ate away at his heart like sulfuric acid.

There was nothing left of his life now but the bitterness and the pain that were tearing him apart. The silence in this house that had once been a cherished home, rich with happiness and love, was deafening. He was drowning in it the same way he'd seen sailors, thrown from a torpedoed ship, drown in the hostile, oily waters of the South Pacific during that other war more than twenty years earlier.

Always another war. Always more purposeless killing and senseless dying. Where was God in all of this?

Without realizing what he did, he brought his fist down hard on the padded arm of his easy chair. If there really was a God, why had he let this happen? What kind of God would tear from a man both the beloved companion of his life and his only son? What kind of God would have let his older brother die a tortured death amid the brutalities of a Japanese prisoner-of-war camp?

None of it made any sense. The Bible spoke of a God of love and mercy, but for all Frank could tell, God remained indifferent to suffering. When one needed help the most, God turned his back. Surely the Bible was nothing but a hollow myth.

From somewhere outside, the throb of a car motor growing closer intruded on his consciousness, followed by the crunch of tires on snow as it turned into the drive, then the muffled slam of a car door. The unexpected chime of the doorbell startled him to his feet. He hardly realized where he was.

The doorbell chimed again.

He became aware of the steady tick of snowflakes, wind-driven against the windows. Outside the light had all gone. The icy wind that had been blowing all afternoon out of the northwest had grown distinctly stronger while he had been occupied with his bitter reflections. He could feel sudden gusts shake the walls of the house.

He glanced at the clock. Nearly seven-thirty.

Who would be out in a storm this late on a Sunday night—especially on the night before Christmas? Julie and Dan would be at the Christmas Eve service at church, and he couldn't think of anyone else who would be likely to stop by that late.

The bell rang once more. Reluctantly he went to the door, twisted the lock and pulled it open. Then he stood blinking into the snowy night, for a moment certain he was seeing an apparition.

On the step before him stood a slight young woman— hardly more than a child, really. Asian. She was small and fragile, her face thin and heart shaped, her complexion turned a pasty ocher by the icy wind that froze her breath to frost and whipped her waist-length black hair into her eyes.

For an instant his attention was caught by the headlights of the taxi probing through the snowy darkness as it backed out of the driveway and disappeared down the street. Then his glance returned to rake over the young woman who trembled before him on the stoop.

She wasn't dressed for the cold. Her quilted coat of padded, embroidered silk was thin and threadbare, and the small suitcase she carried looked battered from a long journey. She was heavy with child, due to deliver at any time, he guessed.

A shock went through him as he realized why she looked familiar. It was the girl in the picture Mike had sent all those months ago. He'd seen it lying on Maggie's dresser. The girl Mike had married. Thi Nhuong.

"Mr. McRae?" The girl's low voice stumbled over the name, trembling as much as her body was.

He nodded, feeling nothing.

"I am Thi Nhuong." She enunciated the words carefully. "Michael tell me that if something happen I am to go to his home, that his family will help me. He worry for our baby and—"

"Mike's baby?" His eyes narrowed. "You expect me to believe that kid you're going to have is his? Well, I don't. I suspect you don't even know who the real father is, so don't think I'm going to be your meal ticket like Mike was. He was pretty naive, but I know all about women like you."

She stared at him, pain deepening in her dark eyes. "Michael and I marry in February in the church. We find out we going to have a baby—"

"I don't know anything about Mike marrying!"

The lie was forceful. In spite of the cold his face burned red, and his voice grew thick with rage as he spat out the words.

"If he did think he married you, there's no way it was legal, not in this country. Anyway, I wrote Mike that if he was fool enough to marry a gook, he didn't need to bother to come home. You took my son away, and you're the reason he's dead. If it hadn't been for you and your kind, he'd be here today. He'd be alive. He's dead because of you, and the sight of you makes me sick!"

Overcome by the pounding in his head, he slammed the door shut.

For some time he stood there, satisfied, letting the full force of his fury wash over him. But gradually the rising howl of the wind outside and the snow beating even more thickly against the windowpanes intruded on his consciousness. A degree at a time, his anger cooled.

At last he took a shaky breath. He didn't feel a bit sorry, he told himself. In fact, he was glad he'd done what he did. That girl represented everything he despised. She was nothing but a gold-digger looking for a free ride to the good life in America.

There was no way she could prove that her baby was actually Mike's. He refused to believe that it could be. A half Vietnamese grandchild! He'd spent more than twenty years despising all Asians for what the Japanese had done in the war, for the atrocities he'd seen, for Bobby's death. To have a grandchild whose blood was mixed with such a race would be intolerable, a monstrous joke.

But the image of the young woman's face, her eyes shadowed with pain and fear, the tentative hope suddenly extinguished, kept haunting him. He couldn't shut out the vision of her, even when he squeezed his eyes shut and rubbed them angrily.

Uncertain, he reached for the door knob, but pulled his hand back almost fearing it would scorch him. At last, his hand moving against his will, he grasped it and wrenched the door open.

There was no one there. The step was empty, swept clear by the wind and the dancing snow.

Staring into the thickly swirling flakes made him dizzy. Had she really been there? Thi Nhuong. Where had she gone? Surely it couldn't have been ten minutes since he had slammed the door. But there was no sign of her in any direction. It was as if she had been swallowed up into the night and the storm.

"LET'S TURN TO THE FIRST CHAPTER of John." Flipping to the passage in his Bible, Dan said, "I'm going to read verses one through five and ten through thirteen."

Julie shifted Amy on her lap as she found the passage. She threw an anxious glance toward the church's stained-glass windows. Behind them she could hear but not see the blowing snow. With no light shining from outside, the brilliant colors of the glass were muted into dull shades of grey and black.

Besides Terry and Angie, only eight other families of the congregation had showed up for the service, even though the weather service had predicted that the blizzard wouldn't strike until near midnight. But it was becoming obvious the forecast had been wrong. Even through the thick limestone walls, they could hear the wind worrying the solid old building the way a dog chews a bone.

Standing below the pulpit, his voice calm and unhurried, Dan began to read.

> In the beginning was the Word, and the Word was with God, and the Word was God. He was in the beginning with God. All things came into being by Him, and apart from Him nothing came into being that has come into being. In Him was life, and the life was the light of men. And the light shines in darkness, and the darkness did not comprehend it. . . . He was in the world, and the world was made through Him, and the world did not know Him. But as many as received him, to them He gave the right to become children of God, even to those who believe in His name, who were born not of blood, nor of the will of the flesh, nor of the will of man, but of God.

He looked up. "In this passage John lays out the most profound truth of the Bible, the central core of our Christian faith."

Balanced precariously on Julie's lap, Amy squirmed. The mystic truth so eloquently described in the scripture passage was the most precious part of the Bible for Julie, but tonight she was finding it as difficult to pay attention as Amy obviously was.

The rest of the service passed by in a blur. Julie hardly heard a word that was said and sang the joyful Christmas carols mechanically. Finally the lights were dimmed, and from a single lighted candle the flame was passed from candle to candle among the congregation gathered in the sanctuary, until the multiplied points of light dispelled the darkness.

Light and shadow wavered before her eyes. Tonight of all nights thoughts of Mike and of her mother kept whirling around her in a storm of grief as all encompassing as the strengthening blizzard outside.

Memories of Christmases when all of them had been together, safe and well and innocently happy, oblivious to the forces that would one day tear them apart. Memories of a young mother working to the point of exhaustion to provide for her small daughter, careful to keep her child from seeing her weariness and fear while her husband was far away at war. Memories of Mike as a tiny baby, a sturdy, happy-go-lucky little boy, and then a serious, intense teenager.

Laughter. Tears. Hugs and kisses that made everything all right after anger or misunderstandings or separations.

But nothing could diminish the immensity of this loss and make the world all right again.

Mercifully, Dan cut the service short. The sanctuary lights were switched back on and the candles were extinguished. By seven-thirty everyone had said their good-byes and hurried out into the snow to make it home before the streets became impassable.

Julie, Dan, and Amy were the last ones to leave. As they went out, banging the front door shut on the warmth behind them, the frigid wind cut through Julie's coat with the force of a knife blade.

She caught her breath, blinking her eyes against the icy blast. It was worse than she had expected. The wind came at them horizontally, driving the snow directly into their faces and making it difficult to breathe. Already she could barely make out the street lights or the bright Christmas lights that decorated the houses on across the street.

Even with Julie and Dan tightly holding onto Amy's hands, the small child could make little headway against the force of the wind. By the time they reached where the curb was supposed to be, she was shaking and sobbing.

"Daddy—Daddy!" she squealed in panic as a sudden gust caught her, tearing her hand out of her father's. "It's blowing me away!"

"I can't hold her, Dan!" Julie cried. Stumbling in the deep snow, she fought to keep Amy in her grasp and somehow catch her breath.

Grabbing Amy up in one arm, Dan engulfed Julie in the other and somehow got them across the street and up the steps onto their porch, where they were out of the full force of the storm. Julie managed to wrench open the door, and the three of them collapsed inside, trembling with cold and laughing with relief.

As Julie turned to slam the door shut, through the driving snow she saw the glow of the church's stained-glass windows spilling into the night. "Oh Dan, we forgot to turn out the lights in the sanctuary!"

Dan came to her side to follow her gaze, then shook his head. "I thought I turned them off. Oh, well, don't worry about it. There's no way I'd make it back over there now, and anyway, they don't use that much electricity. They sure look pretty through the snow, don't they?" he added, smiling. "Like a Christmas card with glitter on it."

She smiled back at him and together they forced the door shut against the howling draft. After the bitter cold and raging storm outside, the warmth of the house gathered them in like a loving embrace at the end of a wearisome journey. Pulling off ice-encrusted coats and hats, mittens and snowpants, they gravitated to the kitchen, where Julie poured milk into a saucepan and pulled out the cocoa.

While the milk was heating, she reached for the phone to call her father. "The line's dead," she said with a grimace as she hung up the receiver.

"I'm sure he's okay." Dan plopped into his chair at the table. "He knows better than to go out in a storm like this one."

She cocked her head to listen to the howl of the wind that buffeted the house, rattling the windows, before grinning back at him. "We certainly don't, do we?"

He chuckled. While she stirred the dark brown powder and sugar into the steaming milk, Amy snuggled into Dan's arms and turned her face eagerly to his.

"Daddy, will you read the story about how baby Jesus was born?"

He smiled down at her and reached for his Bible. When Julie had poured the hot chocolate into mugs and carried them to the table along with a bag of marshmallows, he began to read in a clear, steady voice the ancient story of the birth of a Savior and of angels appearing to shepherds in the night.

Although she had already heard the story several times during the past week, Amy listened raptly. When he finished, she said in a small voice, "I was scared tonight, Daddy."

"So was I," Dan admitted.

"But you took care of us, just like Jesus does."

As he hugged Amy tightly, Julie looked over at him and smiled into his eyes. For the first time in months, joy flooded through her, and for that moment, peace settled deep in her soul.

"Daddy, can we pray for little children who are lost in the storm?"

"We sure can, honey. Let's all hold hands, and you say the prayer."

They clasped one another's hands and bowed their heads. "Dear Jesus," Amy murmured, "please take care of the children who are out in the storm. Please let them know you love them, and send someone to take care of them tonight. Amen."

"Amen," Julie echoed over the lump in her throat.

DESPERATE, FRANK TRIED TO CLAW his way out to the end of the driveway, but it was impossible. Struggling to break through the rapidly hardening crust of the deep snowdrifts that blocked his path, he was repeatedly swept off his feet, battered and bruised by the relentless gale.

He'd been outside less than a quarter of an hour, but in spite of his ski mask, waterproof gloves, and insulated boots, his face, hands, and feet had already lost all feeling. Even his down-filled parka provided little protection against the knifing cold.

Glancing fearfully back toward the house, he could just make out the light from the windows between undulating waves of horizontally driven snow. Terror clogged his throat. He knew that if he went any farther he could become completely disoriented in the whirling whiteness and might be unable to find his way back to safety and warmth.

Suddenly he was weeping uncontrollably, the tears freezing instantly against his cheeks under the wool ski mask. Summoning the last of his strength, he fought his way back inside the house and slammed the door shut against the force of the wind. His breath rasping loudly, he stumbled on frozen feet to the kitchen and clumsily dragged the telephone receiver off the hook, his numb fingers almost dropping it.

I'll call Julie and Dan. They'll know what to do.

But no sound came from the receiver. The phone lines were dead.

SINCE MAGGIE'S DEATH, and then Mike's, Frank had been unable to cry. All the tears had been choked up inside the hard place in his heart. The only emotions he'd allowed to rise to the surface had been bitterness, anger, resentment.

Now it seemed as if a locked door had been violently broken open and all the feelings he had worked so hard to suppress had been torn loose from his control.

Bobby had been a soldier, just as Frank had been. Bobby had known the consequences of falling into the hands of the enemy in time of war. He had known there would be no pity or mercy. All of them had known, and they had accepted this as the price of safeguarding all they held dear.

But this girl had done nothing, except to fall in love with Frank's son and conceive a baby—his grandchild. And she had come halfway around the world to a strange country and to an alien people—to *him*—for shelter against the raging storms that had torn her loose from the fragile moorings she had clung to in her brief, war-torn life. The same storms that had torn Frank away from all that was solid and known and loved.

She had come to him for hope and for healing, this girl Mike had loved even as Frank had loved Maggie. And he had cursed her and turned her away into the howling wind and snow, into the impenetrable darkness of the night.

Olivia's house was next door, but she had gone for the week out to California to spend Christmas with her family in Walnut Creek. The nearest neighbor who might be at home was almost a block away on the corner of Church Street. Dan and Julie's house was more than a quarter of a mile distant on the other side of the park. Through the shadowy trees. Across the icy creek and up a steep hill.

Thinking of the winding path Thi Nhuong would have to thread through the blinding snow to reach a place of shelter if she blundered into the park, his blood ran cold. On a night like tonight the chance of her being able to make it— even if she knew the way, even if she had the courage to knock on the door of yet another stranger—was all but non-existent.

With piercing clarity the realization broke over him that what he had done was as monstrous as what the Japanese soldiers had done to his brother and to the other soldiers in the prisoner-of-war camps. The sheer enormity of it sank into him, breaking apart the cold, hard knot that had encased his heart for so long. Bitter remorse brought the agony bursting from his chest in great, gulping sobs.

It brought him at last to his knees.

The more he thought about the scene that had played out on his doorstep that evening, the more the vision of Thi Nhuong's face haunted him. She had looked so small, so lost, so lonely, so frightened. Grief and weariness had bowed her shoulders: the grief of overwhelming loss, the weariness of her body, heavy with child.

Suddenly he remembered that this was Christmas night, the night the Savior of all humankind had been born. Jesus' mother also had been turned away from safety and shelter and companionship. God's Son had been turned away by the very ones he had come into the world to save.

And suddenly Frank understood his true guilt—the guilt of more than this individual sin of rejection. The guilt of that infinitely more evil sin on that night so long ago. He was guilty as one who hardens the heart and turns the back on the poor, the oppressed, the defenseless who plead for aid in a time of despair. And worst of all, he was guilty of rejecting the Holy One who had shed precious blood to save him.

The revelation of the depths of his own wicked nature broke him now. For years he had prided himself on being a good, just, kind man, one who helped others and needed no help for himself. But by this one act he had revealed himself for what he truly was: cruel, merciless, and proud.

No longer could he deceive himself. If his actions were not atoned for, then justice must surely sweep him away into eternal darkness.

For the first time in his life Frank felt totally helpless to save himself or anyone else. The phone was dead, and outside, the driveway was completely blocked by snow-drifts. As strong as he was, even he could not fight far against the power of the gale or the bitter cold that would extinguish life within minutes. Not even a strong man could survive such a blizzard for long. How could a fragile, pregnant woman?

Stricken, he asked himself if she was already dead. And what of the baby—his own grandchild?

Anguish flooded over him, crushing him under its weight and forcing him at last prostrate on the floor with his face buried in his crossed arms. Hardly knowing what he did, not even hearing the words that poured from his heart, he began to pray with an all-consuming intensity he had not known even amid the terror and chaos of war.

For this battle, he knew absolutely, was greater than that for his physical body. This night his soul weighed on divine balance scales against two wholly innocent lives.

CHAPTER 20

THE MUFFLED ROAR OF A SNOWPLOW laboring down the street jerked Frank out of exhausted, unhealing sleep. Slumped at the kitchen table, he lifted his head from his folded arms and looked through the bay window opposite him.

Faint light was just beginning to tinge the charcoal sky, bringing the leafless trees in the backyard into muted focus. The storm had finally worn itself out, leaving the world unnaturally hushed and pristine its aftermath.

The phone was still out, he quickly discovered. In frenzied haste he collected his sodden parka, gloves, and boots from the laundry room where he had shed them when the storm had forced him back into the house. He pulled them on, insensitive to their cold wetness against his skin, then went into the garage to find the snow shovel. With some effort, he managed to pry the garage door open. Digging with fierce determination through the five- and six-foot drifts that buried the driveway, he reached the street as the eastern horizon brightened with hues of rosy pink and pale yellow.

By then he was lightheaded, his face tingling from the frozen air, gasping for the breath that burned his lungs. But fear drove him on. Dropping the shovel, he followed the one cleared lane up the street as rapidly as possible on unsteady legs, stumbling, sliding, several times almost falling on the snow-coated asphalt in his haste, then around the corner and down the block, until at last he reached Dan and Julie's house.

AMY GOT THEM UP BEFORE DAWN. With unabashed glee she tore the wrappings off her presents one by one and piled them in front of the tree.

Wrapped in a warm robe, Julie snapped pictures with the new Instamatic camera Dan had given her. Finally she and Dan opened the gifts from her mother. Fingering each treasure, Julie was overcome by a flood of memories—and by the unexpected, comforting sensation of her mother's closeness.

Just then someone pounded on the door. Julie went to throw it open, while Dan hushed Judge, who had responded to the commotion with deep-throated woofs.

Julie regarded her father in alarm. His clothing was wet and caked with snow, and he was almost incoherent, windblown, coughing from cold and exertion. She and Dan got him inside, and Julie hurried to bring a cup of hot coffee.

Excited, Amy tried to show her grandpa the sled Santa had brought her. After shooing her off into the living room to play with her new toys, Dan took Frank by the arm and steered him into the study. Julie followed, carrying a steaming cup, and they sat down on the sofa with Frank between them.

Making an impatient gesture, he waved away the coffee Julie held out to him. "You've got to help me find her. My phone was dead all night, and I couldn't get through to the police or call an ambulance—"

"An ambulance?" Dan exchanged a concerned glance with Julie.

When Frank tried to explain what had happened the night before, his words were jumbled. Finally Julie insisted that he drink some of the coffee to warm up.

Just then Amy appeared in the doorway, bundled in a slightly askew snowsuit, scarf, and mittens, with her boots on the wrong feet. Absently Julie wondered how she had managed to pull her snowsuit off the hanger in the front closet.

"I'm going sledding!" she announced.

Distracted, Dan waved her off. "Stay in the backyard," he called after her.

The words tumbling out, Frank proceeded to tell them everything that had happened the night before. They could only stare at him in horror.

"Daddy, how could you?" Julie cried at last. "She came all this way—and she's pregnant! She couldn't survive—!"

Distraught, he buried his head in his hands. "I know. I've been praying for forgiveness all night, praying that the Lord would bring her to a safe haven." He looked up, pleading. "I've done the worst thing a man can do, and I have no excuse, no way to make up for it. I don't know what to do."

Dan reached over and laid a hand on his shoulder. "Admitting that you were wrong and asking for forgiveness is the first step. Now we'd better try to find Thi Nhuong right away. If somehow she survived out there, we'll need to get her to the hospital."

Julie went to the desk. Lifting the phone's receiver, she listened, then shook her head. "It's still dead! How are we going to call an ambulance?"

Just then they heard the front door open and bang shut. Amy came running into the room with Judge trotting behind her.

"Guess what!" She looked expectantly from one to another. "I went to church to see if baby Jesus was born yet. And he was! He's in the manger!"

"Well, of course he is. It's Christmas morning," Julie agreed brightly.

She stopped, then wagged her finger at her daughter. "But you know you're not allowed to cross the street by yourself, young lady. Now up to your room until I tell you you're allowed to come down."

She turned back to Dan. "The two of you had better head over to Dad's house and try to trace Thi Nhuong's path from there. She may have wandered into the park. I'll dig out the car as fast as I can and—"

"But Mommy—!"

"Not now, honey," Dan interrupted sternly as he and Frank got up from the sofa. "Obey your mother. There's something really important Mommy and Grandpa and I have to take care of. Then we'll have a talk about you crossing the street by yourself."

"But baby Jesus—"

"We'll have to see baby Jesus later," Julie insisted. "You heard what Daddy said, so take your toys and go up to your room."

She started for the door. "I'm going to get dressed. Dan, you'd better bundle up. It's really cold out there. Take Judge, too, and—"

This time Amy grabbed her mother's robe and pulled on it forcefully, wailing, "*But Mommy!* Baby Jesus really has come! He's crying, and I can't find Mary anywhere. You have to come take care of him! I'm too little!" Then she burst into anguished sobs.

She had their full attention now. In suspended animation, they stared down at her. Then at one another. And all at once the realization sank in that she was telling the truth.

"You know . . . I didn't put the baby doll into the manger last night," Julie said, suddenly feeling breathless. "We were in too much of a hurry to get home."

Instantly Dan squatted down to put his arms around Amy. "Hush, sweetheart. Tell me—just where is baby Jesus?"

"He's in the manger, Daddy! He's all wrapped up in cloths, just like you told me about. They're real soft and green, with little pictures all over. I think he's hungry."

Julie looked from Dan to her father, who was staring at Amy, his expression registering the same shocked comprehension she was certain reflected on her own face. "Let me get my clothes on," she said hastily. "We'd better go see what she's talking about."

She was quickly dressed. Taking Judge with them on the leash, they hurried across the street to the church.

The building was warm inside, the lights they had forgotten to turn off the night before flooding the sanctuary with a serene, otherworldly glow. As they hesitated just inside the sanctuary's rear double doors, Julie glanced up to the stained glass window above the altar, where Mary held the beckoning infant Jesus amid the clouds.

Then, from just below the altar, echoing in the high-ceilinged space, they heard a soft cry like the sound of a kitten mewing.

Amy ran down the aisle toward the crèche in front of the altar. Propelled by Judge, whose leash she held, Julie followed on her heels, her father and Dan bringing up the rear. By the time they reached the manger, Amy was already kneeling beside it, looking into it lovingly like a small Mary bundled in snowsuit and boots, while Judge thrust his muzzle into the straw, eliciting more wails.

It was the adults who could hardly believe the sight that met their eyes.

For there, bundled in the clean straw that lined the little manger, wrapped tightly in bands of exotically embroidered, deep green silken cloth like the swaddling bands of old, lay the babe.

The cloth was blotted here and there with blood, Julie noted with clinical detachment. Most of the vernix caseosa, the creamy coating of a newborn's skin, had been clumsily wiped away from the small face, but the flecks of coagulated blood still in the folds of the downy skin told her that the baby was probably less than two hours old.

Instinctively she picked him up and cuddled him to her shoulder. He nestled against her neck, his cries subsiding to a whimper. When he had quieted she laid him back down and unwrapped him gently to make sure the umbilical cord had been tied off. It had been secured with a piece of string and cut raggedly with a blunt instrument. Whoever had taken care of it had lacked the proper instruments, but not knowledge or determination.

The baby was a boy. The thick hair on his head was a rich, dark brown, already drying into loose curls. His large eyes, though a beautiful, clear blue, were almond-shaped, and his light ochre complexion and the figures embroidered with gold thread on the swaddling bands made her think immediately that although one of his parents was more than likely Caucasian, the other had to be Asian.

She glanced sharply up at Dan to see that he was thinking the same thing. Together they turned to Frank.

"You don't think Thi Nhuong could have made it this far, do you?" Dan said.

Frank slumped down onto the front pew, his whole body shaking. His voice came in a hoarse whisper.

"Who else could it have been? It's Mike's son. My grandson."

Amy looked up at her mother, her eyes growing big. "You mean, he isn't Jesus?"

"No, sweetie. We think it's Uncle Mike and Thi Nhuong's baby."

Her face puckering with concern, Amy bent down to kiss the top of the baby's head.

LOOKING AROUND, DAN NOTICED a trail of dark blotches on the scuffed wooden floor, as though whoever had carried the child to the sanctuary had stepped in blood. Squeezing Julie's arm, he bolted down the transept, following the trace to the back door that opened onto the parking lot behind the church. He threw it open and looked out across the windswept, snow-drifted parking lot to the park beyond, where the drifts were even higher.

The wind had done its work. Except for a single, icy, blood-edged footprint on the doorstep, there was no sign that anyone had entered or left by that door. His heart pounding, Dan slammed the door shut.

Shivering in the cold he had released into the sanctuary, he raced down the side aisle and through the door into the building's classroom wing. After glancing inside each of the classrooms, he pushed into the women's restroom just outside the fellowship hall.

There he found evidence of the birth: bloody cloths, afterbirth discarded in the waste bin. But not the child's mother.

A small, worn suitcase lay in the corner on the other side of the sinks. Squatting down, he pulled it gingerly open and sorted through the contents, feeling as if he were breaking a confidence, intruding on what was most private. At the bottom, beneath several items of clothing, he found a dog-eared, weather-beaten hymnal.

For a moment he stared at it, his eyes blurring, finally pushed open the cover with a careful finger. There were two names inscribed in ink on the inside front page, one above the other.

The first was badly faded, but he could still make it out. *Frank McRae.*

Below Mike had written his own name, *Michael Joseph McRae.* He had added the date: *November 19, 1966.*

After replacing the hymnal, Dan noticed at one side a small packet sticking out beneath the folded clothing. It was tied with ribbon.

He pulled the ribbon loose and several photos spilled into his hand: Mike with his buddies on the base. Thi Nhuong at her apartment. The two of them together, wrapped in each other's arms, the serene and confident joy of love shining on their faces.

Replacing the pictures hastily, he stood up and took one more look around. From the copious traces of blood on the floor, it was obvious she had been hemorrhaging when she had made her way back to the sanctuary.

Anxiety tightening his chest, he rejoined the others. Julie and her father sat side-by-side on the first pew, Julie cradling the infant, Amy leaning over her lap to gently stroke the head of the tiny boy who stared up at them in puzzled wonder.

At Dan's approach, Frank lifted his eyes reluctantly from his grandson's face. "Did you find her?"

Dan shook his head, unable to conceal his concern. After telling them about the suitcase with the hymnal and pictures inside, he added, "It looks like she was hemorrhaging pretty heavily. I don't see how she could survive very long without medical attention even if she found shelter somewhere else."

"She couldn't have left here much more than an hour ago, if that," Julie estimated.

Frank gathered himself with visible effort. "She's got to be alive. And we have to find her. Julie, take Amy and the baby back to your house. Dan and I will start searching.

She can't have gone far, and Judge may be able to pick up her scent."

Dan instantly agreed to the wisdom of his plan. Holding out a length of the cloth that bound the baby, he let Judge sniff at it, then led him to the church's rear door, with Frank following closely.

BUNDLING THE BABY inside her warm parka, Julie led Amy out the front door and down the steps. When they reached the sidewalk they saw a telephone repair crew at work a short distance down the street. Hoping they would be able to summon aid on their radios, Julie hurried toward them as rapidly as she could while taking extra care not to slip because of the wriggling bundle she carried.

Before she could reach them, a car approached and pulled to the curb beside her. When the driver rolled down the window, she saw that it was Terry. With him were Angie and the children, smiling and waving.

"Merry Christmas!"

"We're on our way to Minneapolis to my folks," Terry said with a laugh. "More presents to unwrap."

Terrance and Shawna stuck their heads out the rear window. "Did you get any neat presents?" Terrance demanded of Amy.

"We got a baby!"

As if on cue, the baby began to cry from inside the breast of Julie's parka.

Hurriedly Julie explained what had happened. Terry turned off the car and got out.

"Baby, take the kids and go with Julie!" he barked at

Angie. Then he took off in the direction of the telephone repair crew.

DAN AND FRANK SPREAD OUT several feet apart and with some effort worked their way along a line a short distance inside the first rows of trees, following Judge. The huge dog wove back and forth, snuffling his way deliberately forward.

Frank heard the crunch of snow behind him and glanced back to see Terry working his way through the snow around the side of the church. He waved his arm back and forth over his head until Terry saw them.

"That line crew up the street is radioing for an ambulance," Terry shouted as he veered toward them.

He had almost reached them when Judge suddenly tore the leash out of Dan's hand and began to bound away through the snow. In moments he stopped under the spreading branches of a towering pine and furiously began to dig into the shallow drift that encircled its broad trunk.

They could see what seemed to be a bundle of clothing dropped against the base of the tree. Then as Judge cleared away more of the drift with his paws and nose, they realized it was a person, huddled there for shelter. Breaking a path through the crusted snow, they circled around.

Frank fell to his knees and began furiously to dig away the snow while Terry and Dan squeezed in beside him and squatted down. Gently Dan turned Thi Nhuong's face up to the light. Her eyes were closed, her skin drained of all color. Putting his face down close to hers, he felt the all but imperceptible warmth of her breath against his cheek.

"Thank God—she's breathing!"

Without speaking, Terry gathered her in his arms and stood up. Her head fell back, and she lay in his embrace as limp and unresponsive as a rag doll.

At a distance they heard the wail of an ambulance siren. With Judge plowing a path through the drifts ahead of them, they hurried toward the sound.

CHAPTER 21

THEY SURROUNDED THE BED, listening to the steady beep of the ICU monitors, their eyes fixed on Thi Nhuong's still face. Some moments passed before Dr. Huston glanced over at Julie.

"Thankfully, the cold lowered her body temperature and caused her heart to slow down. That stopped the hemorrhaging and ultimately saved her life. She has some frostbite on her fingers and toes, but I'm pretty sure there won't be any permanent damage from that."

On her right, Julie's father moved restlessly. "She's been unconscious for almost twenty-four hours. Shouldn't she be waking up soon?"

"Her vital signs are dangerously weak. She lost a lot of blood, and her temperature dropped very low. That and the shock of a difficult birth . . . " The doctor stopped and shrugged. "At this point it's too early to tell if she'll wake up or remain in a coma."

Julie pulled back, her fist pressed to her mouth, and Dan wrapped his arms around her from behind. Terry leaned over the bed, bringing his face close to Thi Nhuong's.

She couldn't make out what he whispered to her. The only thing she could understand was Thi Nhuong's name, repeated softly several times, and his own. Still Thi Nhuong did not stir.

"I checked on her baby this morning," Dr. Huston said. "He's doing surprisingly well. His lungs and heart are strong, and there's no infection. I believe we'll be able to release him within the next couple of days."

"Walking away from her baby must have been the hardest thing she ever did," Julie said softly. "I know it would be for me. And her husband was killed in Viet Nam just a few weeks ago . . . "

Stopping suddenly, she turned to look up at Dan. "Maybe she thinks the baby died too because she abandoned him, and she's given up. If she could hold him—"

"You've always said people often feel or hear even when they seem to be unconscious," Dan agreed with an eager nod.

Julie swung back to the doctor. "If we brought the baby to her, it could make all the difference."

At first the doctor dismissed the idea, but faced with Julie's insistence, backed up by the others, he finally gave his permission for the baby to be brought from the hospital nursery. In a short time a nurse wheeled a bassinet into the room.

Julie gathered up the bundled infant. Bending over the bed, she gently placed him in the crook of his mother's arm, against her breast. He began to squirm, then twisted his head around as though trying to suckle. Frustrated, he began to whimper.

When his whimpers turned into a hiccupping cry, Julie noted that Thi Nhuong's eyelids fluttered briefly. All at once the infant let out a lusty wail that brought an involuntary smile to every face in the room.

This time Thi Nhuong's breathing quickened. As they watched anxiously, she forced her eyes open.

Clearly disoriented, she looked up at the strange faces that bent over her bed and instinctively clutched the baby to her breast in fear. After a moment, feeling him wriggle against her, she turned to press her cheek against his head.

And then she began to weep. Her lips moving against his downy hair, over and over in her native language she crooned words Julie could not comprehend.

Seeing that Terry was fighting to blink back tears of his own, she touched his arm. "What's she saying?"

Terry had to clear his throat several times before he could answer. "She's saying, 'Forgive me, my son. Forgive me, my husband.' "

A sudden movement drew Julie's gaze to her father. With the back of his hand, he awkwardly brushed away the tears that streamed freely down his cheeks. Then he took one of Thi Nhuong's small hands between his own large ones. When she flinched away from his touch as though fearing he would strike her, the devastation in his eyes pierced Julie's heart.

"You have nothing to be forgiven for," he said, his voice breaking. "You did nothing wrong. I'm the one who needs to be forgiven for the great wrong I did to you. Please forgive me, Thi Nhuong. Please forgive me, my daughter."

By slow degrees the fear in her eyes gave way. At last a tentative smile lit her delicate features. Her fingers tightening over his, she clung to him as though she found in him a lifeline.

THE FOLLOWING AFTERNOON, after Thi Nhuong had been moved out of ICU into a private room, Julie sat beside her bed, caressing her hand as she slept. Close beside them in his bassinet, the baby began to wave his arms and legs, and then to cry insistently. Thi Nhuong awoke instantly, and finding Julie beside her, she smiled.

Julie brought the baby to her and helped her prepare to nurse him. When he was cuddled contentedly at Thi Nhuong's breast, Julie leaned on the edge of the bed, watching the tender scene, memories of nursing Amy making her misty-eyed.

"They grow so fast. Amy just turned four in October. I can hardly believe she was ever that little."

Thi Nhuong raised her eyes from loving scrutiny of her son's face. "It is hard to believe one day he will be as big as his daddy."

At the reference to Mike, sorrow closed over her features. Fighting her own emotions, Julie reached to tuck the covers around her.

"I miss Mike so much. I can't imagine how hard it must be for you. We're so glad you and little Michael are finally here where we can take care of you."

"Mr. McRae—" When Julie frowned and shook her head, Thi Nhuong quickly amended, "No—Daddy. He says to me we are to live with him."

Julie brightened. "You're going to have my old room, and little Michael will have his daddy's room right next door. Dad has already started getting things ready. The painters came today, and by the time you're released day after tomorrow, the new furniture will be in the nursery. You'll have my bedroom set. It's very pretty—I always loved it, and I hope you will too."

Thi Nhuong gave a contented sigh. "My heart is so heavy from losing Mike, but your God is good to me. Many years I pray for a family, and now I have one."

For a moment Julie could not speak because of the flood of gratitude and hope that washed over her. Finally she bent to kiss Thi Nhuong on the forehead.

"I always wanted a little sister. I'm glad I finally have one."

Thi Nhuong reached for her hand. "I am so sorry about Mother. I wish I can know her."

"She loved you even though she hadn't met you, Thi Nhuong. She was anxious for Mike to bring you home, and how she wanted to hold this little one! Last summer while she was still well enough, she collected a trunkful of presents for both of you." Dabbing her eyes, she added, "As soon as we learned that Mike had been lost in the battle, Terry and Dan tried to get in contact with you. Terry called everyone he could think of, but no one knew where you were."

Thi Nhuong laid the baby over her shoulder and gently patted his back. "Mike give me and Father Tranh strict instructions what to do if . . . something bad happens. Father Tranh and Sister Chau take me to Saigon for flight to U.S."

"That's a long drive from Nha Trang," Julie said, taken aback.

Absently Thi Nhuong twisted the edge of the baby's receiving blanket around her finger. "The roads are very bumpy, so I start to have labor pains and some bleeding. When we get to Saigon, they take me right away to hospital. The doctors say I cannot go on plane, but I know this is what Mike wants me to do. And I am afraid to stay there alone with my baby in the war. I want a family and a place of peace. I am there almost three weeks, but when the doctors release me, I go to airport."

Julie shook her head. "Traveling that many hours—you might have given birth on the plane!"

Thi Nhuong shifted the baby to her other breast and gazed lovingly down at him. "It is not good," she agreed, her tone sober. "And then I stay in the night at San Francisco, and I am having pains again. By time I come to Minneapolis, snow is coming and wind is blowing hard and no taxi driver wants to drive all this way. One finally says he takes me, but he is in big rush to go back. I give him your address and Daddy's, and he comes to Daddy's first, but he will not wait."

"So he left you stranded."

They sat silent, each lost in reflection. Finally Julie said, "Why did you go into the park instead of to one of the houses near Dad's?"

"All I can see is snow," Thi Nhuong explained. "There are no lights and I see no houses. Mike has drawn a map showing me your house across the park from Daddy's, so I think that is how I go to your house, but the snow is blowing so hard I almost do not find the gate."

"How in the world did you make it all that way up that steep, winding path to the church through the storm— pregnant and in labor?" Julie exclaimed in astonishment.

"Oh, I hear Jesus call my name." Thi Nhuong's face glowed at the memory. "Mike tells me about Jesus, that he is God's Son. So I say, if you are real, Jesus, please help me. Then I hear his voice and I see the light of the windows. They are so beautiful, and there is baby Jesus reaching out for me, and I go to him."

Julie considered her doubtfully. "I didn't think it was possible to see the church from the other side of the bridge."

Thi Nhuong frowned. "I do not remember a bridge. But I do not walk far because I am having much pain, and I am very soon by the great window where baby Jesus is. There is a bright light above a door nearby."

A thrill went through Julie. "That light burned out last month. We still haven't had it replaced."

She hesitated for a moment, but she couldn't help asking the question that haunted her. "You said Mike told you Jesus is God's Son. Do you know if he accepted Jesus as his Savior?"

Thi Nhuong looked at her with a puzzled expression. It was clear she didn't understand what Julie was talking about, and Julie squeezed her hand.

"It's okay. I just wondered if he'd said anything."

Standing up, she took the drowsy child from his mother's arms and laid him across her shoulder to burp him. "Do you know that Amy prayed for all the children lost in the storm that night? It must have been just when you were trying to find your way across the park. And Jesus heard our prayers. He brought you to a safe shelter."

"Mike is in safe shelter now too," Thi Nhuong said, her voice trembling. "And Mother."

Julie smiled down at her. "We will see them again. But we have a lot to do until the Lord calls us home. I have a feeling this little one is going to keep us very busy."

A SHORT DISTANCE DOWN THE PATH that led from the main gate into the park, they stopped near the rustic pavilion on the edge of Shepherd's Creek. Just beyond them they could see the graceful stone arch of the footbridge spanning the narrow, rushing rivulet, its banks now bordered with a jagged film of ice. Brushing the horizon in the pale blue sky, the sun cast a silvery patina over the bare branches of the trees. Long shadows striped the heavy layer of snow that cloaked the ground.

Julie gazed across the creek to where the gently rolling woodland rose gradually to Church Street. "It's hard to make out the church from here in daylight. At night, even with the lights blazing, I don't see how she could possibly have seen it through the blowing snow."

Dan shook his head. "Dad said he looked at the clock when she rang the doorbell, and it was right around seven-thirty. I ended our service about the same time, and we got home a few minutes later. Then I read the Christmas story to Amy, and she asked us to pray for children lost in the storm."

"There's no way Thi Nhuong could physically have walked all that way through the storm, especially when she was in labor." The lump in Julie's throat made it hard for her to talk.

"No. There isn't."

For some moments they stood silent, their hands clasped, thinking about one child who had been lost in the storm that night and how the Savior had brought her to a safe shelter, how he had gathered her and her son beneath the shelter of his wings.

And just as he brought Thi Nhuong safely to us, so too he brought Mom and Mike safely home together.

A quiet assurance eased the grief that had closed over Julie's heart during the weeks of separation. Although they could never know for certain about Mike's salvation until the Lord also took them home, he *had* told Thi Nhuong about the Savior. Surely, Julie told herself, if he had not believed, he would not have done so.

Beneath the layers of turmoil and anguish, she found her feet once more on solid rock, and the balm of peace soothed her aching spirit. One thing the past months of trial and pain had taught her was to trust more fully in the Lord's faithfulness, and for that she was humbly grateful.

It would yet be some time before the heavy weight of grief would lose its dreadful hold, she suspected. But in its season, joy would fill their lives once more.

"I saw Dr. Grove this morning before I went to the hospital."

Dan looked down at her. "What did she say?"

"She thinks it'll be July."

He smiled deeply into her eyes. "If it's a girl, we'll name her for your mother."

"Margaret Louise." Julie said tremulously, then, smiling, "Maggie Louise Christensen. I think Daddy will like that."

He put his arms around her, and she nestled against his chest, drawing his strength into herself.

"There is an appointed time for everything. And there is a time for every event under heaven—a time to give birth and a time to die . . . a time to weep and a time to laugh." Julie's voice trailed away on the evening breeze.

Dan's arms tightened around her. "And we know that God causes *all things* to work together for good to those who love God, to those who are called according to His purpose."

For some minutes longer they stood motionless in the twilight, looking up the hill toward the distant stone walls of the old church only partially visible through the branches of the green-black pines. At length, hand in hand, they crossed the bridge where the clear, icy water gurgled and bubbled over the worn stones of the creek bed. Then together they climbed the winding path through the woods toward home.

FOR A LONG TIME FRANK STARED at the faded photograph of emaciated soldiers liberated from a Japanese prisoner-of-war camp at the end of that other war. He tried to imagine what it must have been like for Bobby—the agony and despair he must have suffered so far from home and the ones he loved.

Had he prayed in desperation for rescue that never materialized? Had he worried that they would never know what had become of him?

Frank's fingers tightened over the picture. He had held onto rage and hatred far too long. Maggie had been right.

All that had resulted from his stubborn anger had been his own unspeakable act against one who was innocent of any wrongdoing. A hard lump tightened in his throat when he thought of what he had almost lost.

It was finally time to set all that aside. To let it go. To forgive. And from his heart, asking the Lord's strength not to turn back, he did.

Getting up, he went around his desk and through into the living room, carrying the photograph. Tonight he had laid a fire in the fireplace for the first time since Maggie's death. Tonight, for the first time also, he would return to the bed they had shared for so many joyful years.

The flames crackled and hissed, sending sparks and smoke up the chimney and giving the room a warm glow. The heat of it felt welcoming on his face and arms as he squatted before the grate.

Pulling open the screen, he glanced once more at the picture he held. Then, taking a deep breath and letting it out, he laid it across the burning logs with relief, as though a burden too great for him to bear had at last been lifted from his shoulders.

As it caught the flames, the edges of the photograph turned a translucent brown and began to curl. White steam tinged with amber rose in twisting streamers from its surface.

For a brief moment, the image stood out with heartbreaking clarity. Then it melted away. And as he watched, the paper disintegrated into thin, charred, black flakes that crumbled to powder indistinguishable from the ashes of the wood.

EPILOGUE

THEY ALL AGREED TO HOLD a memorial service for Mike as soon as Thi Nhuong was home from the hospital and well enough to attend. And after she regained consciousness, the process of healing was swift, greatly speeded by the tender love that surrounded her.

As soon as Olivia returned from California, with practiced efficiency and happy anticipation, she supervised the transformation of the bedrooms that would belong to Thi Nhuong and the baby. That allowed Frank to spend most of each day sitting at Thi Nhuong's bedside cradling his grandson or holding Thi Nhuong's hand, feeling as though their presence in his life and the love for them that flooded his heart were incomprehensible miracles.

The greatest miracle, he knew, was the forgiveness he had been granted in spite of the stubborn hardness of his heart.

He welcomed his new daughter and grandson into his home after church on Sunday, the last day of the year. Thi Nhuong was soon comfortably settled in Julie's old bedroom, and by evening Mike's former room had become the domain of his son.

The next day, the first day of the new year, dawned cold and blustery, with occasional flurries. Early that afternoon all of them gathered in the church sanctuary beneath the stained-glass window that only days ago had led two lost children safely home. Listening to the wind that buffeted the timeless stone walls, it struck Frank that for nearly a century they had stood solid and unyielding against every force that beat upon them.

After reading well-known words of comfort and faith from the Bible, Dan handed out mimeographed sheets to the congregation. "I copied these words from the hymnbook Frank used during worship services aboard a ship bound for the South Pacific," he explained with a nod at Frank as he passed out the pages. "He gave that old hymnal to Mike when he left for Viet Nam, and Mike had it with him when he died. In one of his letters home, Mike wrote that 'Rock of Ages' had become his favorite hymn.

"You'll notice that the words are a little different from the ones we're used to. They're the original words, and I know they brought both Frank and Mike comfort in some pretty dark days. I think we ought to sing them today."

And so together, their voices blending sweetly in that hallowed space, underlaid by the piano's clear tones, they sang the old words with joy tempered by sorrow.

> Rock of Ages, cleft for me, let me hide myself in
>   Thee;
> let the water and the blood, from thy riven side
>   which flowed,
> be of sin the double cure, cleanse me from its guilt
>   and power.
>
> Not the labors of my hands can fulfill thy law's
>   demands;
> could my zeal no respite know, could my tears
>   forever flow,

*all for sin could not atone; thou must save, and
thou alone.*

*Nothing in my hand I bring, simply to thy cross I
cling;*
*naked, come to thee for dress, helpless, look to
thee for grace;*
*foul, I to the fountain fly, wash me Saviour, or I
die!*

*While I draw this fleeting breath, when mine eyes
shall close in death,*
*when I soar to worlds unknown, see thee on thy
judgment throne,*
*Rock of Ages, cleft for me, let me hide myself in
Thee.*

Hearing again the words that had meant so much to
him all those years ago when he also had faced death in the
South Pacific, Frank looked over at Thi Nhuong. She
glanced up, tears welling into her eyes. Instinctively he
wrapped a protective arm around her shoulders, and she
settled trustingly against him.

She's on the right path now, he thought. *And so, finally, am I.*

The baby snuggled, rosy with sleep, in his other arm.
The child knew nothing of the pain this moment held for
the grownups who were responsible for his welfare. He
knew only that his stomach was full, that he was warm and
dry, safe and loved.

With a simple, uncomplicated faith, this little one
trusted in the goodness of those who loved him. He had
not yet learned how not to trust.

In God's mercy, he never will, Frank humbly resolved. *I need to trust the Father just like this child does. There's a lot I don't understand, a lot I probably won't understand until I go home. But God can use even death for our ulti-mate good.*

From Thi Nhuong's other side, Julie's glance met his. She cradled Amy on her lap, and although her eyes were bright with unshed tears, she gave him a crooked smile.

In the pew behind her, movement caught Frank's at-tention. He glanced back to see Olivia dab her eyes and blow her nose, and an unexpected warmth came over him.

The love he and Maggie had been blessed with had been so precious that he couldn't bear the thought of going the rest of his life without it. For the first time he al-lowed himself to hope that, with time and healing, after the pain of loss had softened, both he and Olivia might find love again.

In God's time. For now it was enough that he could acknowledge the possibility.

One thing he knew with certainty was that Maggie would always remain a dear and vital presence cherished in his heart. And so would Mike. Surely a good God would also have held Mike safe in his hand, would allow him to know of his father's change of heart, his sorrow for the in-justice he had done his son, and that he was caring for Mike's wife and child.

But then, Mike had always said that Frank would love Thi Nhuong once he got to know her. How well Mike had known his father!

Turning back, Frank looked up at Dan standing behind the pulpit, the lines of his face showing the strain of grief and weariness. And yet, there was hope reflected there too: hope borne on the firm foundation of centuries of faith handed down from generation to generation. And last of all, as to one untimely born, to Frank as well.

There were, after all, rich blessings amid the terrible losses, and Frank was overwhelmed with the realization. A new grandson and daughter. Julie and Dan and Amy. Long-time friends like the Bringelands. Terry and Angie and their children. Newer friends like Olivia and Ed and Emma Winthrop—and yes, Lily and Sam Chou too. Each of those seated beside and behind him. Family and friends who would always close ranks during times of grief and loss.

He had been blinded for so long, but now it seemed as if scales had been removed from his eyes by a merciful, loving hand. And he found himself unexpectedly grateful beyond measure.

He had the feeling that somewhere Maggie and Mike, his brother Bobby and his parents, too, were looking down at all of them together there, and smiling. A cloud of witnesses cheering them on.

He also had to smile, through his tears. *The Lord giveth and the Lord taketh away*, he reminded himself, remembering a passage in Job that he had read when he had first begun to really study the Bible what seemed like a lifetime ago.

Had only nine months passed since then? The time of healing. The time of a baby's miraculous birth.

Yes, God in his wisdom and mercy always gives back abundantly more than he has taken from us. He took my wife and my son, but he gave me a new daughter and a precious grandson. It's going to be hard for a while, but in the end it's going to be all right.

No—better than all right. Full of joy.

If you enjoyed this story and found its message uplifting, we would appreciate your taking the time to recommend it to others and to post an online review on sites such as amazon.com, barnesandnoble.com, christianbook.com, and other online retailers. On each site, search for *One Holy Night*, click on the link to the book page, and then look for the link to post a review.

STUDY GUIDE

1. Frank's experiences fighting the Japanese in WWII left him with a deep hatred of all Asians. He refused to forgive the evils he encountered during the war. Although his attitude is understandable given the circumstances, was it fair? Why or why not? Who was harmed the most by the hardness of his heart?

2. When Frank decided to be baptized, do you think he was consciously trying to make a bargain with God? Identify the errors in this type of thinking. What does the Bible tell us about God's sovereignty?

3. Frank disowned Mike for marrying a young Vietnamese woman. What effect did his actions have on Maggie and Julie? How did they choose to treat Frank, and why? Ultimately, what effect did their response have on him?

4. What does the Bible tell us about judging others and refusing to forgive when we are wronged? What judgmental and unforgiving attitudes do you hold against certain racial/ethnic groups or against individuals who have directly harmed you in some way? What might Jesus say to you? What might he ask you to do?

5. In Chapter 11, Julie's Bible study group was studying Ephesians 5:22-33. After reading this passage, do you

agree with their conclusions? Why or why not? How does Paul's charge to women to submit to their husbands make you feel? What do you think he really meant?

6. When Dan encountered temptation in Chapter 12, how well do you think he handled the situation? Should he have been more sympathetic to Mrs. Webster? Look up scripture passages about dealing with temptation. What Bible character dealt with serious temptation in a similar fashion? Identify the spiritual weapons Jesus used to overcome Satan's enticements when he was tempted in the wilderness.

7. When Olivia's ex-husband overdosed on drugs, she chose to be at his bedside when he died, in spite of the pain his abandonment had caused her. She offered comfort to his parents and even to the woman he had been living with. Why? What was the outcome of her decision to forgive and to reach out to them with God's love?

8. Why do you think Frank reacted as he did when Maggie and Mike died? Attempting to bargain with God can lead to deep disappointment and disillusionment when God doesn't act as we think God ought to. Think of a time you felt God didn't hold up his side of the bargain in relation to your expectations. How did you feel? What did you do?

9. The consequences of Frank's rejection of Thi Nhuong shattered Frank, but also opened his eyes to his own sin. Have you ever had a similar experience that brought you in humility to the foot of the cross? What changes have

you seen in your life as a result? How is your relationship with God and with others different now?

10. Were all of Frank's and Julie's questions answered at the end of the story? What conclusions did they draw? Have you had experiences in which your questions weren't all answered, but you found God's presence sufficient nevertheless?

ACKNOWLEDGEMENTS

I HAD A SUPERVISOR at Abingdon Press, where I worked as an editor for many years, who often said, "We depend on the kindness of strangers." Indeed we do. And on the kindness of family and friends as well, I might add.

This book could never have been published if it had not been for so many kindnesses so generously offered by strangers I encountered unexpectedly. Acquaintances, close friends, and family members also stepped in without hesitation wherever needed. All of them in one way or another contributed to bringing this story into existence and getting it into the hands of readers, and I am more than grateful. I couldn't have done it without every one of you.

First of all, I can't thank Paul Ellis, webmaster, and Val Sinnott from St. John's Church in Ainsdale, England, enough for providing the exquisite image of the church's Mother's Union Window and securing the church's permission to use it on the original cover. We weren't able to incorporate it in the front cover of the new edition, but you'll find it on the back cover, and also on the One Holy Night blog at *oneholynight.blogspot.com* along with other images I discovered that beautifully illustrate the story.

The center panel of this window is the exact replica of the one I envisioned above the altar in Bethlehem Christian Church that plays such an crucial role in leading Thi Nhuong to her safe haven. I had no idea it actually existed, so you can imagine my amazement when I located it while searching the Web for a stained glass window that was at least somewhat similar. Wow—this was far beyond my wildest expectations!

Thank yous are also due to my daughters Katherine and Anna. While on a trip to Scotland, Katherine took a day trip and stopped by the church in an effort to surprise me by getting pictures of the window. Alas, it was a weekday and the church was locked. So Anna stepped in and made the long-distance call that reached Val, who was graciousness itself in making sure we got beautiful high-res images and the permission for use we needed. Thank you, thank you to all of you!

Just as astonishing, I could never have imagined I would find a photo from the Vietnam War that would stand in so well for Mike and Terry. But there it was on Rob Kopan's The War Page Web site (www.thewarpage.com) in a photo album contributed by Marine Sgt. Donald Goodwin. Many thanks to both Rob and Don for permission to use this photo on my blog. You guys are the greatest! I pray this story will be a blessing to many soldiers and their families.

More thanks go to my daughter Jennifer, who stepped in to quickly and carefully proofread the text before it went to the printer, and to author Kaye Dacus, another dear friend from Middle Tennessee Christian Writers, who did an excellent job of copyediting the original text, and then provided a lovely endorsement as well. I am also deeply indebted to Tamara Leigh, Kathy Harris, Kathi Macias, Jackie Cooper, Kacy Barnett-Gramckow, Michelle Sutton, Kim Ford, Christy Lockstein, Linda Mae Baldwin, and many others for their very kind endorsements and reviews.

And what can I say about my designer, Marisa Jackson that would do justice to this lovely, evocative cover? Marisa has designed many covers for me, and each one has been better than I could ever have expected. Marisa, you're a treasure, and a delight to work with!

If I've left anyone out, I apologize profusely. There are simply too many kind folks who have had a hand in this project and not enough space to mention them all or to detail their contributions. Please know that I am grateful for each one of you.

Most of all, I thank God, who gave this story to me as a precious gift. I did my best to translate the vision I was given into words on the page, but I know that my efforts are imperfect. At times it seems that the harder I try to grasp what I see, the farther it slips from my fingers. So any flaws you find in these pages are solely mine. But if this story touches your heart and communicates even a faint impression of how very much God loves each one of us, then the glory is all my Lord's.

J. M. Hochstetler
July 2013